THE SECOND SON

•

D. W. Linden

AVALON BOOKS
NEW YORK

Published by Thomas Bouregy & Co., Inc.
160 Madison Avenue, New York, NY 10016

Library of Congress Cataloging-in-Publication Data

Linden, D. W.
The second son / D.W. Linden.
p. cm.
ISBN 0-8034-9811-X (acid-free paper)
1. New Mexico—Fiction. I. Title.

PS3612.I53274S43 2006
813'.6—dc22

2006018077

PRINTED IN THE UNITED STATES OF AMERICA
ON ACID-FREE PAPER
BY HADDON CRAFTSMEN, BLOOMSBURG, PENNSYLVANIA

This book is dedicated, *con mucho cariño,* to the
Alvarado family of Safford, Arizona, and to
the memory of Jose Juan Garcia y Alvardo, *mi hijo*.

Chapter One

On several occasions, while seated at meals or before a winter's fire, I have related incidents of my life and that of my forebears to members of my family. Most, I fear, have only feigned interest out of courtesy to an old man, but one, my great-grandson and namesake, has shown a genuine curiosity about the people and events that have preceded him. Therefore it is to you, *mi bisnieto,* that I address this narrative, on condition that you read these, the ramblings of a very old man, with charity toward the shortcomings of my humble efforts. I do not recall having ever read a like work, so I have no model by which to guide my pen. Having been born with this century, I have neither hope nor expectation of seeing the next. However, as only two years remain until that epoch, I feel constrained to preserve the history of our family while I have the opportunity. You will forgive the vanity of man if I begin with my own story and then proceed, in such time as remains to me, to tell you about those who came before me.

I, Jose Juan Garcia y Alvarado, was born the second son of Don Benito Esteban Garcia y Baca to his wife Doña Maria Elena Alvarado y Chaves. This unremarkable event occurred in the spring of the year of our Lord 1801, at our family's residence in The Royal Town Santa Fe in His Spanish Majesty's Province of New Mexico. Our family, through both my father and my mother, traces its lineage to Extremadura in Spain. Our ancestors from that harsh but beautiful land were among those who marched with Capitan Hernan Cortez in his conquest of the Aztec. Still later, an Alvarado rode with Coronado in Spain's first exploration of this country, and a Garcia was among those brave settlers who, with Don Pedro de Peralta, lay the foundations of Santa Fe in the winter of 1609 to 1610.

As a young man, my father, Don Benito, marched with the *gobernador,* Don Juan Bautista de Anza, in his campaign against the Comanche leader, Green Horn. In later years, my father stood beside the governor as they battled Apache, Navajo and Ute. Though my father was a man capable of violence when necessary, he was not a violent man. Perhaps a more accurate way to describe his temperament would be to call him a passionate man, fierce in his loyalties and antagonisms. One of my earliest memories may serve to illustrate this trait.

While I was no more than five or six years of age, our family owned a home in the western part of Santa Fe adjacent to the *Santuario de Nuestra Senora de Guadalupe*. Don Benito decided to build a wall to divide our property from that of the church. The good fathers of the church, however, claimed that he had expanded his own boundary and usurped land belonging to the church. Don Benito ignored these clerical protestations for several weeks until one day word came to him that, unless he removed the offending wall, a pronouncement of excommunication would be made against him following the homily on the Sunday next.

I still remember that Sunday. It dawned marvelously clear and calm with the sound of birdsong and church bells shimmering in the chilly air. My mother, silent and grim, dressed us quickly and herded us closely behind my father as we walked the short distance to the chapel. Father's back was stiff and his expression somber as he strode purposefully from our front gate. There he was joined by several of my uncles, all equally grave. It was only then that I noticed that they all, my father included, carried firearms cradled in their arms.

The only sound was our scuffling feet as we moved to the front and stood—the men with arms folded comfortably around their weapons that pointed meaningfully up toward the heavens, as if to defy even God Himself should He be so imprudent as to dispute a New Mexican's land claim. Our neighbors arrayed themselves at a safe distance—not so close as to appear allied with our audacity, but not so distant as to miss any nuance of what might transpire.

A bell chimed as Padre Timoteo appeared before the altar. To his credit, he did not stumble as he saw the Garcia armaments bristling from the congregation, but his face paled visibly and he cleared his throat frequently during the celebration of the mass. Nor did Don Benito's expression change as Padre Timoteo stepped up to the lectern, but the sound of five muskets cocking echoed eloquently in the silence. I don't recall the topic of the sermon but I do remember its brevity. It seemed but an instant from the good priest's prefacing cough to his stammering dismissal. Excommunication was never mentioned.

The service concluded, and the people waited as our family walked unhurriedly out of the cool gloom of the sanctuary into the warm glare of the dusty street. From that day, my father never again set foot in the church, and the church never again mentioned my father's wall.

Like most New Mexican land-holders, Don Benito raised cattle and sheep on our family's land grant. It was situated in the valley of the Pecos River to the east of Santa Fe. The upper reaches of this property were sheltered by the peaks and pines of the Sangre de Cristo Mountains but, as the river flowed south and east, the valley opened like an invitation to the morning sun as it rose across the open plains. But those plains held danger. Both the Indian pueblos and the Spanish settlements were severely buffeted by the horse tribes of the flatlands. By the year of my ninth birthday, Don Benito was losing so many animals and herdsmen that our family was nearly destitute.

As I have mentioned, Don Benito spent many years fighting the Indians of our country, but despite the wounds and hardships, my father, a fair man, respected his opponents in battle and none more than the Comanche. Therefore it seemed to him only reasonable that if our men and arms alone could not protect our property, then some allies must be found.

I should point out that most of the depredations to

our flocks were not being perpetrated by the Comanche. Following the campaigns of Governor de Anza, an understanding was reached whereby the Spanish would no longer pursue the Comanche and, in return, the Comanche would no longer attack the settlements of New Mexico. The two peoples would henceforth meet for trade rather than combat. That was the agreement, but of course in practice, neither the Spanish nor Comanche authorities could entirely restrain the predators from among our respective nations. This imperfect peace with the Comanche did serve to enrage their ancient enemies, the Apache, the Ute and the Navajo. As a result, the Spanish, now the friend of their enemies, received the brunt of their anger.

At the time, of course, I was too young to understand such things, but New Mexico was particularly vulnerable. The sparks of the American War for Independence, and the writings of Jefferson, Franklin and Paine, had ignited a conflagration in France, and the King of Spain was fearful that his far-flung territories might also be consumed in the fires of revolution. In addition, Napoleon's invasion of Spain drew troops away from the new world to the old. As a result, the Spanish frontier was woefully underarmed and undefended. The thinking in the Spanish bureaucracy seemed to be that arms might be used in a war of independence. As it turned out, their fears were as justified as their methods were foolish, but in the meantime, pragmatic men such as my father had to devise some means to preserve our tenuous existence.

There were among our household servants, two young men of the Tarahumara tribe of Mexico who had been captured by the Comanche as children and, after a season or two among those people, had been brought to Don Fernandez de Taos and traded for a royal ransom. My father, having taken them into our home, now struck a bargain with them. In return for their seeking out the Comanche of the Antelope group and bringing them to a meeting with my father, he, Don Benito, would see that they were returned to their own people in the Sierra Madre.

I later understood that it required great courage for the young men to agree to such a scheme. Success in their endeavor would mean a return to all that they held dear, while failure could mean a slow, tortuous death at the hands of people skilled in such arts. So it was in the year 1810, when the last of the winter's blizzards had spent itself upon the plains that the two gentle Indians, known to us as Jaime and Juan, rode out in search of the war chief, Red Hand, and his band of Kwahadi Comanche. If they succeeded, the Comanche would meet in peace with my father outside the crumbling walls of the Pecos pueblo in one month's time. If they failed, we would probably never know their resting place.

The appointed day arrived. At sunrise, Don Benito had stood on the eastern roof of the pueblo with two of the elders of that place. At one time, this village had been the largest and strongest of the Indian pueblos. Then called Cicuye, Coronado had camped there on his long search for the Gran Quivira. But when the Comanche acquired the horse, they burst out of the mountains and altered the pattern of life forever. As the Apaches were forced off the eastern plains by the Comanche, the pueblos became the target for raids by both the desperate vanquished and the arrogant victors. For over a hundred years, the herds and weapons of the Comanche increased and so did their audacity until the great pueblo of the Pecos, Cicuye, sheltered only a handful of people who remained out of a sense of duty. They were the firekeepers who every morning stood to greet the rising sun with prayer. This day my father stood with them, his eyes searching the eastern horizon, a different prayer in his heart.

The shadows grew shorter, the hours passed, and still my father watched. Inside the walls, also watching, I stood with my uncles and our remaining herdsmen. Every man was armed, and even I had been given a precious pistol with which to defend myself should events go badly. All were silent and tense. All except my elder brother Esteban who grew increasingly impatient. Four years my senior, Esteban was the second pillar of my world, the first being Don Benito. I alternately basked in the light of my father and hid in the shadow of my brother.

Esteban was tall and sturdy, broad-shouldered and handsome, made in the image of my father. Like the Sangre de Cristo Mountains, Esteban's moods could change from sunshine to storm cloud and back without warning and sometimes, it seemed, without reason. The day before, as we rode through Glorieta Pass on the way to this anticipated appointment, my brother rode beside my father.

"Why must I come on this trip, Father?" Esteban scowled. "I care nothing for savages!"

Don Benito eyed my brother for a moment before replying. His face was without expression. "You are my first-born son, Esteban. To you will fall the responsibility for our family's property. What occurs tomorrow could well determine if you will have an inheritance at all." He turned his face forward again and my brother knew that he should say no more.

But now, as flies buzzed in the warming air, Esteban scuffed his feet in the dust of the pueblo and complained. "This is stupid! We sit here and bake like *adobe* in the sun and wait for *Indios*." He spat noisily in the dirt.

Without turning, my father snapped, *"Cállate!"* Don Benito rarely had to repeat himself. When he told us to be quiet, we would be quiet.

Esteban fell into a sullen silence, jabbing his knife into a crack between the bricks.

When the sun was directly overhead, my father spoke quietly. *"Hay vienen."* He pointed with his chin toward the horizon. "They're coming."

Indeed they were. Slowly, ever so slowly, dark specks became colorful figures. My heart beat faster. There was an excitement about The People, as they called themselves, that I could neither explain nor resist. There were twenty-five or thirty riders, all men. Some were stripped to the waist, some wore shirts made of hide. Several wore what appeared to be short capes made of leather. These, I later learned, could be used to shade them from the fierce summer sun as they rode across the treeless earth. All were painted with designs that seemed inspired by fever.

We New Mexicans, like our Spanish ancestors, pride ourselves on our horsemanship, but I had never seen such unity of man and beast as these Comanche displayed. When they were but a hundred yards from us, they split into two columns, their horses changing from walk to trot to canter with sinuous grace. Each column circled the pueblo in a different direction until they rejoined and turned, forming a half circle before my father, who stood exposed before the pueblo's walls. There was silence then in which you could almost hear the dust settle. We crouched within, hidden and hushed.

Don Benito, his musket cradled in his arms, slowly and deliberately scanned the full line of the warriors, staring intently at each of them. His eyes returned to the center of the line and he nodded a silent greeting to the two Tarahumara who sat nervously astride their mounts. The young men glanced furtively from my father to a broad-chested warrior whose horse pawed impatiently between them.

Too much violence and conflict had passed between our two peoples to make this a comfortable meeting. Time passed and tension grew until my father finally walked forward and laid his hand on the knee of the young Tarahumara to his right. "You have done well, Juan," he said calmly. Looking up at the Comanche to his left he said, still speaking to Juan, "Will you bid welcome to Red Hand, in my name?"

When this had been translated, the Comanche turned to look disdainfully down at Don Benito. He said something that caused the other warriors to laugh. With embarrassment, Juan translated. "Red Hand says that your welcome is unnecessary, as he has been in this place many times before, without an invitation."

I could see a shadow pass over my father's countenance and a muscle in his jaw begin to throb. But before he could reply to this deliberate rudeness, he stopped and turned to see what had distracted the attention of Red Hand.

I was that distraction. So absorbed was I by the exotic appeal of these Indians, that I had unthinkingly drifted out from the concealment of the pueblo walls. Heedless of the hissed warnings of my relatives, I slowly walked forward to stand beside my father.

Red Hand held up his hand to restrain his warriors, who seemed ready to ride forward and search the pueblo for a possible ambush. He looked down at me with a mixture of amusement and curiosity. My father laid his hand on my shoulder with apparent lightness, though his grip was painful. In Don Benito's eyes there blazed a flicker of fury and concern.

"You disobeyed me, *mi hijo,*" he stated with a calm that greatly concerned me. Disobedience was at the top of his list of cardinal sins. In the past, such a transgression had caused me to eat several meals standing, it being too painful to sit.

His eyes still on me, Red Hand asked a curt question of Juan. The Tarahumara answered in a word. Red Hand nodded and considered the reply for a moment then looked at my father with a changed expression and quietly said something else to Juan, which caused the warriors to visibly relax.

There was relief in Juan's voice. "Red Hand says that he knows now that you have come in peace. One does not go out to make war accompanied by a son so small . . . particularly an unarmed son." To compound my ignominy, I had left my pistol behind.

Red Hand nodded at the translation, then added

through Juan, "We will camp here with you. We will talk with you—you and the little Spaniard." Perhaps only I saw the twinkle in his eye.

Red Hand and his warriors did not stay with us that day. Instead, they rode east again promising to return with the rest of their band who were waiting a safe half-day's ride away. When they came the next day, I was further captivated by the People. There were about two hundred men, women and children in the band. Virtually everyone rode except for the very young or very old who, along with all the other material possessions of the band, were dragged behind horses on skins stretched between two poles, an arrangement which the French trappers had called a *travois.* Horses far outnumbered people. Each warrior kept a private herd of horses. Indeed, a man's prestige was often measured by the size and quality of his herd.

The talks between my father and the Comanche went on for two more days. Being only nine years old, I was not privy to these conferences, nor was I very interested. To a nine year old, the sights, sounds and smells of Indian camp life were infinitely more alluring. On the third day, however, as the Indians struck camp and prepared to leave, I was extremely interested to learn that I had played a part in the negotiations.

The accord which my father had reached with Red Hand involved several stipulations. In return for their help in protecting my family's herds, Red Hand agreed to return to this site on the Pecos twice yearly—in the spring and in the fall. At that time, my father would bring trade goods such as kettles, knives, blankets and silver ornaments—for their horses, not their women—

in return for buffalo robes and horses. I'm sure my father realized that the horses he'd be dealing in would probably be stolen from other settlements, but such was the expediency of life on the frontier in those days. Besides, Don Benito could always ease his pangs of conscience by reasoning that the horses were as likely to come from American settlements as Spanish.

The part of the agreement that concerned me was not revealed until the last day. When my father roused me from my blankets into the cool gloom before dawn, I sensed sadness in his silence. Don Benito was a reserved man, not given to showing his emotions, but his stoicism that morning barely concealed turbulence in his soul.

Walking with me until we were some distance from the camp, he stared at the thin strip of dawn's first light across the eastern sky. He cleared his throat and spoke quietly without looking at me. "Life is often very difficult, my son," he sighed. "But the true mark of a man is that he confronts those difficulties directly, not turning aside or running from his responsibilities." He glanced at me to ask, "Do you understand?"

"Si señor," I assured him, though I didn't.

He nodded and returned to his study of the sunrise. After a deep breath, he continued. "You are now nine years old and today I must ask you to become a man." With that, he turned to look at me directly. "In order to obtain the help of these Indians, I have had to agree to certain things—difficult things. You know, Jose, that it is very important for our family that we have this assistance?"

I nodded. Even though still a child, I could appreciate how our fortunes had declined. It seemed that every year we had to sell some property and move into a smaller house.

Don Benito placed his hand on my shoulder. "Red Hand has agreed to help us and, to cement that alliance, our families will be joined. He is giving us his little daughter to raise in our home. When she is fifteen years old, she will marry Esteban and thus the peace will continue for generations. This is a good thing." He nodded, persuaded by his own words.

"And to ensure the safety of his daughter, I have agreed that you will live with his family, but only for half the year." Don Benito looked very weary as he spoke the word. "This is a hard thing, *mi hijo*."

It took a moment for the import of his message to be absorbed by my brain. A hard thing, I thought. This is a splendid thing! For six months out of the year I would be able to ride and play with these *Indios broncos* and not have to listen to the droning catechisms and grammar lessons of Father Alonso. But seeing my father's doleful expression, I betrayed no excitement. Nodding solemnly, I said, "As you wish, *Papi*."

Such filial devotion nearly brought a tear to Don Benito's eyes. He embraced me quickly and tightly, then turned away. "Get some things together, *mi hijo*," he ordered, his voice thick with emotion. "A change of clothes, a blanket, and your *sombrero*. Don't forget your *sombrero*! We can't have you returning to your mother this fall as dark as these *Indios*." A pained expression crossed his face. "*Ay*, your mother!" he groaned, imagining her reaction when he told her what he had done.

By the time the sun was fully up, the People had already struck camp and were ready to travel back onto the plains. Father stood beside my horse, facing Red Hand who was already mounted. At a gesture, Red Hand's wife came forward with a somber-looking little girl of about four. She had a small bundle in her hand and her buckskin dress was plain and unadorned. Her black hair was cut short and formed a line just above her dark eyes. At a nudge from her mother, she marched bravely forward to stand beside my father. Looking down at the ground, her lip trembled, but she refused to cry.

Don Benito scooped her up into his big arms and announced, "We shall call you Amada, little serious one. You will be fine with us." Still stiff, Amada continued to look at the ground, but her little hand gripped my father's collar tightly.

Turning to me, my father patted my leg and said softly *"Vaya con Dios, Torrito."* It had been many years since he had used that nickname. When I was very little, I was solid and short and scowling most of the time, so I came to be called the little bull. Such a sign of affection from Don Benito had me blinking back tears, but I resolved to shoulder the responsibilities of my newly bestowed manhood, and responded, "And equally with you, *señor.*" I urged my horse forward beside Red Hand.

Through Jaime, Red Hand said, "We shall meet again, Don Benito, when the geese fly." Glancing at me, he added, "The Little Spaniard will be fine with us." Turning his horse's head we, the People and I, the Little Spaniard as I came to be called, rode off toward the open plains.

I'd vowed to myself that I would not look back, but after a hundred yards, I stole a glance while pretending to adjust my stirrup. My father was mounted now, with Amada seated before him in the saddle. I could barely hear his *"Vámanos!"* as he turned and led my kinsmen back up the valley, back to Santa Fe, back to my home.

Chapter Two

From the distance of nearly a century, it may seem to you a monstrous thing for a father to do, entrusting his youngest son to a people renowned for their merciless warfare. But from this remote vantage, you can not appreciate the harsh realities that confronted us at that time. We, the Spanish of New Mexico, were nearly two thousand miles from the seat of government in Mexico City. The six hundred miles from Santa Fe to Chihuahua were so sparsely settled and hostile as to be a veritable wilderness. We were isolated and alone, fewer than ten thousand in number, just another tribe, so to speak, among many sharing this beautiful but unforgiving land. As in the vying kingdoms of medieval Europe, alliances were formed and hostages were exchanged, not to establish dominance, but merely to survive in a cruel world.

I never doubted my father's love, but it was understood that the Spanish community and the family Garcia, both present and future, must take precedence over any individual member. Indeed, for the individual to survive, the community that sustains him must survive, that much remains true. Although not explicitly stated I, as the second son, was the more logical one to be put at risk. To the first born went the responsibilities of stewardship. The younger sons were expected to either act as loyal lieutenants to their elder or to remove themselves to the priesthood or elsewhere so as not to challenge or interfere with the authority of the first born. Thus has it always been among our people and I have no quarrel with it.

While Red Hand might not have understood the system of primogeniture, he would have appreciated my father's subtlety in presenting me, the more expendable of his sons, as hostage to their alliance. As I learned, Red Hand and Don Benito had much in common. The daughter my father had named Amada, was also expendable. She had been born a twin. Among the Comanche, the birth of twins was so unusual as to be considered unnatural. Frequently such children were left to die after birth to prevent any misfortune befalling the People by their presence. Fortunately for Amada, Red Hand dearly loved his wife, and his wife, She Who Walks Far, was far more tender-hearted than the average. Red Hand grudgingly acceded to her request to spare the children, but at some cost.

The boy was treated as if he had no twin sister. He was given a name, trained by his mother's uncles and spoiled greatly by his parents, while poor Amada was scorned by all except her mother. Indeed, my father's bestowing of 'Amada' was the first name she had ever had. Once entrusted to my family it was as if she had never existed among the People. They saw her departure as a stroke of good fortune since it meant the burden of the curse of twins had been lifted from them. The evil of twins was thus exorcised from among them to great advantage.

On that first day, of course, I knew none of this. I was on my own. A man of his word, my father had released Juan and Jaime from service, so that I had no one to even interpret for me. Red Hand, like many Comanche, knew a few words of Spanish but preferred to conceal that fact when dealing with most Spaniards. As it happens, I discovered that I had been blessed by our Creator with a facile ability to learn languages, so it required only a few weeks of miming and mistakes for me to become passably conversant in the Nermernuh tongue—Nermernuh being their name for themselves while Comanche is derived from a Ute word for enemies.

Looking back, I can compare our ride down the valley of the Pecos to a sort of second birth experience for me. From that time, I passed beyond the self-absorption of infancy and the unfiltered perception of childhood, to an awareness of myself in relation to my surroundings. In other words, I went from being an observer of life to being a participant in it.

We traveled until a short time before sunset, moving at a slow but steady pace out onto the sun-drenched plains to the east. When the peace chief signaled that it was time to make camp, I went with Red Hand and the other men to tend to the needs of our horses, but my fascination was captured by the efficiency of the women. In less than a quarter of an hour, I would estimate, they were able to erect the lodges and have the cooking fires burning. First, they would raise the four foundation poles that were some ten to twelve feet in length, lashed together at the top. Once thus properly anchored, other poles would fill the framework in between. Then, standing on each other's shoulders, the women would lift the buffalo hide outer covering up over the poles, fastening it at the top. Finally, an inner tenting of hides would be suspended to shield the sleeping robes. While it may astound some of the more cultured of my countrymen, I must say that a Comanche lodge is a very comfortable shelter—cool and breezy with the sides rolled up in the summer, snug and warm and well ventilated in the winter.

All of the lodges opened to the east to greet the morning sun. One did not move about the interior of a Comanche lodge in a haphazard manner, as we might move about a room. Rather, upon entering, one always moved in the direction of the sun, from east to south, to west, to north, being careful to step around, rather than over, individuals. As I discovered, there was a certain amount of ceremony involved in virtually everything that the People did.

After currying the horses and turning them out under the watchful eyes of the young sentries, Red Hand took me to his lodge for the evening meal. I must confess that I was famished. In my excitement, I had eaten very little that morning and the Comanche were not accustomed to taking a midday meal. Their main meals were morning and evening with otherwise no more than a Spartan handful of jerky or pemmican while in the saddle. Thus it was that I joined the family meal with an appetite that gratified Walks Far who, like most women, liked to see her cooking appreciated.

Mealtime etiquette would probably seem rude to us, with each family member reaching into a common pot, but it began with an expression of thanks to the Creator and was accompanied by laughter and mundane conversation as with any happy family. Huge amounts of food could be consumed at a sitting. The People led a hard and demanding life and everything they did, they did robustly whether joyfully in good times when there were great feasts or uncomplainingly in the hard times of famine. Unlike some tribes of my acquaintance, the Comanche were quite particular as to what they would eat, having certain proscribed animals that they considered unclean. For example, they would generally avoid eating turkey despite that bird's abundance on the eastern ranges of Comancheria. They feared that eating turkey would make a person timid or cowardly. Similarly, they would avoid fish or other animals associated with water. Nor would they eat dog, a custom for which I was grateful. The dog was too near a relative of the coyote, for whom they had great respect and admiration as 'God's dog.'

At that first meal, I met my adoptive family. Seated about the cook fire, first and foremost, was Red Hand. The best way to describe Red Hand would be to call him strong. His broad face was divided by a straight, if prominent, nose. His wide mouth was most expressive, ranging from a terrifying scowl to a luminous grin. His normal expression was one of suppressed mirth. He possessed wide shoulders and an extremely broad chest upon which tattoos circled and highlighted the scars he had received in combat. His vanity centered on his hair, which hung in two long braids to his waist. He gathered his topknot into a smaller braid from which hung a pair of eagle feathers. He kept his hair well oiled so that it shone with the blue-black luster of a raven's wing. The part in the center of his hair was painted red, and from his ears hung an assortment of wires and shells. The only other remarkable thing about his appearance was the contrast between Red Hand mounted and Red Hand afoot. When astride his horse, his massive upper body made him appear a virtual giant, while dismounted, his short, bowed legs gave him an awkward, rolling gait. Perhaps for this reason, he conducted most of his business, even visiting around the camp, from horseback.

Red Hand's wife, She Who Walks Far, was of quite a different appearance. Unlike the men, Nermernuh women tended to disdain their hair, clipping it short at the shoulders and straight across above their eyes. During my time among them, I must say, the women were always extremely modest, clothing the nakedness of even the infant girls. Like the men, women were fond of painting themselves in a variety of colors, but most of their effort went into adorning their blouses and skirts with beautifully colored porcupine quill work or shells. The mother of Walks Far had been a captive from another tribe somewhere to the east and the result had been a daughter of quite delicate proportions. Her refined features and slender limbs were as different from her husband's as it was possible, and yet the affection between the two was always evident.

Walks Far and her younger sister served the men at meals. Seated beside Red Hand was his father, who looked remarkably like his son, except for his clouded eyes, the result of some unknown ailment, and a twisted leg that had been shattered in combat some years before and had not healed properly. When I knew him, Four Bears hobbled about the camp with the aid of a branch and required the assistance of his son to mount his horse. Despite his constant pain and poor eyesight, Four Bears was valued for his ability to make arrows that flew truly, his talent for telling stories of the People's history, and for his wisdom. For these qualities, he was the band's peace chief.

Beside me, the fourth male at that first meal was Amada's twin brother. He was quite a handsome little boy, taking the best features of both parents. It was the custom among the People to bestow names quite casually on small children, realizing that some time around their twelfth or thirteenth year, they would receive a vision that would form the basis of their adult name. When I first met this young boy, he was known by a most unflattering name which I shall translate as He Who Breaks Wind. In the Nermernuh tongue, it is shorter and far more crude. I shall refer to him as Windy.

I have already devoted more space to my time among the Comanche during those years than I intended, but let me relate briefly a few incidents and perhaps the Lord will permit me adequate time in the future to relate more of my numerous experiences among the Indians.

The arrangement with my father was that, in return for the exchange of children and the twice yearly trade fairs, the band of Four Bears would come to assist my father in punitive raids against other tribes who might try to steal livestock from our herds. During the first month I spent with the People, no such call came, so we set about the business of hunting the herds of buffalo that were drifting north with the springtime grasses. Only a few years ago, I had occasion to cross some of that same country and, I must say, that my heart was heavy as I compared the past with the present. Where once lush grasslands stretched unbroken to the farthest horizon, and every kind of wild animal lived and flew in abundance, now there is only silence and emptiness, the earth dusty and bare beneath the hooves of cattle. Looking back on my memories, I felt somewhat as Adam must have felt looking back on Eden.

I and the other children could not take part in the actual slaughter of the buffalo. This was something the men did under the direction of a hunt leader, but we came along with the women to butcher and clean the mighty beasts. Each family would descend on the animals marked by their warriors' arrows. Dragging the great animals onto their bellies, all four legs splayed out, the hide would be cut along the spine and carefully peeled away from the carcass. Then, every part of the creature would be carved and packaged, nothing going to waste. The meat racks of camp were filled with sun-drying morsels and every pot, even those of families who had no able provider, were filled. Each evening, the drums would sound and the People would sing and dance for joy at the bounty of the earth shared with them. I was only vaguely aware of the revelry during that first hunt, so exhausted was I by the grueling work of butchery. Never before had I worked so hard, but by the end of the month my muscles had developed to where I would sit in the firelight, as brown and happy as my adoptive tribe.

Sometime in May, my father sent word to Red Hand that Apache raiders had swept down on our lands, killing sheep and stealing horses. These same high plains which the People now roamed, had once been home to the Apache, so it was with glee that Red Hand prepared to do combat with the old enemy on behalf of the new friend. Before leaving, he moved the camp to a protected canyon and left a few disappointed warriors behind to guard us. And so it went over the next three years. I was too young to go, but two or three times each year, the Comanche came in force to assist my family against the Apache, the Navajo or the Ute. Each fall, before the first snowfall, I would be delivered back to the pueblo on the Pecos and each spring I would rejoin the People.

In the third year, certain events changed my life forever. It must have been early in September when the warriors left to aid my father against the distant Navajo. We were left in camp near the *Rio Colorado,* or Canadian River as it is now called. Red Hand had been gone only a few days when we were startled from our sleeping robes by the excited barking of the camp dogs and the rumble of hoof beats.

"Pawnee!" someone yelled. We heard a crackle of gunfire and everyone started scrambling from their lodges. The Comanche had only a few firearms at this time, but some of the ancient enemies of the People to the east had acquired many weapons from traders who came to the plains from Canada, St. Louis and New Orleans.

Walks Far struggled to help Four Bears up and out of the lodge, calling for me to help their son. "Little Spaniard! Grab Windy and bring him quickly!" Her sister was gathering *parfleches* which resembled our modern saddlebags and were filled with dried food.

Windy was still quite small, so I picked him up in my arms and ran with him up the canyon to a grove of scrub oak and cottonwood. People were screaming behind us as the enemy rode through the camp, shooting indiscriminately at all who moved. The few Comanche warriors left to protect the camp had been diverted by the initial enemy assault on the horse herd, so that there was virtually no resistance to the attack on the People.

Reflexively, I dropped Windy and covered him with my body, peering back through the underbrush in the hope of seeing my family. To his credit, Windy did not cry or complain at my rough treatment, he merely punched me in the ribs until I shifted enough to allow him breath. He was a true Comanche.

In horror, I watched as Walks Far tugged desperately at Four Bears. The stubborn old man refused to move. Planting himself in front of the lodge, he stood facing in the general direction of the oncoming enemy and calmly strung his bow. Although nearly blind, his hearing was excellent and he must have assumed that anyone on horseback would be an attacker. He let fly half a dozen arrows in the direction of the sound of hoof beats. Remarkably, he killed one and wounded another but, before he could nock a last arrow, a screaming rider rode him down, striking him with his hatchet. Walks Far was also knocked down by the charging horse. She lay stunned and helpless on the ground as the rider reined his horse and whirled for another charge.

Before I realized what I was doing, I was on my feet and running toward Walks Far. My heart pounded in my ears and my lungs screamed a long continuous "No!" as I strained to reach her before the enemy. God must have blessed my short legs that day because, just at the moment when the warrior raised his arm to strike, I launched myself wildly into the air. My body struck his just beneath his raised arm and carried him out of the saddle. He landed heavily on the ground with me on top of him, pummeling his face furiously with my fists. This brief combat was interrupted by Walks Far's younger sister who had snatched up Four Bears' bow and arrows. Knocking me aside with her hip, she coolly loosed an arrow into the throat of the hapless raider. He lay pinned to the ground, bleeding to death even as he drowned in his own blood. Formidable women, these Comanche!

Younger Sister was helping Walks Far to her feet. Around us the chaos continued. Several lodges had collapsed on their own cooking fires and were now ablaze. Everything was happening much too fast.

"Kiyi!" We three turned as one at the sound of Windy's childish war cry. He had run from the shelter of the brush, with rocks in his little hands, to do battle with the enemy, true to his warrior heritage.

Walks Far gasped, "My son!" her words pitching up into a scream as an enemy raider reached down and snatched the child off of the ground, tossing him face down across the saddle in front of him.

I was stricken by my failure to protect Windy, so I

ran off after the horseman, perhaps hoping to repeat my earlier feat. But before I could reach him, the sound of hoof beats thundered up behind me. I half turned in time to take a glancing blow from a rifle butt on the side of my face. I heard a roaring in my ears and the bright light of pain faded into a gathering darkness of red, as I lost consciousness. I was only distantly aware of rough hands lifting me and throwing me like baggage across the withers of a horse, then all became black.

Chapter Three

The harsh and demanding existence of most Indian tribes was particularly hard on women and children. It was difficult for a woman to bring a child safely to birth through the full term of her pregnancy and it was difficult for those born to survive the rigors and hazards that confronted Indian children, a point that I very nearly illustrated. In any event, it was a common practice among the tribes to slaughter their adult adversaries without mercy while seeking to capture small children to raise as their own.

It was my good fortune to be small for my age, so I was not killed but was considered young enough to be taken, as a slave, back to the enemy village near a river to the east. Neither then nor now was I certain of the exact location. I regained consciousness within a few hours but it was several days before the throbbing pain in my head subsided. We rode on through the night and then another day before making camp. Even then, the raiders dared not light any campfires for fear of being seen by possible pursuers. That night I lay with my arms around Windy as two other Comanche boys huddled close for warmth. The object of the raid had been horses and they had taken hundreds from our herd. We children were an incidental benefit.

The next morning, our captors spent some time in grooming and applying paint so that they could look properly resplendent when they entered their village in triumph. They plucked hairs from each other's faces and combed and stiffened the hair at the crown of their heads into roaches that they wore as a kind of taunt to their enemies, daring them to try to take their scalps. When they were satisfied with their appearance, we mounted and slowly pushed the horses the last few miles. Coming up on a bluff overlooking the river, our captors began to howl in triumph as they kicked into a canter and swooped with their prizes down into their village.

By now I had discovered that my captors were not true Pawnee. Rather, they were members of a people known to us as the Taovayas, although the French would refer to them as Black Pawnee. While related to the Pawnee, they had split off from that tribe at some earlier time and, under pressure from the European-armed Osage, had been drifting south toward the *Tejas* settlements ever since.

For many years, these Taovayas had earned great wealth and distorted their own society by capturing other Indians and selling them as slaves to the French in Louisiana. But when the Spanish took control of Louisiana, Indian slavery had been outlawed. Still, the poison had entered the body of the tribe and slave holding had become a means of achieving status and wealth.

Unlike the Comanche, the Taovaya were not wanderers. Rather, they lived in villages protected by walls and moats. Their houses were round and made of woven grasses and willow poles over a solid cedar framework. Sleeping platforms encircled a central fire pit. A brush arbor provided a shady place for housework during the heat of the day. Curiously, unmarried young women were closely chaperoned and placed in a small hut of their own to sleep. This hut was elevated on stilts and the ladder used for access was taken down every night by their protective parents, leaving the girl in lofty and, it was hoped, lonely isolation until morning.

The villages were surrounded by quite extensive fields of corn, pumpkins, melons, beans and squashes. Beyond the fields, though, lurked a formidable array of enemies—Osage, Tonkawas, Apache and the pressures and diseases of the Europeans.

Certainly, at that point, I was feeling no great affection for them either. Rather than giving into despair, however, I had tried to keep track of the distances we covered each day and the landmarks we passed in the hope that somehow we might find our way back to the People again. I say 'we' because I had determined to take Windy, at least, safely back with me. He had, after all, been my responsibility.

After the war party's heroic entrance to the village,

there had been much boasting and reenacting of their exploits. A feast and a dance were planned for that evening to celebrate the great victory. My particular captor dragged me by the arm to his house where he presented me to his wife. That gentle lady then picked up a piece of firewood with which she proceeded to beat me about my arms and shoulders all the while lecturing me, I presumed, on the perils of disobedience. After that, a leather thong was pulled tightly around my neck and I was tied like a dog to the base post of the 'maiden's tower.' It was clear to me that I was not to be adopted as a son, but rather, used as a slave.

Although hardly endearing by her manner, I must admit that Taovaya women were, on the whole, quite handsome. Small and quite dark complected, they sought to enhance an otherwise winsome appearance by extensive tattoos on the face and body.

This will no doubt sound quite barbaric to you, my grandson, as a modern reader, but I would urge you to consider the cosmetic lengths modern women will go to achieve a less indelible, but no less artificial, effect intended to allure and enhance whatever natural beauty they might possess.

I might add that Taovaya men were not averse to tattoos. Many of the men were tattooed on both eyelids, with a short line extending out from the corner of their eye. Not surprisingly, their name for themselves was 'raccoon-eyed people.' Tattoos also decorated the corners of their mouth and the backs of their hands, arms and chest. The effect was completed by several ornaments dangling from each ear.

Over the next two days, I tried very hard to act as

docile and obedient as I could. By the third day, the lady of the house decided to test me by taking me with her to haul water and gather firewood. She kept a long willow switch readily at hand in case she cared to emphasize her instructions. The next day we spent harvesting crops from the garden, shucking corn and again fetching wood and water.

For three more days, I maintained my servile demeanor until, finally, after a week of hard usage, she pointed me toward the fields with only some harsh sounding instructions. She intended to take her leisure that day. My patience had been rewarded. I completed my chores faithfully over the next few days but each day I would explore the village a little more. Soon I learned where each of the Comanche children had been placed, where the horses were pastured and noted something of the village routine. The other boys had been more kindly received than I and, though closely watched, were being groomed for adoption.

At that time of year, in that country, thunderstorms were frequent and violent—great crashing, flashing tempests that I hoped I might use to some advantage. I made my plans, and prayed that God would somehow lead us home.

We had been there two weeks when I decided we must try to escape or be trapped there all winter. During the course of the day, I managed to approach each of the Comanche children and whisper instructions. If a storm occurred that night, I told them to slip away and meet me by the corn fields after their captors were asleep. As the sun set, clouds formed on the horizon and the muttering of distant thunder could be heard.

I had one immediate concern. I had been tethered every night to the posts supporting the daughter's aerie and though it was an easy matter to cut the leather thong with a sharp rock I'd found by the garden, I could see the daughter's eyes watching me through a crack in the floor every night. She was a dark, pretty girl only slightly older than I. I did not know if she would raise an alarm, but I had to risk it. When night had fallen, her watchful eyes merely blinked as I cut the thong and slipped away to the fields. I can only assume that she felt pity for me.

After what seemed an interminable wait, first one, then a second child joined me and, finally, after a period of anguish, Windy also crouched beside me. I thanked God that these were Comanche boys and not Spanish. They waited for my instructions in disciplined silence without questions or comments.

We could do nothing without horses. On foot, we had little chance of survival and far less of escape. We crept along the river to near where the horses were pastured. By now the thunder was louder and the dark clouds were filled with lightning. The charged air had made the horses skittish. They stirred and nickered as they nervously watched us approach.

I particularly hoped to reclaim a painted stallion that belonged to Red Hand. By good fortune, I spotted him near the edge of the herd. Several Comanche mares crowded near him. The sentries seemed more intent on studying the weather than their charges. On our bellies, we crawled slowly among the horses. I spoke softly in Comanche and patted them reassuringly on their shoulders and chests.

When I reached the stallion, rain began to fall in big, cold drops. I grabbed him by his halter and boosted Windy onto his back. Reaching for the nearest horse, a large and placid mare, I placed the next boy on her back and repeated it with the last child on a second mare. Through the increasing deluge of rain I led the stallion slowly through the herd to the side furthest from the village. Just then, the storm gave a deafening clap of thunder and a bolt of lightning crashed into a tree on the far side of the river. Instantly, the tree was ablaze.

Swinging up on the halter, I clambered behind Windy and kicked my heels as hard as I could into the horse's flanks. Already nervous from the storm, he needed little urging. Like an explosion, we burst from the herd and flew up the bluff above the river, the two of us clinging desperately to his mane and to each other.

The moment we emerged from the herd, two things occurred. The first was a tremendous thunderclap and a bolt of lightning that actually struck the village council house. Made of wood and grass, the building was immediately engulfed in flames. The attention of the entire village was absorbed by the conflagration. The second occurrence was equally remarkable. Perhaps it was the noise and confusion that caused a stampede, but the stallion we were riding was followed by the two mares bearing the Comanche boys, which were followed by the rest of the Comanche horses which, in turn, were followed by the entire Taovaya herd.

It was a ride I have never forgotten. The lightning flashed and the thunder boomed and there were we four children riding at the head of a huge *remuda* of horses like corks on the crest of a mighty ocean wave. Thus we charged through the turbulent night for what seemed an eternity. We finally outran the storm and emerged into the gentle light of a bright, full moon. The wet grass looked like molten silver as it rippled in the night winds. The shadows cast by the trees in the ravines were dense and inky black.

Our pace slowed as the storm receded behind us. I quickly oriented myself by the few landmarks I could recognize and by the familiar twinkle of the North Star at my right hand. We loped along in a westerly direction above the river. We rode, without stopping, throughout the night. Fortunately, Comanche children are taught to ride almost before they learn to walk. Even as they nodded in fatigue, the little horsemen clung steadfastly to their mounts.

By the next morning, a few of the Taovaya horses began to slow and turn back. Thinking like a Comanche, Windy looked up at me through bleary eyes of exhaustion and said, "Elder brother, we should ride at the back so we can keep all the ponies as our prizes."

Because our stallion was the leader, I did not dare take him to the back lest he turn the herd. Instead, we rode alongside another horse and I leaped to its back leaving Windy on the paint stallion. I then drifted to the rear and managed to prevent any further defections.

At mid-afternoon, we saw a most welcome sight. Actually, the other three saw it first while I was choking on the dust of the herd. Riding down off a ridge came Red Hand and the other warriors, who had returned from war and immediately taken up the trail of their lost children. When I finally saw the Comanche warriors take up position to drive the herd, I nearly wept with joy and relief. But at such a time, a Comanche warrior does not weep, he rides on. I rode on.

Chapter Four

Our return to the camp was the occasion for great celebration. Not only had the lost children been recovered and all of our horses, but our honor had been redeemed by the plunder of the Taovaya ponies. The joy was tempered by sadness, though. Four Bears was dead, as were two women and one of the other warriors.

Four Bears had lingered for nearly two weeks after the attack. He had known that his death was inevitable and had begged to be placed on his horse one last time so that he could ride out on the plains alone to die. Ordinarily, such a request from an old man would have been honored but Four Bears, as peace chief, was the most respected member of the People and a council would have to be called to find his replacement. With the majority of the warriors away, this decision would have to be postponed, so Walks Far nursed the old man faithfully until impatient death intervened the day before Red Hand returned.

According to the custom of the People, Four Bears was bathed and clothed in his finest apparel, then his legs were bent up to his chest and his head tilted forward to rest on his knees. A rawhide rope was used to bind the body in this position. He was then laid on a blanket to await the return of his warrior son.

Walks Far and Younger Sister then mourned the passing of the noble old man by gashing their legs and arms with a knife, cutting off their hair, and painting their faces black. Four Bears' name was never spoken again. The burial could be delayed no longer. On the day of our return, the body was wrapped in a blanket and placed on his favorite pony. Younger Sister sat behind to hold the body in place. With Red Hand riding alongside, we all followed as the body was taken to a crevice in the rocky wall near the head of the canyon. Gently, Four Bears was propped in a sitting position facing the sunrise and a pile of stones was assembled to seal the body off from scavengers. The camp was struck that same day as the People moved off for deeper canyons further south where they would make their winter camp.

Despite their grief at the loss, my family was overjoyed at the recovery of their only son. Walks Far embraced the boy and gripped him so fiercely it seemed as if she would never let him go. Looking over his head, she gazed at me as tears washed through the paint on her cheeks. I became embarrassed by the unwavering gratitude of her stare so that I had to look away to keep from weeping myself. In Windy's account of our adventures, he'd given me far more credit than I deserved.

Red Hand stood before me and placed his hands on my shoulders. Speaking with great gravity, he said, "Little Spaniard, I give you a new name this day. You are the Little Spaniard Who Leads the Children of His People and the Horses of His Enemies Home." Fortunately, such a ponderous label would ordinarily be shortened in daily usage to something more manageable such as He Who Leads or Little Horse or simply Leads. In future years, I continued to be known mainly as the Little Spaniard.

Leading me a little distance away, Red Hand informed me that the time had come for me to return to my family in Santa Fe. The next morning two warriors were appointed to take me as far as the Pecos pueblo where my father was no doubt already waiting.

The morning meal was quieter than usual as each of us tried to contain a welter of emotions. The usually reserved family embraced me each in turn then, after I had mounted, Red Hand led his prize pinto stallion forward and handed me its lead rope.

"It is a small thing for the life of one's son," he said solemnly. "But now I have two sons." He looked at me closely to be sure I understood. I nodded, unable to speak. "My heart will be heavy until I see you in the time of green grass." So saying, he slapped my horse on the rump and sent us on our way, with me leading the beautiful horse that had carried me to freedom.

I looked back once as we were about to cross the ridge. Red Hand was still standing with Windy and

Walks Far at his side. He raised his hand in a final salute and then he was beyond my sight. It was the last time I ever saw him.

It seems that we brought back more than horses from the Taovaya village. Through contact with the Europeans and Indians to the east, smallpox had entered the Taovaya camp. From what I could later learn, one of the Comanche boys had been taken into a Taovaya family that had only just lost a son to the dreaded disease. He had probably slept beneath the same blankets that had covered the dead boy.

Red Hand's people were part of the Antelope, or Kwahadi, branch of the Comanche and were considered the most aloof. They rarely came into contact with Europeans. They seemed to have no resistance whatsoever to any of the ailments common among us. Something as deadly as smallpox, could wipe out entire bands in less than a week.

One of the warriors accompanying me, Yellow Eagle Circling, was the father of the infected boy. In his gratitude for my part in returning his son, he had asked to be allowed to escort me to my family. We camped that night in a shallow arroyo that had two live cottonwood trees and one lightning blasted one that now stood hollow and ghostly white. We hobbled our horses and rolled into our sleeping robes beside the glowing embers of our fire. In the morning, Yellow Eagle was dead and my other companion delirious with fever.

Fighting panic, I wrapped Yellow Eagle in his buffalo robe and, with difficulty, dragged him a short distance away. On horseback, I located a small spring about a quarter of a mile up the arroyo and filled my buffalo gut canteen with water. I raced back to camp. My companion, whose full name I don't recall but who was known as Kills Something, was aflame with fever, his face a mask of livid pustules. Struggling against my horror, I bathed his ravaged face and poured a few drops of water into his mouth. Finally, I soaked his hair with what was left of the water in a desperate attempt to extinguish his fiery fever.

In a few moments, his eyes opened and sought my face. In a raspy voice, he said, "Little Spaniard, young one! My *puha* has abandoned me." *Puha* was the spiritual power bestowed on a man through a vision. "I will die now," he continued. "Follow the sun to your homeland. Be strong-hearted!" His voice was fading, choking, but he repeated, "Be strong-hearted!" He was gone.

I sat back on my heels and wept. My tears burned like acid. I felt weary and pained. I was unaware that the fever was beginning to rise in me. After a time, I stopped crying and struggled to my feet. I now had a raging thirst, so I staggered to my horse and, with difficulty, remounted. We plodded back to the spring where I drank and bathed my head. The other horses, despite their hobbles, had made their way up to drink as well. I filled my water sack and, oblivious of my horse, trudged on foot back to our charnel camp.

I do not know how long I sat there, my body flushing with fever, my back leaning against the trunk of the dead cottonwood. My mind would wander far away and then return to some kind of numb awareness again. I was conscious of the warmth of the sun on my face but could find no energy to move to the shade of the other trees. At one point, I had the sensation of waking to a perfect stillness. Red Hand stood before me once again, his hands on my shoulders, looking benevolently into my face. Behind Red Hand, stood Walks Far, Windy, Younger Sister, Four Bears, and all the rest of the People in a line that stretched beyond the horizon.

I could feel other hands that I knew to be my father's holding me firmly from behind. I could not see, but I knew that an innumerable host of people were lined up behind him. My left and right hands were gripped by warm and gentle hands, but I was unable to turn my head to discover their identities. Again, though, I knew that other people were beside them, stretching to infinity and that each person in every line was connected to his neighbor by a tender touch.

Red Hand spoke a single word, paused and repeated it, with a smile. "*Paz*," he said. "Peace." In my dream, he spoke the word in Spanish. I do not know if the Comanche have a word for the kind of peace which I understood him to mean. Certainly, even Spanish is inadequate to express, not just an absence of conflict, but a rightness, a balance, a harmony of all things. Such a peace must have reigned on the sixth day of creation when God declared, "It is good!"

"*Paz*," he kept repeating until finally, it was drowned by a roaring in my ears that reached a crescendo and I awoke to a terrible crashing. Night had fallen, and was alive with thunder. Serpents of lightning writhed across the sky. With unbearable weariness, I crawled inside the hollow trunk of the cottonwood, seeking shelter from the storm, the Taovaya, and all the tragedy and sorrow of life. I wept again as I thought of the peace that Red Hand and all my relatives had sought to bestow on me in the vision. Soon, the very heavens broke down and cried with me. Great, drumming drops of rain beat against my hollow shelter.

I remember very little else. Apparently, concerned that I was so long overdue, Don Benito had left the Pecos and ridden out on the plains in the desperate hope of finding me somewhere at the bottom of that awesome sky. A Pecos Indian who accompanied him, guided him to the spring where the horses continued to linger. Searching the arroyo, they found the bodies of my friends but almost failed to find me in my dead tree. According to my father, my delirium and a merciful God had induced me to begin reciting the *Pater Nostre.* The whisper of the Lord's Prayer led them to my sanctuary.

In a few days I was back in Santa Fe, not in my own room for fear of infecting the rest of the family, but on a pallet quickly devised in a horse stall behind our house. Later, the straw and blankets were burned. My father personally tended to me during my illness. As a young man, he had survived the smallpox and was now immune to its evil. From the time he found me in the tree, he kept everyone away from me and carried me in his two strong arms night and day on the journey home. Actually, during my childhood, an immunization program for smallpox had begun in New Mexico, but I had been out on the plains with Red Hand and had not been inoculated.

Somehow, I lived. For nearly a week I lay, drifting in and out of consciousness, not able to distinguish one state from the other. Finally, the fever broke. I opened my eyes to discover myself lying on my side looking out the entrance of the stall. The sun was not yet up, but the yard was suffused with the grey pre-dawn light. My father sat with his back against the rough plank wall, his knees pulled up and his head resting on his forearms. He was asleep.

"Pápi!" I whispered through a throat that was dry and raw. *"Señor!"* My voice was a more audible croak the second time.

With a start, Don Benito looked up. His eyes were bloodshot, his face drawn and haggard. For the first time in my life, I think, I looked at my father and saw, not his strength and authority, but his age and humanity. At that time he must have been over forty years old.

"Torrito?" He knelt beside me and studied my face closely. What he saw must have reassured him for he smiled and sighed in relief.

"Don Benito?" a small voice called from outside the stall. "I have brought you food."

"Wait there, *mi hija!*" my father instructed. To me he explained, "It's Amada. Every day as I tend to you, she tends to me." He threw off my blankets and, wrapping me in his own *serape,* he lifted me up and carried me outside. Birds were beginning to sing in the trees, conferring on their southbound plans for the day. "My own daughters still lie asleep in their beds, but Amada," he smiled down at the child who stood with a stack of cloth covered *tortillas*, a serious expression on her dark face, "*aqui esta!* Here she is, the faithful one." Speaking to her, he said, "Today we shall eat inside. Jose too! We shall all eat inside."

"Will Jose be alright now, *señor*? Will he live?" Her dark eyes were opened wide.

My father laughed with relief. "Yes, Amada, by the

mercy of God, he will live for a very long time. Death has taken the measure of my son and found him to be a most worthy opponent. Yes, he will live." Don Benito laughed again. "He will live!"

And so I have, perhaps longer than I should have wanted. It seems that I have outlived practically all that is familiar and dear to me. But God has His reasons and He does not need to consult me on such matters.

I was very weak that winter, spending much time in my bed. The months that I spent at home were usually devoted to my education. My mother would send me to the priests to be instructed in my grammar and catechism, but this year, I was not even able to leave the house for a long time. Instead, my mother would have me read to her from the few books that we had in our home. Although she herself could read only with great difficulty, she made me swear by the Virgin that what I was reading to her was correct and she would then judge me by my speed and fluency.

Amada too, spent a great deal of time with me during those months. She was a lonely child. My sisters were all quite a bit older than she and had no time for childish play, and I am afraid that the other children of our *barrio* were rather cruel to her, taunting her for her dark skin and scorning her as an Indian. In children, it seems, both the best and the worst of our human nature are most readily apparent.

Amada would spend her time helping with the housework and the cooking, doing any task without complaint. At first, she would peek shyly into my room. When I would speak to her in Nermernuh, her eyes would sparkle. Soon I was teaching her to read Spanish as well. Since my parents did not object, we soon became good friends. She looked so much like her brother, Windy, except that where his features appeared strong and chiseled, despite his youth, hers were delicate and clear. Her hair had grown quite long and shone blue-black, persistently tumbling across her face as if she were hiding behind it. Something about her made me continually try to make her smile. There was a sadness that seemed to accompany her like a shadow.

One day in March of the year 1813, Don Benito sat me down and spoke in a serious tone. "You are nearly a man now, Jose, and I feel that you are old enough to live with truths." He placed his hand on my shoulder. "You will not be returning to Red Hand. The truth is, that we have heard from some of the Indians who have come in to trade, that the same smallpox that sought to kill you, has claimed Red Hand and all of his people."

We sat in silence. Against my will, a single tear escaped and rolled down my cheek. Pretending not to see it, my father nonetheless squeezed my shoulder softly. "He was a good man, and a true friend to our family."

Don Benito stood. "Now we have decided that you must have more education. Your mother is very impressed with your reading. However"—he cleared his throat—"I do not think that these local priests are capable of teaching you properly." My father had never forgiven them for the incident of the boundary line, an offense he held against all members of the Franciscan Order.

"For this reason, we are going to send you to your mother's relatives in the capital in Mexico. We will provide them with some gold and ask them to place you in a suitable school where you will learn all that there is to know." My father, being himself uneducated, could not, of course, fully appreciate the magnitude of the assignment he had given me.

And so it was that in the spring of that year, I again left my home and family, this time heading south on the Royal Highway from Santa Fe to El Paso del Norte, from El Paso to Chihuahua, to Parral and then to Mexico City. I traveled in the company of a squad of dragoons who were carrying messages and taxes from the governor to the viceroy in the capital.

In the splendid home of my cousins, the Alvarados, I was made to feel very much like a poor, rustic relation but they took their familial obligations seriously. It was not easy, however. In those years, following the uprising of Hidalgo, Mexico was in great turmoil. Education was in the hands of priests, and some priests like the lamented Father Hidalgo sided with the aspirations of the people seeking justice through independence from Spain, while others sided with the Spaniards and *Criollos* who wanted to maintain Spanish, or at least non-Indian or Mestizo, rule. To further complicate the matter, Don Benito's prejudice against Franciscans, who were everywhere in Mexico, made it virtually impossible to find a suitable school for me.

So it was that in the sweltering month of September, I found myself embarking on a ship bound from Vera Cruz for Havana and from there on to the United States. It took well over a year and many adventures but in the year 1815 I landed in the City of Baltimore in the United States of America. From there, I proceeded by a small coastal trader up the Potomac River to the city of Washington. From the malodorous dock at Georgetown, I could see a spire rising through the trees on the bluff above. The Jesuit College in Georgetown was to be my home for the next four years, until tragedy should again call me home to Santa Fe.

Chapter Five

The college at Georgetown was founded for the express purpose of educating the sons of planters and of Indian Chiefs. I was neither, but educated I was, regardless. The Jesuit Fathers were a mixture of nationalities. There were fiery Irishmen, banished from their homeland, urbane French, refugees from both the reign of terror and that of Napoleon, and there was my own mentor, Father Saavedra from Castile in Spain. Though they were of different temperaments and cultures, they were united in their love for God and for the truth. It was their conviction that the search for either would lead to the other. Both by education and experience, I too share that conviction for, truly, to embrace the tragedy of truth without the love of God would be unbearable.

Washington City at that time was a city of mud in a truer sense than is Santa Fe despite our *adobe* construction. The nascent capital had suffered at the hands of the British in the recent war, but I suspect it had not been very splendid even before the destruction that included burning the President's house. The elegant dream of L'Enfant had a far different reality in those days. The streets were little more than cattle tracks, convenient for sewage if not for transportation. The seat of government consisted mainly of a collection of boarding houses where the senators, representatives and other officials stayed—convenient to their attendant taverns and brothels. In the summer, the place would steam like a kettle and in the winter the cold would pierce like an icy lance to one's very marrow. While there were periods in the spring and fall when the countryside was quite lush and lovely, I must confess that I was homesick.

News from my family came rarely. There was the initial difficulty of getting Esteban to write on my parents' behalf, and then the letter itself would have to travel thousands of miles and several months before arriving. I recall that it was at Christmas of 1819 that the last letter reached me. As was my custom, I climbed with it up into the tower where I could read it apart from the other boys. Beneath me, the Potomac River was a ribbon of ice and the Virginia countryside was white with snow. The stark leafless trees made a fitting backdrop for the chilling news. My father was dead. His horse had shied from a snake and thrown him onto some rocks. His leg was badly broken and, despite the surgeon's best effort, gangrene had developed. In a matter of days, he had died.

I could picture Don Benito, propped up on his mattress, methodically tending to his final responsibilities, ignoring his pain, giving directions through clenched teeth. Esteban must do this, Doña Maria Elena must remember that, and, oh yes, write to Jose. *Mi torrito* must come home now.

I remained in the tower for a long time that day. My usual habit was to wait for the night and search for the North Star. From that I could orient my face toward the west and home and imagine what my family was doing, traveling there in my mind. But that night, the clouds were too thick and I could see no stars. Thoroughly chilled, I climbed back down the stairs to find Father Saavedra and tell him that I must go.

I do not remember much about the journey beyond my own sense of frustration. It seemed that everything from weather to politics conspired to delay my passage. And yet, I reasoned, there was really no need for haste. It was already too late. The expressions of love and respect must wait for a later and much different kind of homecoming. And God was wise in that, for it is only now, when I have lived more than twice the span of my father's years that I am able to truly appreciate the heroic qualities of Don Benito's character, his determination to do what must be done, and to forgive those human frailties common to us all.

It was late in August when I again rode the Royal Road beside the Rio Grande. At Albuquerque, I could no longer contain my impatience. I left my companions and traveled north alone. The western sky smoldered like a blacksmith's forge when I finally came in view of the lights of Santa Fe shimmering in the clear air. The peaks of the mountains were tinged by the sun to the color of blood. It had been a dry summer and my horse's hooves stirred the dust as we plodded through the streets of my memories. Our family had its home along the Canyon Road at this time. As I turned off from the Water Street, a single rider pounded past me turning north. I caught only a glimpse of buckskin and beard as he galloped by.

I tethered my horse and stepped through the open doorway into the central courtyard where all was noise and confusion. There was the sound of wailing women and shouting men. I grabbed the arm of a man who sought to pass, leading a crying woman whose face was partly covered by her *rebozo* shawl.

"*Señor*, what has happened here?" I implored.

He paused and shook his head. "Death has visited this place again. Don Esteban has been murdered."

My senses reeled. My brother, Esteban, dead! I leaned against the wall to steady myself. The *adobe* felt cool and gritty and real, unlike the nightmare I had come upon in my own home. After a moment, I recovered and shouldered my way through the crowd to our sitting room where a trio of women, my sisters, stood solicitously over my mother. She sat, ashen and stunned.

"*Mama*!" I called above the noise.

Dona Maria Elena looked up, startled. A frown creased her brow, then both hands flew to cover her mouth. She pushed herself out of the high-backed chair and staggered into my arms. In a choking voice, she cried, "Jose! *O, Dios mio! Dios mio*!" Her body trembled in anguish.

Frantically, I looked around the room until finally I

recognized an old man who had been with our family for many years. "Paco! For the love of God, tell me what has occurred here!" I handed my mother back to my sisters, who patted my face and shoulder in wordless greeting.

"It happened down here, Jose, just a little time ago." Paco led me from the crowded room. Like many homes in Santa Fe, ours rambled and grew as the need of the family grew. It was more a compound of connected rooms and buildings than a single edifice.

As we walked, Paco explained. "Today was the *quinceniera* of Señorita Amada. A *fandango* was held, a celebration to which all were invited. After the dancing, Senorita Amada returned to her room. Don Esteban must have heard her distress and entered to aid her when he was struck and killed." Paco shook his head. "The poor child cannot even speak. She can not even weep. She just sits."

The image of that room is in my mind today just like one of those photographs. The candles seemed to cast more shadow than light as they flickered and sputtered in the breeze through the open window. Esteban still lay crumpled on the floor, his hair matted with blood where he had been struck. Beside his body lay an iron candlestick.

I knelt beside my brother and touched his throat. There was no pulse but the flesh still had warmth to it. I jerked my hand back as if burned. "Paco, when did this happen?"

"Only just a very little time ago. Some men have gone to tell the authorities. The *alcalde* should send the *capitán* very soon, Don Jose."

"Jose?" The whisper of a woman's voice startled me. Turning to my left, I saw Amada. She was dressed in the fashion of the time in a dress of flaring skirts and a blouse that was cut low—lower than would be deemed proper today. A lace *mantilla* flowed from a comb in her black hair, and her face was a mask of white makeup which, also, was the fashion at that time. She sat as if frozen in a stiff wooden chair, her hands clenched its arms. Only her eyes moved, searching my face.

"Amada!" I moved to her chair and took her hand in mine. Her fingers were icy cold. "What has happened, *hermanita*?"

A heavily accented voice from the shadows behind the chair caused me to jump. A short, solid woman stepped closer. "A man. He come. He kill. He go now." The woman's face was expressionless, but her tone was emphatic.

"Who are you?" I asked.

Paco interceded to explain. "This is Lupita. She is the *acompañante* of the *señorita*."

His answer surprised me. Our family's fortunes had indeed improved if we could afford a chaperone for Amada. I studied the woman's face. "What tribe are you?" I asked, using both hands to make the sign for 'people.' I had learned sign language from Four Bears many years before.

She considered me for a long moment. "I am Yaqui."

How appropriate, I thought. The Yaqui were nearly as ferocious as the Comanche, and hated the Spanish far more.

"Did you see the man?" I asked.

She shook her head and would say no more.

In a tiny voice, Amada announced, "I feel sick."

Lupita wasted no time. She pulled Amada from the chair and practically carried her from the room. Amada seemed unable to walk unassisted.

Frustrated at getting so few answers to my questions, I turned to study the room. The sight of Amada had a strange effect on me. I felt more rational now, but there was an excitement in me as well. "Bring me more candles, Paco. Please."

I had been taught to track and read sign by Red Hand. As he had explained it, no creature is so small or insignificant that it does not make some kind of an impact on its surroundings. The art of tracking is simply to read the mark of that impact the way you are reading the mark of my pen's impact on this page. I tried to keep my mind off the fact that this was my brother growing cold on the floor at my feet. I had to think clearly and unemotionally as the Jesuit Fathers had instructed me.

There was little I could learn from the body. It appeared that a single blow with the candlestick had killed him. The blow had been delivered with great force just above the left temple. He lay now on his back, his legs bent to the side. On his jacket lapel there was a smudge of white similar to the makeup that the ladies wore. Perhaps he acquired that while dancing, I thought. There was about him the smell of alcohol as if he had been drinking *aguardiente*.

Finding nothing else unusual, I turned my attention

to the floor beside him. Most rooms in Santa Fe had only packed earthen floors in those days, but my family's new affluence was reflected in the wooden floor of this room. Too bad, I thought. The earth would tell me more. Taking care not to step on the space between my brother and the window, I directed Paco to hold the candles as low as he could. With my eyes as close to the floor as possible, I scanned the boards. I sighed with disappointment. My mother, or Amada, continued to be an efficient housekeeper. There was practically no dust on the floor. I could only faintly make out the mark of two different pair of feet, one small and one large. The larger ones appeared to match the shoes of my brother.

The walls and window sill were of *adobe* but I read nothing unusual from their surface. I glanced around the room again, noting the coverlet on the mattress appeared rumpled. Climbing through the window, I leaped well away from the area just beneath it. I was struck by the unusually large window with its real glass panes, a luxury in those days when most windows were small and made of mica. Glass had to come from far away and was very expensive. I was later told that my father had indulged Amada's love of openness and light. The window looked out onto a narrow space between the building and the wall that surrounded our property. The branch of a pine tree extended over the wall a few feet to the left. There was little reason for anyone to pass by this window.

As Paco leaned out with his light, I studied the dusty ground. Immediately, I was rewarded. There was a clear set of footprints beneath the window. It appeared that someone had climbed across our wall and dropped down to the ground from the branch. With his back to the wall he had stood looking in for a while without moving. The image of some shadowy figure staring at Amada through that window sent a rush of anger through me. I quickly pushed it away and continued to read the signs written on the earth.

The watcher had moved forward to the window. His weight had shifted to the balls of his feet as if he had leaned forward or climbed through the window. There was a light sprinkling of *adobe* on the ground where his body had rubbed the wall. Then there were longer strides, the weight forward like someone running, as the man returned to the tree limb and over the wall. There was a clear scuff mark where his foot had hit the outer wall in his haste to escape.

I climbed back into the room, dusting myself off as I pondered. "Paco," I asked, "this may sound odd, but were there any Indians at the *fandango* this evening?"

"Of course not!" Paco sputtered. "Why do you ask such a thing, *señor*?"

I considered for a moment longer, frowning. "Well, the person who was out there was wearing moccasins."

Capitán Rodriguez, who had arrived while I was examining the scene of the murder, seemed angry. Two of his men stood at the entrance to our house, their iron-tipped lances grounded but ready. My family and our servants were gathered in the *placita*, seated on wooden benches beside a pool made of mortared stone. Torches flared to light the night and the women clutched at their *rebozos* against the chill.

The captain had been questioning my mother when Paco and I stepped out from the *sala*. His eyes flashed and his voice snapped. "Who are you, *señor*?"

I bowed formally. "Jose Juan Garcia y Alvarado, at your service, *Capitán*."

He nodded, his lips compressed in his black beard. "You are the second son of this family, yes?"

"I am. Captain, I have examined the tragic scene and I found the mark of footprints outside the window. The person wore moccasins." This in itself was not remarkable, as many people in New Mexico wore moccasins, which we called *teguas*. But it would be unusual to wear them to a *fandango* in a good home, despite the fact that all classes of people were welcome at such a celebration.

Captain Rodriguez drummed his fingers on the hilt of his sword. To the family in general, he asked, "Does this mean anything to anyone?"

They were shaking their heads, when my eldest sister, Juanita, suddenly inhaled. "Oh no!" she exclaimed. Turning to the others, she asked, "Don't you remember that man who was here earlier? The *Norteamericano* mountain man who wanted to dance with Amada?"

Paco responded with a slap to his forehead. "*Tonto yo!* Of course, I had forgotten." He turned to me. "Yes, this *Norteamericano* was wearing moccasins like an *indio*."

"What happened?" the captain and I asked in unison.

"Well, he was good and drunk," Paco noted. "*Bien*

borracho! And he wanted to dance with the *Señorita* Amada."

"Dance!" Barbara, my youngest sister sniffed. "He just wanted to paw at her."

"Yes, it is true," Paco agreed. "She seemed very frightened by this pig. You know how shy she is. Well, Don Esteban and some of the other men, they threw him out. He stood outside the wall and shouted some things in *inglés* for a while, but then he left."

"What did . . . ?" The captain and I spoke together again.

"*Señor*, please," he snapped, holding up his hand. "If you will permit me to ask the questions, it is, for now, my responsibility." He turned back to the others. "What did this *Americano* look like?"

"He was pretty ugly," Paco nodded, looking to the others for agreement. They too nodded.

"Be more specific, please." The captain tried to restrain his frustration.

Olivia, my middle sister, found her voice. "He was very large, *Capitán.* Maybe two hands taller than you, I think. His hair was long and dirty, as was his beard . . . the color of straw."

"Very good," the captain bowed slightly. "And his attire?"

"Like an *indio*," Olivia nodded. "You know, animal hide shirt with fringe on the sleeves. His pants the same, I think. And moccasins, yes." She glanced at me. "He wore moccasins."

"With your permission, *Capitán*," I interrupted. "Was there any design or decoration on his clothing?"

"Why yes. Along the shoulders and sleeves."

"Could you describe it?"

"No, Jose!" she said in exasperation. "I was not so interested in this man."

Captain Rodriguez frowned at me. "I fail to see why any of that is relevant."

"Just one question more, please," I begged. "This design, was it made with beads or with quills . . . colored porcupine quills, that lay flat?"

Paco interceded. "They were beads, Don Jose. I remember, I grabbed his arm to help expel him and it felt bumpy, like beads."

I nodded and indicated that I was through. The captain then said, "Well, I suppose the final thing we must do is question the little *India*."

Doña Maria Elena, who had been staring bleakly at the water in the pool, stiffened and snapped, "Capitán, I am the *comadre* of Señorita Amada. She is a refined young lady and a member of this family. You will remember that, please."

"As you wish, señora," the captain bowed indifferently.

A servant was sent and in a few minutes Amada stepped from the house into the torchlight. I had not really been aware of her appearance earlier, but I will describe it now. She still wore the low-cut dress from the *fandango* but her face had been washed clean of the makeup. Her hair hung down like an ebony waterfall flowing to below her waist. She was slim and fawn-like without the full figure that some of our Spanish women possess and which would have spilled from such a dress. I noticed that she still had the habit of tilting her head slightly forward, hiding in her hair.

Amada seemed reluctant to move forward. In fact, she looked like she wanted to run away. Her eyes searched the faces in the *placita* that were all turned toward her. When she looked at me, her eyes filled with tears.

"*Señorita.*" Captain Rodriguez bowed with exaggerated deference. His sarcasm was wasted on Amada, who curtsied gracefully in response. "Please come forward. I have some questions which I must ask you."

My mother took her hand and indicated that she should sit beside her on the bench. Lupita, like a distorted shadow of the girl, stood right behind her.

"So," the captain said, "I am sure that you are still upset, but you have only to confirm what my investigation has already discovered." His right hand smoothed his mustache and scratched meditatively in his beard. "This *Norteamericano* wished to dance with you. He offended your honor." The corner of his lip curled sarcastically. "And the gentlemen threw him out into the street. This is true?"

Amada looked puzzled, but she nodded. "Yes, that did happen." Her voice was barely audible.

"Later," the captain continued, "when you returned to your room, this besotted creature intruded and accosted you. When Don Esteban entered to rescue you once again, the Saxon pig struck him and fled. Is it not so?"

Amada closed her eyes and swayed. Before she could speak, Lupita interjected, "Yes. That is how it happened." She placed her hands firmly on Amada's shoulders.

Captain Rodriguez looked annoyed. "I was asking the *senorita*, unless you too were present?"

Lupita remained silent, but I noticed her grip tighten on Amada.

Her eyes still closed, Amada nodded. "Yes," she said, and began to cry with great racking sobs.

"No more, *Capitán*! She has lost her betrothed. We have lost our son." My mother turned and clasped Amada to her ample bosom, rocking her slightly like a baby. "Now, *mi hija*, it's over, it's over," she cooed, though she too was crying. Soon my sisters and the servant women were bawling, and even Paco was knuckling away tears. Only Lupita appeared unmoved, her face devoid of expression.

Captain Rodriguez sighed and, turning to me, arched his eyebrow and nodded toward the entryway. "May I speak to you, *señor*?"

Outside in the darkness of the street, he said, "I regret to tell you, *Señor* Garcia, that I doubt very much if we will arrest this assassin. If he had been a New Mexican . . ." He shrugged. "We will, of course, make some inquiries and try to identify the man, but he has no doubt already fled to the mountains." He shook his head. "We would never catch a man like him. I am sorry." The captain placed a comforting hand on my shoulder. "And besides, it may be that I will not have the authority here much longer. You have just come from the capital, you know how turbulent are the times. I have orders to report to Chihuahua. I leave tomorrow. I have a feeling I will not be back."

He walked a step or two away from me, turned, and added, "Spain is losing Mexico, I think. I must decide whether to go with Spain or cast my allegiance with this new country." He nodded as if agreeing with himself. "I must decide."

Looking at me once again, Captain Rodriguez bowed formally. "My condolences to you, Don Jose, and to your family. May God comfort and help you." He straightened and turned to his men. "*Vamanos hombres!*"

"*Vaya con Dios, Capitán,*" I called as they disappeared into the night. I was alone in the darkness. It was then that the tight rein I had kept on my emotions began to slip away from me. My body began to shake. I leaned my shoulder against the wall and slid to my knees in the street. I was crying and trembling like a man with ague. I wept for my brother. I wept for my father. I wept for Amada. It seemed that I would never be able to stop my heart from breaking for all the losses of all the creatures of this earth. And, yes, I wept for myself.

I do not know how much time passed before I could regain some control. A large, orange moon was beginning to rise above the mountains. Like a child, I wiped my face on my sleeve and staggered to my feet. I thought that I knew what I must do. I reentered the house and called for Paco. "Paco, we must prepare my brother for burial." I felt calm and decisive in the wake of my purging tears.

"*Si, patrón,*" he nodded. "It is already being done."

"Very good, old friend. In the morning, I will make arrangements with the *padres* at the *parroquia* of Our Lady of the Conquest for the funeral mass." I was pacing restlessly, my hands behind my back. "I must make some inquiries tomorrow. While I am gone, I would like you to get me the two strongest horses we have. Make sure that they are both well shod."

"Are you going somewhere, Don Jose?"

"Yes, Paco. I am now the head of this family." I had to suppress the panic which I felt at the significance of those words. "It falls to me now. Justice and the honor of our family require that I find the man who did this and bring him back to the authorities."

"But how will you find him?"

"You said that he wore a bead design on his clothing, not quill," I explained. "And I saw the mark of his moccasins. They are not made like the Comanche or any other tribe that I have seen. The beads are something the *Norteamericanos* trade with. Therefore, logically, this man will probably retreat back to where he is secure, among the tribes that trade with the *Norteamericanos.* I will talk to some people and see what I can learn about him."

Paco straightened his old body to its full height, his shoulders back and his chin proudly jutting. "Permit me to accompany you, *patrón.* Your family is my family and I would like a part in this justice."

For the first time that evening I smiled, and embraced the old man. "Yes, Paco, you are indeed an honored member of this family and it is for that reason that I must ask you to fulfill a most noble position."

"Anything, *patrón*!"

"You must guard and keep my family well, while I am gone, Paco. It may be several days. You are the *mayordomo*. Into your care I entrust them all."

Paco's eyes brimmed with tears and his mustache

quivered with emotion. "With my life, Don Jose! With my life!"

"Thank you. I will rest assured. Now we must sleep. Tomorrow it all begins."

It is well that I could not see 'all' that the future held for me or I would not have rested at all that night.

Chapter Six

I arose early the next morning. After making arrangements with the *padres* for the funeral, I went to the blacksmith's shop to begin my inquiries. That gentleman directed me to a carpenter, an American named James Pursley, who had been living in Santa Fe for many years. From him I learned that a small group of mountain men were encamped to the north of Santa Fe, just off the road to Don Fernandez, as Taos was then called. I rode out in the late morning.

The camp was small, consisting of only a handful of tepees, most in the three-pole foundation style of the northern tribes. Two Indian women were tending to a kettle, suspended over a fire. From a distance that I hoped was beyond the range of a rifle, I hailed the camp. The women glanced my way and then ignored me. I sat a moment considering, then urged my horse forward.

"That be far enough, greenhorn, or I'll make meat of ye!" The voice came from my right, but I could see no movement in the trees. With what I hoped was a casual gesture, I let my right hand rest on my thigh, a few inches from the pistol that I had cocked and ready on my saddle. Thanks to Red Hand's training I was not a complete fool!

"I would like to talk with you," I called in English.

"Let drop that pistol on the ground, easy like, and it might be we could palaver a spell," came the reply. Obviously I was not dealing with a complete fool either.

Slowly, I eased the hammer back down and dropped the pistol to the ground. That done, a tall, lanky man materialized at the edge of the trees and began to move cautiously toward me. He held a long rifle nestled in the crook of his arm. His finger, however, rested on the trigger guard.

"Ease yourself on down from there on my side of the horse," he instructed.

He stood about ten feet from me, relaxed and ready. "Didn't bring no companyeros with you?" He looked around despite my answer.

"No." I studied the man. His copper-bearded face was gaunt and sharp-featured, the complexion burned by the sun to the tint and texture of leather. His thin frame was clothed in greasy, unadorned buckskins. He stood much taller than I, in knee-high moccasins which I was sure had not stood outside Amada's window. I relaxed a bit.

The man noticed the change and allowed the muzzle of his gun to lower. "Come ahead on into camp. There's meat on the spit." He turned and started away. "Leave your pistol set, though," he added over his shoulder.

I left the pistol and led my horse to the camp. The mountain man sat cross-legged to the north of the fire, his back to the lodge. One of the women handed him a wooden platter piled high with meat. It smelled like elk. I too sat, to his west, unconsciously observing Comanche manners. A sideways glance told me that it did not go unnoticed. I too was handed a plate and we both ate in silence.

After a while, the trapper laid his plate aside and wiped his hands on his stained leggings. Fishing tobacco and a corn cob pipe from a buckskin bag, he took his time filling, tamping, and lighting while he examined me. "Where'd ye catch yer English?" he asked.

"I have just returned from four years of school in the United States," I explained. I was eager to question him, but realized that it would be considered a breach of mountain man hospitality, even as it would have been among Indians. A certain amount of preliminary small talk was required to satisfy the demands of etiquette.

"Four years of schoolin', you say!" He shook his head, marveling at such rarefied heights of education. One or two puffs more, and he asked, "What do they call ye?"

I bowed my head slightly. "I am Jose Juan Garcia y Alvarado, the son of Don Benito Esteban Garcia y Baca and Doña Maria Elena Alvarado y Chaves, at your service."

He took the pipe from his mouth. "Waugh! They call you all that, do they?" His eyes twinkled, though his expression remained serious. "Me, I'm known as Lodge Pole Pete Ross." He extended a large, callused hand. We shook.

His eyes studied the horizon while he resumed puffing noisily. "Reckon I know why yer here, but let's hear it."

"I'm looking for a man who was at my family's home last night. There was a celebration and, well, he assaulted my younger sister." I thought it best not to tell all. The truth was that I liked this taciturn American, but I did not know if I could trust him.

"Yer sister?" Lodge Pole Pete raised his eyebrows. "I hear'd ye Spaniards was a touchy lot when it come to family."

"The man is about your height, but heavier, with light-colored hair. He wears beadwork on his clothing. Would you know a man like that?"

"I reckon." Unhurriedly, he knocked the ashes from his pipe into the fire. "What do ye aim to do with this here feller once't you rendezvous with him?"

Realizing that I sounded pompous, nonetheless I said, "Teach him some manners!"

"Manners? Waugh!" Pete rocked with laughter. "That hoss wouldn't know manners if'n they was to bite him in the ass! Manners!"

"I just want to administer the lesson." I forced myself to smile. "I do not care if he learns."

Pete slapped my knee with glee. "Sirree! That's well spoke, Joe, it surely be!" His laughter subsided to a smile while he eyed me. "I reckon maybe you could teach him somethin', even if'n ye are a might runty."

"What is his name?" I asked, diplomatically ignoring the disparaging comment on my stature.

Pete was serious now. "That be Jake. Absaroka Jake he's called, and he's no kin to me. Don't rightly know his last name."

"I don't suppose he is still around?" I asked, waving to the other tepees.

"Naw," Pete shook his head. "He lit out of here 'fore sun-up like Old Nick hisself might be comin' callin' on him." He studied my disappointment before saying, "This ain't about yer sister, is it?"

I shook my head. "No."

"I didn't figger it. Ole Jake skeddadling like that just didn't figger." When I did not volunteer any more information, Pete continued. "Though I will say that hoss is a bad'un, 'specially where there's women in the mix. I've knowed him nigh on five years now, and ever time we'd rendevouz, he'd be trying to sneak my punkin's into the bushes." He indicated the two Indian women now cleaning an elk hide a short distance away.

"Arapaho?" I asked, looking at the women.

"Ye've a good eye, Joe." Pete squinted at me. "Sisters, they be, and two finer 'sposas ye ain't likely to find. Cost me a heap of horse flesh, I'll say," he confided. "I'm down here Santy Fe way to do some horse tradin'. Them friends of Jake's near put me afoot. Crows, they was, stole most of my herd."

"Which way did this Jake go?"

"North. I 'spect he's changed his plans 'bout winterin' in these parts. Bragged about how he'd had women from every tribe from here to Canada and wanted to sample some spicy Spanish stuff." Pete's eyes widened and he held up both hands. "No offense, friend Joe. Them's Jake's words."

I nodded and stood up. "No offense taken. I appreciate your information, but I had better get started. Jake has almost a day's start on me." I mounted my horse. Pete's wives looked up from their work. With my two hands flat and palms down, I signed a thank you to them. They quickly lowered their eyes, giggling, surprised that I knew sign language.

"Thank you, Mr. Ross." I extended my hand and we shook. "If you are looking for good horses, come to my family's home, east on the Canyon Road. I'll tell Paco. He will be fair with you.

Pete looked pleased. "Spoke like a white man!" he said, intending a compliment, I suppose. He frowned up at me though, and added, "If'n yore plannin' on ticklin' ole Jake's hump ribs, ye'd best keep yer nose open. Absaroka Jake is a bad'un. He'd as soon take hair, as look at ye." Then, in the undemonstrative way of mountain men, he turned and walked away calling over his shoulder, "Watch yer topknot."

After retrieving my pistol, I returned to my home as quickly as I could. As soon as I stepped through the door, I called for Paco. "Are the horses ready? I must hurry. I leave immediately."

"Where are you going, *mi hijo*?" my mother asked, as she stepped out from the kitchen. My sisters and other servants were coming too, attracted by my shouts.

"The man who killed Esteban is escaping. I must catch him before he loses himself in the mountains."

My luggage had arrived while I was gone. Hurrying to the trunks, I flung them open. Inside, wrapped in oiled flannel, was a rifle I had purchased in the United States. Long-barreled, accurate, and beautiful, it was the artistry of a Pennsylvania German gunsmith. I began to assemble it.

Dona Maria Elena was horrified. "And what will you do when you find him, Jose? Kill him? Will this bring my Esteban back to me?" She began to cry.

I gave her a hurried embrace and kissed her bowed head. "No, *Madre*. I only intend to capture him and bring him back for the authorities."

She gripped my arm tightly. "But such a man will kill you, and I will have lost all!"

I could make no reply. Had I been more rational, I would have had to admit that it was quite possible, even likely, that Absaroka Jake might kill me. But there was an urgency inside of me to do something, to make some effort, to embark on some action that would take me away from this scene of sorrows. I had to go. I turned away without a word, and went to my room to gather some clothing.

Spreading a blanket made by the Ortegas of Chimayo, I tossed an extra shirt or two onto it and began rolling it to tie behind my saddle.

"Jose?" I turned at the whisper of my name. Amada stood in the doorway. She was dressed more plainly now, and more modestly. For once, Lupita was not attached to her.

"Amada, how are you, little one?" I had not seen her since the night before.

She ignored my question. "You are leaving." It was a statement, not a question. She had turned in the doorway as if to leave. "This is all my fault. I am to blame for all of this." Her head tilted forward and she hid within her hair.

"No!" I asserted. Striding across the room, I grabbed her firmly by her shoulders, turning her toward me. She seemed so terribly thin beneath my hands. She would not look up at me. "Listen to me, Amada! You have suffered a great deal. First the death of my father, and now Esteban, to whom you were to be married. Just because your beauty inflamed that drunken *Norteamericano* does not mean that you did anything wrong." She looked up at me when I said the word 'beauty.' Emotions seemed to pass across her face like the shadows of clouds across the earth.

"Beauty?" There was surprising bitterness in her voice. "Do you forget, Don Jose," she asked in a mock, haughty voice, "that my face is dark, that I am Comanche, *una India bronca*?"

Frowning, I stared intently into her eyes. I could read nothing in their black depths. Quietly, I said, "I forget nothing, Amada. I could not forget. In five years away, I could not forget you, your people"—I paused, feeling a strange tightness in my chest—"your beauty." I continued to hold her at arms length. She had not moved. It was as if movement would be too painful for her, or too futile.

She closed her eyes. "I have no place here." She let her head fall forward. In a barely audible voice, she pleaded, "Take me with you, Jose!"

"Amada!" my mother gasped. I had forgotten that she was there with us. "Go with Jose? You forget yourself! You are no longer a child, you are a young woman now. What would people say?" Doña Maria Elena moved alongside Amada and placed her arm around her shoulders. "Besides, *mi hija*, right now I need all my family with me." She glared accusingly at me. "I need you here, Amada." Amada's arms went around my mother's waist and held her tightly.

"And you!" my mother snapped at me. "If you feel that you must leave, you had better get about it quickly and stop pestering decent women!"

We all went outside where Paco had the horses ready. My mother sighed wearily. "I suppose this has something to do with pride and family honor and other such masculine nonsense. Well go!" I tied my blanket roll behind the saddle as she continued. "We women will stay and pray and see that what survives continues."

Doña Maria Elena had surprised me. I had never suspected her of philosophy before. I kissed my sisters and embraced my mother. Lastly, I turned to Amada. "God bless you, Amada. I will return soon."

Reaching out, Amada clutched my hand tightly in both of hers. Her eyes explored my face for something as she pleaded, "Come back, Jose! Please, come back!"

I could only nod. Mounting my horse, I shook hands with Paco and clattered out of the yard. As soon as I was clear of the town, I pushed my mount to a canter. I wanted to ride fast and hard and keep on riding. My mother was wrong. It was neither pride nor honor nor justice that drove me north. It was fear. In less than twenty-four hours, I had gone from being the second son to being the head of *la familia* Garcia. I was now *Don Jose*. The responsibility terrified me, as did something in the way I felt around Amada. So there I was, at nineteen years of age, fleeing from something nameless, toward something unknown, up the road to Taos as the sun plunged toward the western horizon.

In my numerous years of life, I have met many men of the breed known as mountain men. All were resourceful, many were brave, some were honorable and a few were scoundrels. The one thing they all sought in the mountains was freedom, but each defined that concept differently.

I had the honor of knowing Jedediah Smith. This good man, well versed in both Shakespeare and scripture, sought the freedom to exercise his several God given abilities to their fullest. His courage, intelligence and capacity for leadership, would have been stifled in the society of sedentary men. However, in his very first year in the wilderness, he went from a novice to a legend.

Many mountain men simply could not conform to the expectations and limitations imposed on a common working man. But there were the few, like Absaroka Jake, who sought to escape the dictates of both civilization and conscience. The liberty they sought was license to indulge their basest nature. In time, these were often exposed and reviled by both the other mountain men and Indians. In later times, they formed alliances with other outcasts and became bandits, raping and pillaging as the notion took them. Living in a geographic and social nether land, they preyed on the weak and defenseless of both societies, white and red.

Jake apparently did most of his trapping for beaver and otter in Crow territory and made a point of staying on good terms with them. They knew themselves as Absaroka, the Sparrowhawk people, and boasted that they had never harmed a white man. It was to them, therefore, that I assumed that he was fleeing, to spend the winter in the security of their lodges. It was my intention to catch him long before he could reach that refuge.

To accomplish that, I rode like a Comanche. A true Comanche usually had a surplus of good horses and, to cover a great distance quickly, he would ride first one horse until the animal was nearing exhaustion and then switch to another, keeping them all going at a rapid pace. I had only two horses, which was somewhat limiting, but I maintained a punishing pace as long as the horses could stand it, leaping from the back of one to the other without stopping or slowing.

Pojoaque, Nambé, Chimayo, Truchas, Las Trampas, all passed as I rode by the light of the full moon. Finally, my mounts required rest. I camped in a grove of trees below the pueblo of Picuris. I gave each of the horses a measure of grain and turned them loose to graze with only a loose hobble. Disdaining a fire, I rolled myself in my blanket and was instantly asleep.

At first light, I was awakened by magpies squalling in the trees above my head. Saddling the horses, I resumed my pursuit before the sun cleared the mountains. The breakfast fires of Peñasco were still burning as I thundered through the village. It was late morning when I arrived at Don Fernandez.

The environs of Don Fernandez de Taos had become a favorite wintering locale for many of the mountain men. Taos was as close to the Spanish settlements as most mountain men cared to venture, like the sandpipers that forage at the edge of the ocean's surf. This was in part due to their natural aversion to settled places, and in part because Spanish officials regarded all outsiders with understandable suspicion.

I passed by the dirt and grass plaza and continued north toward the Taos Indian pueblo, near which the mountain men camped. I had no real plan in mind, but I loaded and primed both my pistol and rifle, in case Jake was anticipating my arrival. I loosened my knife in its sheath. Red Hand had taught me that, in a close fight, the knife would be far more useful than a firearm.

I approached the encampment cautiously. There seemed to be many people about. Indian wives and Spanish from San Fernandez mixed with the mountain men, who kept busy repairing their gear or visiting from tepee to tepee. Two mountain men were walking in my direction, one talking animatedly to the other. I was only dimly aware of other people around. Neither of the approaching men resembled the description and brief glimpse I had of Jake. Reining in my horse, I hailed the men. They paused, looking up at me suspiciously, while one spat a long, brown stream of tobacco juice into the dust.

Leaning toward them, I spoke in a voice loud enough to be heard above the babel of the camp. "I am looking for a man above middle height, light-colored hair. He wears Crow beadwork on his shirt. He is called Absaroka Jake. Do you know him?"

As I think back on some of what I did in my youth, I am amazed that I have survived to such an old age. I have reviewed what happened next many times over the years in my memory. The tobacco chewer considered my question, then launched another stained stream, this time near my horse's front feet. This caused my horse to back up just slightly, but enough to save my life. To retain my balance, I had to straighten up in the saddle. Next to where my head had been, a blossom of blood suddenly appeared in my horse's neck.

Screaming in fright and pain, the animal reared up so far that it lost its balance, falling back and to the right. Even as I kicked my feet free from the stirrups to avoid being crushed under the stricken creature, I caught a glimpse of the smoke and muzzle flash, followed by the crack of the rifle being fired from about twenty feet to my right.

I landed on my feet, still holding the reins, but was nearly toppled by the frantic thrashing of the horse. Blood was everywhere and it was clear that the wound was as mortal as it was painful. Grimacing in sympathy for its anguish, I jerked my pistol from my belt and thrust it to the horse's temple. Its final torment was cut short by the bullet. As the noble head thudded to the earth, I sprinted around the corner of a tepee in time to see my quarry riding from the far side of the camp, flailing his horse to a run.

"*Diablo maldito!*" I hissed. Running back to my fallen mount, I discovered that my second horse had bolted in the confusion. Stomping my feet in frustration, I looked in every direction, but it was no use. Jake had escaped me.

The two mountain men still stood where I had left them. Another spit of tobacco preceded the laconic observation, "Reckon you found Jake!"

The men helped me get my saddle and gear from the fallen horse. I was relieved that my rifle had been unharmed by the incident. I donated the animal to a grateful Ute woman who had butchered and removed everything but the bloodstains by the end of the day. It was not until much later, much leaner times, that the Comanche would even consider eating horseflesh, but the horse was not such a critical part of the Ute economy as to give rise to such diffidence.

The two mountain men invited me to their lodge to share a meal. After a time, my other horse was returned to me, lathered and wild-eyed. As I groomed and curried the animal, I learned from the men that Jake had preceded me to the camp by only an hour or so. They nodded without surprise as I narrated the incident with Amada, omitting my brother's murder.

"Yep, if that Jake weren't born fer shootin', then why was beaver made?" The tobacco chewer did all the talking. I never heard more than an occasional grunt from his companion. "Seems like a heap of trouble to go to jest fer gettin' frisky with yer sister, but if'n that's the way yer stick floats, friend, yore gonna have to make up yer mind to rub ole Jake out. Track him and hunt him down and make meat of him, 'cause he ain't likely to let you trap him alive."

I think I must have been slightly insane at the time, because I do not recall even considering turning back, and the details of what exactly I planned to do with Jake I refused to think about. I was grieving for my brother, angry about my horse, wounded in my pride, and *loco* without a doubt. "Do you think he will try to winter with the Crow?" I blandly asked.

The man looked at me and shook his head in amazement. "Thar's grit in ye, Spaniard, and a hair of the black bear at that, I'll say!" Spit! "Here's damp powder and fire to dry it, and ye still aim to keep on. Yep, I reckon Jake will skedaddle for the Crow. They're 'bout the only ones'll have him."

I confess that I had to strain to understand some of what he said because his vocabulary was unlike any form of the English language which I had studied at the college. "What route is Jake likely to take?" I asked.

"If'n he wants to make good time, he'll likely head up east of the foothills to the Bighorns country. But if'n he wants to kill ye or just shake you off his tail, he might head into the mountains."

I had a few pieces of gold still with me, so I purchased another horse and left by the middle of the afternoon with the mountain man's benediction on my journey. "Watch yer topknot!"

By this time, I had learned the proper reply. "Watch yorn!"

Obviously, my precipitous tactic of riding up and making polite inquiries was not the best course of action. As my tobacco chewing friend advised, I would have to treat it as a hunt for a dangerous animal and, as

I knew from my Comanche experience, a hunt required equal measures of skill and patience.

I spent some time studying the track of Jake's horse, so that I would recognize it again, then I set out at a slow but steady pace up the valley of the Rio Grande. I resolved to be alert at all times lest the hunter become the hunted.

Chapter Seven

There is little about grief to commend it, but it does resemble an anchor that holds you in the present moment. Thoughts will drift from memories of the past to hopes for the future, but the ache of the present loss always brings one back. At my present age, grief is a familiar visitor, but at nineteen years of age, I barely recognized it.

As I rode north beside the Great River, the burden of sorrow was like a heavy pack on my back. I tried to focus my attention on the hunt, but as time passed my mind would swing from thoughts of Esteban to thoughts of my father. Unbidden, the words of the *Coplas* of Jorge Manrique would fly through my mind like the flocks of southbound birds above me.

Thither the mighty torrents stray,
Thither the brook pursues its way,

And tinkling rill.
There all are equal. Side by side,
The poor man and the son of pride
Lie calm and still.

With just one horse, Jake could not outdistance me, yet neither could I press ahead too rashly for fear of ambush. I never saw him, only his tracks. By that sign, I knew when his horse grew weary by the scuff marks of its tired hooves. I could see that Jake, like me, had to make cold camps for fear that a fire might reveal him. Like me, he slept hidden and at a distance from his horses to prevent surprises in the night.

The pleasures and delights which mask
In treacherous smiles life's serious task,
What are they all,
But the fleet coursers of the chase
And death an ambush in the race,
Wherein we fall?

As I thought of my brother, I was disturbed by the ambivalence of my feelings. He was my brother! Surely my thoughts should be sweet remembrances of youth shared! But, in fact, my memories were only bitter. Esteban was strong, competent and confident, with little tolerance for those more awkward or unsure. Neither had he any patience for a younger brother who wished to tag along, so Esteban had lived in a world of his own, while I lived in mine.

His imperious attitude with our family's servants embarrassed me, for I considered them my friends. His casually cruel treatment of those weaker than he, including myself, were to be avoided, not condemned. Actually, I rather envied Esteban and assumed that his strengths were also virtues, until an incident in the spring before I left for school.

In those days, as in years before, some of the young men among the Spanish would make raids on some of the hostile tribes of the region in order to acquire children to sell or keep as slaves. All this was entirely against the law of Spain, but Spain was very distant, and the mines of Santa Rita and northern Mexico much closer and willing to pay. Although I had not been aware of it, I imagine that my brother had been on similar expeditions before, but that spring morning as he was saddling his horse, I stood in the shade and watched.

As he tightened the cinch, one of his companions said, "Esteban, they say that your brother can ride. Why doesn't he come with us?"

Esteban threw a glance at me and rolled his eyes. "Jose loves the Indians too much. He wouldn't want to come."

"Where are you going, Esteban?" I asked naively.

Esteban strapped his musket to the saddle. "We're going to a *fandango* with the Navajo, little brother." Esteban paused to cast a cold smile my way. "If you like, we will bring you back a little playmate. I imagine you miss your Indians, don't you?" His friends all laughed heartily.

I felt my face flush hotly. I realized then that he was proposing to kidnap and enslave children. "No," I replied stiffly, "I don't want to go with you. It's not right!"

It was Estaban's turn to laugh as he swung into the

saddle. "You don't know what you're missing, Jose. You've no idea what fun these Indians can be." His gaze went from me to the doorway behind me, and his smile broadened. *"Vamanos, muchachos!"* He turned his horse with a jerk and spurred it to a canter, leading his friends clattering from our yard.

I spun around, angry at my brother, and stopped in surprise. Amada stood in the doorway, her eyes wide, her hands clutched across her stomach.

No foe, no dangerous pass, we heed,
Brook no delay, but onward speed,
With loosened rein;
And when the fatal snare is near
We strive to check our mad career,
But strive in vain.

Heading east of Blanca Peak, Jake lead me through the Mosca Pass. It appeared that he was going to choose the faster, eastern route to the Absaroka country, but fear of Cheyenne and Arapaho hunting parties or his search for the best sites from which to ambush me, caused him to turn west up the Wet Mountain valley to the Arkansas River—the Nepeste, as we knew it—and then upstream.

Thus we traveled for days, as summer turned to autumn. The daytime sun was warm but at night the cold air would flow down the mountainsides like icy rivers and engulf me, shivering in my blanket. In some ways it was for the better. The cold helped me to stay awake. As I had feared, Jake doubled back and tried to attack me.

It was long after midnight of the fifth day of my pursuit. The moon had set at least an hour earlier when I became aware of someone approaching. I did not actually see or hear anything, but the sum of my senses warned me that something in the night had changed. My horses were picketed in a copse of aspen near my hiding place in a jumble of rock. As a further precaution, I had rolled my saddle and tack in my nearly useless blanket, in such a way that it resembled a sleeping person. I never heard even a single footstep but, about twenty minutes after I had become aware of someone in the area, I detected a restlessness in my horses. Someone was near.

I heard a thunk as something struck my saddle tree, a faint grunt of surprise, and then he was gone. I marveled at Jake's sharp night vision for it was far too dark for me to respond. To fire my gun would have only revealed my position and I could see no target to shoot at anyway. In the morning, I found the cut where a knife had plunged through the blanket. I found what little sleep I could while swaying in my saddle as we plodded along during the day.

By now I was very hungry. I had brought woefully little food with me, so confident had I been of retrieving Jake in just a day or two. Yet I dared not divert the time or attention necessary to properly hunt, although the signs of game were everywhere. Early snow in the high country was forcing the animals down to the valley. The best I could do as I followed the rugged banks of the Arkansas, was to grub a few handfuls of berries and *pinon* nuts. At one time that river had formed our northern boundary, but I knew of no Spaniard who had traced it to its source as I now appeared to be doing.

Where the river began to turn north and the valley

climbed in dry steps to the mountains, I was fortunate enough to kill a sage hen with a thrown stone. I was sufficiently famished to be able to relish every bite as I ate it uncooked. I could not risk a fire. As Jake and the river drew me further into the mountains' embrace, I had begun to see signs of Indians. The track of the moccasins made me guess that they were Ute, and my Comanche-instilled prejudices shrank from the thought of an encounter. Jake was not the only danger I faced.

And yet, Jake had made no move against me since that dark night. As I wavered, weak and worn, in the saddle, I tried to fathom what his plan might be. The river was narrowing to a stream. Surely we must come to its source soon, and since it sprang from the mountains, that must mean a confrontation soon, for I could see no passes through the snow-clad ridges that surrounded us.

The forage was sparse and my horses were tired, one beginning to favor a hind leg. I was exhausted from lack of sleep and my hands trembled with hunger. While in the United States, I had acquired the habit of shaving every day, but now, my face bristled with beard and I was sure that my sunken eyes must burn like embers from above that dark mask. It occurred to me that perhaps Jake did have a plan after all. He would not kill me himself, he would merely lead me deeper and deeper into the wilderness and allow folly and youth, often synonymous, to do the work. Hunger, or accident, or Indians might yet achieve his purpose.

Behold of what delusive worth
The bubbles we pursue on earth,

The shapes we chase,
Amid a world of treachery!
They vanish ere death shuts the eye,
And leave no trace.

The day began with a sky as pure and deep as the eye of God. There was little wind as I lurched up from my rocky bed. Surely I was at the top of the world. There was little vegetation for my horses to graze on and they hunched and complained like spoiled children as I struggled to saddle them.

I knew how they felt. My head was light, there was a buzzing in my ears, and I would catch myself after long moments of staring into nothingness. We had passed the modest source of the river and climbed the rugged valley to the north. Ambush would have been much easier here, but I was beyond caring and did little to protect myself.

By midday, I crossed a ridge and began to descend into another valley where a creek ran to the north. The cramping in my stomach and the tremors in my hands kept me from appreciating the grandeur that surrounded me. The Creator must have intended that mountainous wilderness for someone greater than mortal men. The scale was much too large. The heights, the depths, the distances, and the splendor served to humble, elate, and overwhelm.

Such was my detached state that I was oblivious to the changing weather. Milky streams of clouds flowed from the north and dimmed the sun. As the light faded, a single wet snowflake stung my eye, and startled me back to awareness. I was cold. My breath was visible. I scanned the northern sky and recognized the gathering snowstorm. I was still too high on the mountainside. There was no shelter anywhere. Dismounting, I led my weary animals over the rocky ground toward the trees below. Around me the snowflakes began to swirl, heavy and wet, stirred by a rising wind.

By the time we reached the trees, the ground was dusted white, covering any tracks there might have been. Pressing on through the trees, I emerged into an alpine meadow created by some ancient fire. I stopped abruptly. In the middle of the clearing something dark lay on the ground. It took my eyes a moment to focus and another moment before the information registered in my exhausted brain. It was a horse—Jake's horse.

Slowly, like one in a dream, I turned back to grope for my rifle secured to the saddle. As I did, there was a sharp, burning sensation along my cheekbone and I felt myself falling sideways like a felled tree, helpless to even cushion the impact. My saddle horse reared and bolted for the trees while its tired companion merely stood in numbed defeat.

I could not move. I lay on my side, my ears roaring and my vision red. Through a scarlet haze, I saw a bearded figure emerge from the trees, rifle in hand, and come to stand over me. There was no real interest in the bloodshot eyes that studied me. I realized that my face was covered with blood. After a moment, Jake turned and walked to my pack horse. Taking it by the halter, he plodded out of my sight without a second glance.

From my vantage, Jake appeared as hungry and listless as I. He did not see the need to expend any more energy on killing me. Wounded and afoot in an early mountain snowstorm, he was confident that I would not survive the night. In all honesty, I shared his assessment of my situation. My Jesuit mentors might have been pleased that my last thoughts as I sank in unconsciousness were of a scriptural nature. I recalled King David's lament for Abner—*Como muere un villano*—He died like a fool.

Chapter Eight

But I did not die. The bullet had plowed an angry furrow along the cheekbone and across the side of my head just above the left ear. Like all scalp wounds, it bled profusely, but no real damage was done beyond the creation of the scar which I still wear. The cold air helped stanch the flow of blood and, within a few minutes, I swam back into consciousness, surprised and slightly disappointed to find myself yet living.

But life means work so, with great effort, I pushed myself to my knees, my empty stomach heaving at the pain. There was no sign of Jake. The snow had already covered his tracks. I sat back on my heels and closed my eyes, my thoughts a prayer for guidance. Clearly the pursuit was over, the quarry fled. Therefore, my goal was to grow strong again and resume the chase at some time in the future. My immediate challenge, however, was to simply survive the stormy night ahead. But how—alone, unarmed, starving, wounded and cold? When no celestial voice replied, I opened my eyes and had my answer. The first thing I saw was Jake's horse, dark and still, through the veil of snow. I began to crawl painfully toward the fallen animal.

I could see that snow had not yet settled on the horse, which meant that the poor creature was so recently stricken as to still have the warmth of life in it. Arriving at the body, I lay my ear against its side, but could detect no heartbeat. The storm was increasing. The snowfall was now so thick, that I could not even see the surrounding trees. I was alone in a world of white.

My knife was still in its sheath against my hip. The throbbing in my head was so great, I feared my eye would leave its socket but, with a desperate cry, I plunged the blade into the horse's belly and began to saw a line up toward its breast. The effort had me panting and gagging but the cold was like a rising flood which I had to escape. With both hands, I reached deep into the animal and wrenched at its innards. As they emerged, I cut them off and threw them away. I set aside those portions which I thought would be edible.

The storm was a full blizzard by now, moaning in my ears and snatching at my coat. Finally, the animal was nearly hollow, the ground around it strewn with gore. Frantic now for shelter, I squeezed myself into the horse's carcass, for once grateful for my small size. I was sobbing with disgust but almost immediately I began to feel the warmth. As the early night fell, I plunged into a deep and troubled sleep, my dreams filled with the howling of the wind, and the tearful face of Amada.

There was something warm and wet on my face. I

opened my eyes and found two other eyes looking back at me. They were yellow and as startled as I am sure mine were. With a snort, the wolf jumped back. Several more wolves looked up from their feasting on the entrails which I had scattered the evening before. I reached up and touched my face. The wolf must have been licking the caked blood from my wound.

I struggled to free myself from the now frozen carcass. My movements caused the wolf pack to retreat to a safe distance. Despite their reputation, I have never known a healthy wolf to harm a human being. Fortunately for me, these were healthy wolves. Looking around, I noticed with pleasure that the storm was over, the sun was shining, the wind had died, and I had not.

At that moment, I felt like a swimmer who has sunk to the very bottom of the waters and, turning, pushes off the ocean floor toward the sparkling surface. Considering my appearance, I had definitely touched the bottom. My clothes, hair, and beard were matted with blood, my own and that of the horse. I swayed on my feet from hunger and hurt. There I stood, ready to fight a pack of wolves for a dead horse, but I was alive and determined to remain so.

"*Discúlpanme, amigos,*" my voice croaked at the wary wolves. "I will take my share, and then you may have the rest." I waved my arms and the pack sprinted for the trees where they remained, watching. The organs I had set aside the night before were gone, delicacies for the wolves. Slowly, laboriously, I carved several pounds of meat from the hams and flanks, piling them in my coat.

When I had finished, I tied the ends of my garment to

form a sack, then tied the arms together to form a strap to carry it by. Glancing back at the skulking wolves, I waved good-bye. "Thank you, my friends. I hope you will appreciate this sacrifice as much as I do." I looked a last time at the mutilated remains of the creature that had saved my life, then with lead in my steps but iron in my heart, I plodded off down the valley, toting my awkward satchel of food.

As the sun rose, and I descended, the day warmed and my clothing began to steam and stink. I reached a creek which flowed to the north. Laying my precious burden on a rock, I stripped off my clothes and squatted in the frigid waters. Taking care not to open my wound, I scrubbed myself all over with handfuls of sand until my skin burned. When I felt clean, I turned my attention to my filthy clothes, spreading them to dry on the rocks.

I would have been easy prey for any hunting Indians, but I did not care. I lay back on the rock and let the sun warm me. I think I even slept. When the sun indicated mid-morning, I drank my fill of the icy creek then set about cutting the horsemeat into strips to dry for jerky. If I had felt stronger, I would have built a drying rack but I settled for the sun-warmed rocks.

My clothes were dry now, so I dressed and walked a little distance downstream hoping to find some berries to eat. Rounding a slight bend, I stopped and crouched instinctively, for my eye had caught a movement. There before me, drinking from the stream, was my horse, the saddle askew and the reins trailing. Somehow it had survived the blizzard, sheltered in some trees and, this morning, had followed the scent of water. Slowly, cautiously, I approached him.

His nostrils flared, his ears twitched and a ripple ran along the muscles of his neck, but he did no more than shift his weight as I grasped his reins. This was one of the two horses I had left Santa Fe with and he was not afraid of people. My relief was so great, that I buried my face in his mane and wept, my arms around his neck.

Composing myself, I removed the saddle and blanket and led the stallion into the stream. Talking to him in a soothing tone, I scrubbed his hide with water and sand, then dried and groomed him with grasses and pine needles. Finally, resaddling him, I mounted and rode triumphantly back upstream to my cache of meat.

I ate some of the strips, still nearly raw, and turned the others to dry evenly. I do not know when I have felt so exhilarated. Listing my blessings, I felt like the richest man in the world. I was alive, and had in my possession a supply of food, a horse, a knife, flint and steel, and my prized rifle from the Pennsylvania gunsmith. Sometimes since, when I have felt myself weighed down by cares and concerns and unfulfilled desires, I have reminded myself of what a gift from God it is to merely be alive and have a chance to go on.

I had only the vaguest notions of where the Absaroka country might be, and that was somewhere to the north. That afternoon, I followed the creek and camped where it joined a larger stream. I had seen no sign of Indians since I had left the Arkansas, so that night I indulged in the luxury of a small fire. The warmth was marvelous.

I followed the valleys north. Where the stream met a

river, I managed to shoot a deer, a large buck. I was ecstatic. I spent an entire day jerking and smoking the meat, and tanning the hide with brains. My heart was overflowing with gratitude to Creator and creature both. Across another pass, I found myself in a wide and gentle valley that emptied to the north. For days I rode. Jake thought that I was dead, so I felt a sense of liberation from fear of him. Instead, I could concentrate on hunting, and caring for my horse, relishing an intoxicating sense of simply being alive. Around me, the ridges were capped in white and rivers of golden aspen flowed through the dark green pines on the hills.

Despite my awareness of my surroundings, I was surprised one morning to see three riders sitting on their horses watching me from a rise to my left. They were Indians, I could see that much, but I had no idea from which tribe. Three was too few for a hunting or a war party so I assumed that they must be scouts for a larger group. That would probably make both fighting and fleeing a futile gesture, which left me only one option.

Stopping, I turned my horse to face them. Leisurely dismounting, I sat cross-legged on the ground facing south, my rifle across my lap, and waited for them to come to me. I knew that they would be intrigued. Either they would kill me or they would talk with me. Life was really very simple at that moment. I waited.

Cautiously, the riders came down the hill, approaching me from over my right shoulder. I tried to look relaxed and indifferent, though I was assuredly neither. Two of the Indians remained on their horses behind me, while the third circled around to face me. For at least a minute he studied me from a safe distance while I studiously ignored him, staring at the far horizon like a philosopher.

I had hoped that he would address me first, but he seemed as unsure of how to proceed as I. Uncertainty is an unwelcome sensation in anyone, but in Indians, for whom most of life is clothed in ceremony, it could be dangerous. Looking at the man now, I greeted him and, by the sign language of the lowered fist, I invited him to sit with me.

The man facing me was probably about my own age, taller and handsomely built. His face was painted, but that was typical. I saw no paint on his horse, which I took as a good indication that this was not part of a war party. He ignored my invitation and asked me something in a loud voice, accompanying it with the signed question asking my people.

I considered for a moment and replied, making the sign for Spaniard, and offering my Comanche name, "Little Spaniard," as I touched my breast.

He nodded and said nothing more, but I could detect no relaxing of the grip which he kept on his bow. Behind me, a horse pawed impatiently. We seemed to be at an impasse. Holding my right hand palm down in front of me, I signed for him to wait. Carefully, I rose to my feet and approached the young man. He tensed. I stopped about five feet from him and, holding my rifle forward in my left hand, I made the sign for giving with my right.

His eyes widened and he studied my fine weapon. In his hand was a bow with arrow nocked. He did not appear to have any firearms. I repeated the gift gesture and finally, gracefully, he brought his left leg over and dropped lightly to the ground. Stepping close to me he looked from my face to my weapon and back. I continued to hold the rifle out and tried to maintain what I hoped was a calm gaze at his eyes.

Reaching out, he grasped the rifle. I relinquished it and stepped back. He balanced it in his hands, examined the fine wood of the stock and then, putting it to his shoulder, he sighted down the barrel at my heart. I smiled and forced myself not to flinch. He lowered the gun, and nodded at me, saying, "*Ah-hi-e!*" which I later learned meant that he was much pleased.

Like most people, Indians love to receive gifts and, like gentlemen, they love to appear generous. I had purchased my life for the price of a Pennsylvania rifle and now, the man must respond to my gift in some way. With dignity, he presented me with his bow and quiver. As he had done, I balanced the weapon in my hands and tested the strength of the string. I used both hands to make the sign for "Thank you."

His companions could no longer resist. Dismounting, they came forward as if to remind me of their presence. Gravely, I walked to my horse while my mind feverishly considered all that I did not have to give. Searching in my saddlebag, I found a small mirror which caused me to wonder why I had packed it and not my razor. I also unstrapped my knife.

Approaching the two, I quickly decided which was the more vain by the attention given to his hair and presented him with the mirror. To the other, who appeared the youngest, I gave my knife. In return, I received a bag of arrowheads and a pair of moccasins right off the youngster's feet. I expressed my gratitude and again indicated that we should sit. The man who had received my rifle produced a pipe and he and the others removed their moccasins before they sat. I too removed my shoes in emulation. I later learned that this was a gesture of sincerity.

Like many peoples, Indians relish ceremony. The comfort of traditions is quite profound. Therefore, there was no rushing the deliberate pace of the pipe ceremony. After its presentation to the directions, earth and sky, to witness the truth of our speech, we shared the smoke for about twenty minutes before any information was exchanged.

At last they asked me why I was there. Using the universal sign language which most of the tribes shared, I explained that I was pursuing the man who had killed my brother and that he was seeking refuge with the Crow. As I brought my fist up to my forehead to imitate the pompadour hair style of the Absaroka, the Indians caught their breath in alarm.

As they explained, they were Shoshone who lived most of the year to the west of the great mountains, and lived on small game and fish. But now, in September, the Hunting Moon, they rode east to hunt the buffalo. They would no longer be *agaideka'a*, salmon eaters, they would for a season be *kutsendeka'a*, buffalo eaters. To do this, they must ride into the territory claimed by the wealthy, well-armed Sparrowhawk people, the Absaroka.

This settled the matter for them. If my enemy was an ally of their enemies, then they would be allies to me. This led to embraces from each of the warriors, and the announcement that I would accompany them, hunt with them and share their lodges.

So it was that in September of 1820, I joined the Shoshone tribe of Indians. While the sun stood high in the cloudless sky, we mounted and rode off in search of the buffalo that would feed 'our' people.

Ordinarily, I do not consider it wise to allow your enemies to choose your friends, nor your friends to decide who your enemies should be, but in this instance it proved felicitous. During my time with them, I found the Shoshone to be a fine people, honorable and brave and far less inclined to warfare than my Comanche brethren were.

In fact, the Comanche and the Shoshone were closely related. At some time in the past, probably at about the time that Cortez was conquering Mexico, the Comanche and Shoshone had been one people. The Shoshone were often called the Snakes and indeed, in sign language, the Comanche were also symbolized by the sign of the snake. At that time they were living much further north on the eastern side of the mountains in what is today Canada.

Following the Pueblo uprising of Pope against the Spanish in New Mexico, the horses taken from us had been bred and traded widely by the Indians. Those horses, which the Spanish had brought to this New World had radically altered the lives of the Indians. The Snakes acquired the horse quite early and used this advantage against their rivals, such as the Blackfeet. However, the Blackfeet soon improved their situation by acquiring guns from the French and British to the east. In time, European diseases and weapons drove the Snakes southward where they split into the Comanche who went southeast and the Shoshone who went northwest.

Meanwhile, another split was occurring further east among the Hidatsa. After a conflict over a buffalo, a group split off and headed west, soon calling themselves Absaroka, and thus the Crow nation was born. The Crow and the Blackfeet, better armed than the Shoshone and themselves now mounted, pressed those people westward into the mountains and beyond, claiming the rich buffalo plains for their own.

On our ride in search of buffalo, I became acquainted with my new friends. The youngest, who gave me his moccasins, was a shy, serious adolescent who, by virtue of his vision, was called Hawk Striking. His carefully groomed cousin was known as Wolf's Tail and the third man, to whom the others seemed naturally to defer, was called Rattler. He was to become famous later when he unified the People. His name in Shoshone was Washakie and, as far as I know he, like I, continues to live.

Rattler had the inherent qualities that make for a leader among the Indians. He was courageous and unselfish and an eloquent orator. His father, Paseego, was a Flathead, who had been killed by the Blackfeet. When Washakie was about five years old, he and his brothers and sisters rejoined his mother's Shoshone people. He was still sometimes called Quanah by his older relatives who remembered his childhood name, Pina Quanah, which means Smell of Sugar, but he had acquired his adult name after his first buffalo hunt. Taking the skin from the head of the buffalo, he had taken the hair off, puckered it up like a gourd and allowed it to dry. Putting small stones in it, he tied it to a stick to make a rattle. When the Sioux came to raid his people, he had ridden among them scaring their horses with his rattle even as his lance decimated the enemy warriors.

As we rode, we talked, and I discovered that Shoshone and Comanche were not unintelligible to each other despite the years of separation. It did not take me long to learn Shoshone. In fact, limited contact between the Shoshone and Comanche continued. One of the foremost men among the Shoshone while I was with them was a Comanche named Yellow Hand, who had joined the Snakes some twenty years earlier.

By mid-afternoon, we had located a sizable herd of buffalo and turned west to notify the main encampment. There was joy among the People that night for their survival that winter depended on a favorable hunt. I spent that night with the uncle of Rattler, where I was made very welcome, and slept warmer than I had been in weeks.

The next morning, the *buhagant* or medicine man, foresaw a successful hunt and the people cheerfully followed the hunt leaders to the east. The scouts returned and reported that the herd was still where we had found them the day before, now just the other side of a low ridge. At the leaders' directions, we spread out behind the hills, forming an open-ended square into which we would drive the animals.

There were very few guns among us. Like me, most of the hunters were equipped only with lances or bows. Frankly, I was concerned. Buffalo hunting from horseback is a dangerous endeavor for both man and horse and requires great skill from each. It had been many years since I had hunted with the Comanche and my horse, though strong and swift, was not trained for this. Still, I felt that I had to earn my place among the People, so I strung my bow, nocked an arrow and patted the neck of my nervous mount.

Beside me Hawk Striking grinned in anticipation and pretended to bite and chew an imaginary piece of buffalo meat. I wanly returned the smile, but my stomach was aflutter. We were along one of the arms of the square. Those at the base would rush into the herd first, then we would angle in from the sides.

We heard the pounding of hooves, then the signal was given and fifty horsemen were launched across the plain. I still consider the Comanche the finest horsemen anywhere, but these Shoshone were nearly their equals. It was incredible to watch the horse straining forward to within inches of a maddened buffalo, its rider stretching out over his prey with bow pulled taut, all the while balancing on his pitching pony with only his knees.

Unfortunately, I could spare little attention to the others. My horse was more than a little reluctant to get too close to the desperate animals, which meant that I had to compensate by making sure my arrows flew true and hard. My arms trembled with the effort of pulling the bowstring to its extreme. Miraculously, my first arrow found its mark and my target pitched forward to skid in the dust. With relief, I eased my horse off and drew another arrow.

At the approach of danger, the herd arranged itself with the cows and young on the inside and the bulls on the perimeter in an attempt to provide a shield. At this season, we were after the females, because the meat of the bulls was particularly tough and stringy. This meant weaving between the thrusting horns of the furious bulls in order to get at the panic-stricken cows.

Before I could select another animal, my eye was caught by Hawk Striking. The youth was a magnificent horseman, graceful as a swan and dexterous as an acrobat. But just as he was leaning out over his chosen cow, an enraged bull turned in and hooked his pony with a vicious jab. Horse and rider were both unbalanced and went down in the midst of the dust and stomping hooves.

I slipped my bow over my head and shoulder and urged my unhappy horse through the torrent of brown fur. Hawk's pony was back on its feet, eyes bulging in terror, a scarlet gash along its side, but I could not see its rider. Closer I pressed until suddenly he was there, standing, but hurt, barely ten feet in front of me. Calling his name, I spurred my mount, reaching my hand out toward the injured hunter.

He spotted me, our hands grasped, and he spun up behind me, his arms grabbing around my waist. I wasted no time getting out of the herd. Once safely clear, Hawk Striking dropped to the ground, clutching his ribs. I suspected that he had broken at least one. His face was clouded by more than pain, however. In words that sounded similar to the Comanche, he indicated that he had only gotten one buffalo. It took me a moment to appreciate the significance of that information.

The Comanche had so dominated the southern plains that they could ride to the buffalo hunt virtually any time that the weather permitted, in much the way that a modern American would walk to his pantry. But for the

Shoshone, dashing onto the buffalo plains only once a year, there would be no second chance. A poor hunt now could mean a winter of starvation ahead. My recent hungry experience made me more than sympathetic.

I nodded my head in understanding and indicated that I would hunt for him. I swung back up into the saddle, wishing that my enthusiasm could match my determination. But God was again gracious to me, and I managed to bring down three more fat cows before the herd escaped us.

Because I was using Rattler's arrows there was some discussion as to which were my kills and which were his, but since he was such a successful hunter, there was no problem receiving credit for my efforts. My first animal, I gave to the lodge of Rattler's uncle with whom I was staying, and the other three went to the family of Hawk Striking.

The whole chaotic, clamorous hunt was over in less than half an hour, but I was utterly exhausted by the strain. As the women and children swarmed over the field to begin the butchering, I walked my lathered horse back to the knoll where I had left Hawk. His father and uncles were with him, wrapping him tightly with a buckskin. When I informed them that there were three animals for them, each of the men embraced me with great dignity, pressing their cheek against mine in the Shoshone manner.

That evening, there was dancing and gladness in the encampment. Many of the hunters stood to tell and reenact their exploits. Because the hunt had been successful for everyone, there was much praise heaped on the notable hunters. I sat with the family of Rattler, a rabbit fur robe about my shoulders, trying not to doze in the warmth of the congenial fire. I was not too successful though, because Rattler's elbow in my ribs woke me.

He nodded toward the fire circle where the father of Hawk Striking now stood. For my benefit, he accompanied his speech with signs. With many colorful embellishments, he described how I had plucked his son from certain death and placed meat in the mouths of his family. For this reason he wished to let all the People know that, from this day forward, the Little Spaniard was to be considered as one of his sons.

I was truly dumbfounded at the honor. It was required that I respond. I have never been comfortable in public situations, but I rose to my feet. Mixing the few Shoshone words which I had learned with Comanche, I signed that I was not worthy of the distinction, that I had done no more than what any human being should do for another human being. My meaning was not completely conveyed, I'm afraid. The Shoshone, like all Indians, and indeed, all peoples anywhere, limit the definition of human beings to include only those like themselves, members of their society, and place all others in some other, lesser status. In any event, the People were pleased by my words. I concluded by saying that I should be honored to call the noble warrior, Horse Dancing, my father, touching my breast in the sign for father.

As I resumed my seat, there were many shouts of *"Ah-hi-e!"* to show approval. The celebration went on for quite some time but I soon retired to my robes and fell quickly into a deep sleep, my dreams crowded with jostling buffalo, with fathers and brothers, living and dead, and with Amada.

Chapter Nine

Rising the next morning, I found that Rattler had already left to search for more buffalo. After helping myself to breakfast from the family's hide cooking pot, I went to the lodge of Horse Dancing to see about Hawk. The morning was chilly, so the entrance to the tepee was still closed. Scratching on the lodge skin, I announced myself to whoever might be inside. I was not prepared for the person who stepped out to greet me.

The flap went back and out stepped Amada, or so I thought. My stomach tightened and my senses reeled. I must have staggered from my shock, for I became aware of a small hand on my arm and a lovely, concerned face staring into mine. I stared back for what must have been an unseemly length of time, for the expression changed from concern, to embarrassment, to alarm. With great effort, I shook myself from the spell.

"I am sorry," I said, trying to give a reassuring smile.

"You look so much like my sister, it came as a great shock to me." I then realized that I had spoken in Spanish, so I repeated in sign language.

With an impish grin, the girl signed, "I am your sister. I am the daughter of Horse Dancing and now you are his son."

I could only nod. Physically, she bore a remarkable resemblance to Amada but, where Amada was shy and reserved, this girl shone with confidence and enthusiasm. Seeing this young woman, I realized, perhaps for the first time, how beautiful Amada was. But Amada was a diamond in the shadows, while this girl was a jewel sparkling in the sun.

I had been staring again. "I came to see how Hawk Striking is today."

"He is very stiff and should not ride today, but he is strong," she explained. Moving gracefully to the cooking fire, she lifted a sheep's horn ladle full of stew. "Are you hungry? We have some very good buffalo meat. But then, you know that, don't you!" Her laughter tinkled like a bell.

I started to say, "I have already eaten," but caught myself. Even if one has gorged himself, it is impolite to decline an offer of food in an Indian household. "Thank you," I said instead. "It does smell good."

She smiled. "If you would like to go in and visit with our brother, I will bring you both some food." She lifted the flap and I stepped through into the lodge. It was dark inside. A small sleeping fire had already been banked for the day. I stood for a moment to let my eyes adjust. I saw movement on the opposite side. Hawk Striking was trying to sit up.

Moving in the direction of the sun, around the fire, I cautioned, "Do not try to get up, younger brother. I will just sit with you for a while."

There was a painful sigh, as the young man sagged back down onto his sleeping robes. Only his head was propped up. "You're learning Shoshone very quickly, aren't you? You sound like a Comanche, but you're getting the words almost right."

I sat cross-legged at his feet. "The lodge of Pash-e-co sends greetings," I said. Pash-e-co, or Sweet Root, was Rattler's uncle, my host.

"You should live here with us now, my elder brother," Hawk said. "You are of this lodge now—a son of Horse Dancing." He smiled warmly.

The entrance flap opened and the girl stepped through, two wooden bowls in her hands. Kneeling beside her brother's head she handed me a bowl and started to feed Hawk Striking. He caught her by the wrist.

"I can feed myself, younger sister." His tone was stern but his eyes were appreciative. "You should not be here, you know. It's not proper."

She tossed her head and put the bowl down where Hawk could reach it. "Proper!" she scoffed. "What's proper is often silly and very impractical." She pretended to pout a moment, then smiled and stood. "But I will leave. I don't want to make a bad impression on our new elder brother." She looked at me mischievously from the corner of her eye. "Don't tire my old brother, new brother!" she scolded me, then left, trailing another radiant smile.

Hawk rolled his eyes at me in exasperation. "My sister! Our sister, actually. She is very strong-willed."

"What is her name?"

"Chilsipee, the antelope. Our mother died a few years ago and my father has so far refused to take a new wife. So Chilsipee takes care of us like a little mother."

"She seems very good-hearted," I said and Hawk appeared to appreciate my tolerant nature.

Just then, the cry came from the center of camp, "Buffalo! Buffalo!"

Hawk looked up with frustration in his eyes as I stood and prepared to leave.

"Do not worry," I assured him. "If the Creator permits, we will have another successful hunt today." I emphasized the word 'we.' Hawk took his responsibilities seriously, which was good, but I wanted him to know that the responsibility was not his alone. "Rest and grow strong. We will leave some buffalo for you to hunt."

Stepping out of the tepee, I was treated to another smile from Chilsipee who was working on a buffalo hide. I could think of nothing to say, so I simply nodded and started to leave.

"Hunter!" she called to me. "You should use my father's arrows, that way I will recognize what is ours." She pointed to a quiver of arrows on a stand by the entrance. I retrieved them, and, as I left, she called after me, "I hope that you will make much work for me, Little Spaniard."

I hurried to the *remuda* to catch my horse, but my mind was not on buffalo. Instead, it swung like a pendulum from Amada to Chilsipee and back again. The sight of Chilsipee had caused me to think about my feelings for Amada, and my thoughts of Amada caused me to feel very warmly toward Chilsipee, and this both confused and embarrassed me. Confused because I had not realized, or admitted, how far my feelings toward Amada went, and embarrassed because those feelings were toward the young woman who was to have been my brother's wife.

I decided to concentrate on the hunt instead. My horse was no more eager to hunt this day than he had been the day before, but I managed to bring down two more buffalo, though it took several arrows for each.

From the plains we could see that the snow was building up in the high country, effectively cutting me off from any chance of returning to New Mexico before spring. Though I thought often of Absaroka Jake, I was certain that he was safely encamped with his Indian allies and I could think of no way to safely pursue him into their midst.

Therefore, I spent my days engaged in hunting. After the kill, the long hard job of butchering, tanning and preserving the meat filled the daylight hours. Among the Shoshone, everyone worked at it, not just the women. The campsites were crowded with drying racks and hides were pegged to the ground all around.

I do not recall how many days went by this way. The Shoshone have no concept of time analogous to our week. They keep track of months, seasons and years, but the week is for them an unnecessary unit of time. Every day is to be lived in a sacred manner and, for a tribe surrounded by armed enemies, a day of rest is a luxury that they can seldom afford.

It must have been nearly a dozen days after my arrival among the People, that the Crow came. We had just finished another successful hunt and were walking our weary ponies back to our fallen prey, when a column of riders came shrieking down on us from a ridge to the north. Their timing was nearly perfect. Most of us had empty quivers and exhausted horses. Still, with lances and knives, we leaped back on our mounts and closed with the enemy.

To our surprise, the Crow seemed to shy away from a direct confrontation. After one pass through our midst, they turned and headed east followed by most of the angry Shoshone braves. I, however, had spotted Rattler. I watched as he broke off the pursuit and came riding swiftly back toward me. "The camp!" he shouted as he galloped by.

I understood then, and spun my horse to follow. Rattler had surmised that our attackers had been only a diversion to lead us away while another group fell on the camp. His suspicions proved correct.

Rounding the shoulder of a hill, we could hear the camp dogs barking madly and see smoke and confusion in the camp. Crow vandals were knocking down drying racks and toppling tepees while they chased any Shoshone left in camp. This was to be the punishment for what they considered our trespass on to Crow hunting grounds.

Rattler wasted no time. With cold efficiency, he bore down on the heedless marauders. With lance and tomahawk, he began exacting vengeance on the invaders. I still had one arrow in my quiver and my knife at my belt, but I felt as close to unarmed as I could imagine.

But I was then young so, armed with a young man's sense of invulnerability, I pitched in behind my friend, doing little more than covering Rattler as he did his lethal work.

My head swiveled in every direction, as I tried to avoid being taken unaware. I crashed my horse headlong into an unsuspecting Crow who was charging on Rattler's right flank. Warrior and horse went over. Taken so suddenly, the Crow was unable to leap free and the full weight of the horse rolled onto him. By his screams, I assumed that his leg was broken.

I let fly my arrow, catching another warrior in the shoulder before he could loose an arrow at Rattler. I felt a certain satisfaction at how adept I had become with a bow. Spying another rider bearing down on a Shoshone child, I charged up alongside and, as he was leaning down to snatch up the little boy, I cut through his saddle cinch, causing him to tumble head first to the ground. His erstwhile quarry, who could not have been more than eight or nine years old, then turned and began to beat the fallen raider about the head and shoulders with a piece of firewood.

I was almost beginning to enjoy myself, when I spotted a rider with straw-colored hair and beard. Absaroka Jake had decided to join his Crow brethren in a little vicious entertainment, pillaging a defenseless village. At the moment, Jake's attention was fastened on a young woman, fleeing toward the creek—Chilsipee.

Although at an angle, I was closer to her than to Jake. I only hoped that my tired horse could capitalize on the advantage. Stretching his neck like a champion, the stallion fairly flew across the ground. I could see that Chilsipee, the antelope, was aptly named, for the girl could run marvelously fast.

If I had to slow at all, Jake and I would collide at full speed, for he was so intent on the girl that he was still unaware of me. At a dozen yards I called her name, praying that she would understand what I intended and respond in time.

Hearing her name, Chilsipee turned and crouched in fear, but immediately recognized me and stood up, her arms above her head, stretching as high as she could. At a dead run, I caught her with my right arm across her chest, my hand under her left arm. The air exploded from her lungs, but she brought her arms down to clasp mine tightly as I curled her up onto the saddle in front of me.

All that Jake saw was a brown blur erasing his prey from before his eyes. Jerking back on the reins, his horse nearly sat as it skidded to obey. Almost comically, Jake looked first to the right where I had been and then to the left where I was turning my horse to face him. His expression went from shock to horror as he gazed on the ghost of the callow young Spaniard he had left for dead in the snowy mountains.

Never before had I felt the murderous rage which I felt then. Had I been able to reach him, I would have taken pleasure in killing him with my bare hands—this man who murdered my brother and tried to kill me, who assaulted both Amada and now Chilsipee with the basest of intent. I take no pride in confessing this emotion which had me trembling with wrath. Later, as it ebbed, it left me feeling sick and unclean.

Jake spun his mount about and fled. In my mindless anger, I nearly flung Chilsipee aside in order to pursue him, but the rasping sound of her breathing brought me back to my senses.

"Chilsipee! Did I hurt you?" Naturally, she was in no condition to reply. She struggled against my too-tight grip and slumped to the ground where she fell on all fours, desperately sucking in air. I knelt beside her, my hand on her back in a useless, but I hoped, comforting gesture.

After a few moments, she slumped down on one hip, her breathing more normal. Pushing her hand against my shoulder, she gasped, "I'm all right. Go back to fight!"

I did not really want to fight anymore, but she was right. I swung back up on my horse and cantered back to the camp. Like the aftermath of a thunderstorm, only a few faint rumblings of the fight remained. Others had seen Rattler and I ride back to camp and had followed. They had quickly routed the Crow who had counted on uninterrupted plunder.

Characteristically, the Crow had tried to retrieve all their wounded and fallen brethren, but two or three unfortunates remained to experience the anger of the People. These were dispatched with far more merciful alacrity than some tribes would have accorded, but their scalps were taken sometimes sooner than their lives.

One of the fallen was the warrior I had shot. My arrow indicated that the honor should go to me, and Wolf's Tail presented me with the scalp. By now I was feeling drained and wanted only to rest. I shook my head at the proffered trophy, and suggested that he give it to Horse Dancing with my compliments. Impressed by my apparent modesty, he smiled and left to bring the glad news to my adopted father.

I sat, quiet and sad, on my trembling horse. Around me the once prosperous camp was a shambles. The Shoshone were calmly cleaning up, counting themselves lucky because none of the People had been killed and little of the meat ruined. My thoughts were more on myself, appalled at the fact that I had felt myself capable of hot-blooded, even gleeful, murder. My dark ruminations were interrupted by Horse Dancing, who rode up beside me to thank me for the scalp and to inquire, with forced casualness, if I had seen Chilsipee.

I nodded and waved toward the creek. Horse Dancing turned to his son and directed him to ride quickly to see. Indian fathers were not supposed to show such concern for mere daughters, but Horse Dancing was of an unusually tender-hearted nature which he stoically tried to conceal. In a few minutes, Hawk returned, leading his horse, astride which rode Chilsipee, ashen-faced but smiling. At the sight of her, relief flooded her father's face, but he quickly looked away. Patting my shoulder he simply said, "We have meat to gather. Come." He turned his horse at a walk back toward the hunting ground. I took a deep breath, trying to shrug off my black mood, and followed.

Gradually, after putting some order back into the camp, all the People followed to complete the butchering. That night, the mood was more somber. It had been a good hunting moon but it was clear that the Crow would not now leave us in peace. The People must take what meat and robes they had and retreat back across the mountains to their winter camp grounds.

That evening, there was some boasting and story telling but most of the people were subdued. The sentimental Horse Dancing rose, scalp in hand, to extol my virtues in riding quickly to the defense of the camp and, incidentally, in saving his daughter from the foul, yellow-bearded Crow. I, however, was distracted from his praises. Across the camp circle, the firelight flickered in the eyes of Chilsipee—eyes that were looking only at me.

Chapter Ten

The Shoshone were a migratory people anyway, so the retreat from the gun-wielding Crow was hardly a disaster. In the spring, the People would head to the west to dig the camas roots on what became known as the Camas Prairie, then they would move on to the salmon streams for a summer of fishing, and then ride east for the fall buffalo hunt. Now it was time to complete this thousand-mile cycle by withdrawing to the shelter of the mountain valleys for the winter. Some of the young men, like Rattler, wanted to strike back at the Crow, but the elders counseled restraint, arguing that everyone was needed to safely bring the food supplies into winter camp.

I rather suspect that it was this variety of diet that caused women to have a higher status among the Shoshone than they enjoyed among the buffalo Indians of the plains. Roots, nuts, and berries formed a significant part of the People's diet and, unlike hunting which required greater strength, women were as important as men in providing this essential food.

The camp was quickly struck and the *travois* were piled high with meat, robes, infants and old people. With the morning sun warming our backs, we followed the river called the Sweetwater as it led us to a broad, gentle pass through the mountains. Around us the prairie grasses glowed in the autumn sun like burnished brass. The dark mountains wore helmets of white. Above us, clouds of birds hastened to their winter homes in the south, carrying my melancholy thoughts to Santa Fe.

Despite the active life I had been living, I had done a great deal of thinking during my sojourn with the People. The Jesuit fathers would encourage us to search our hearts, but I had discovered only emptiness and longing there. I knew that I was welcome among the Shoshone, but that I was really just a visitor in their lives. Indeed, as I brooded on it, I felt that I was a visitor everywhere I went. I could fit in among the Shoshone, or the Comanche, or the Americans, but I was not really a part of them.

Had I become merely a visitor even among my own Spanish people in New Mexico? Certainly more than half of my life had been lived apart from them. But then, perhaps what I felt was not unique to me but simply a recognition of the human condition. Alienated from our Creator, we were at odds with creation, even our own kind. Searching for that spiritual home that we lacked the eyes to find, we were strangers in Eden, pilgrims in Paradise, still hiding from God in His own garden.

Self pity is a virulent cancer, *mi bisnieto*, and not to be indulged. Focusing on myself, I was oblivious to the beauty around me, except when it forced itself upon my attention, as Chilsipee finally did. The others had left me to my moody solitude, but after several days of virtual silence Chilsipee could stand no more. Urging her horse alongside mine, she addressed me with characteristic bluntness.

"Will you return to your family in the spring?" she asked.

I felt like someone shaken from a deep sleep. "No," I replied in a cracking voice. "I must pursue that man who chased you."

She cocked her head like a curious magpie. "But, he did not catch me!" Then a faint, teasing smile crept onto her lips. "Or are you so fond of me that you must avenge his insult?"

I blushed furiously, visible I am sure despite my tanned and bearded face. "No!" I blurted. "I mean, yes, I am fond of you but . . ."—my face was aflame now—"I mean . . . he is the same man who killed my brother."

Her laughter at my discomfort ended abruptly. "Oh, I understand," she said in a subdued voice. But the sly expression quickly returned. "Do you have a woman in your homeland?"

"No." Beads of perspiration were forming on my forehead, though the day was really quite cool.

"Oh," was all she said, hiding a secret smile. We rode for a while in silence.

"What river is this we're approaching?" I asked in order to say something.

"The Seedskeedee." She was not to be distracted, though. "You said I looked like your sister. Is she married?"

"No. She was going to marry my brother but, as you know, he was killed." When her hand flew to her mouth in horror, I realized what I had said and hastened to explain. "Actually, she is not really my sister, although we treated her as if she were. She is Nermernuh," I said, using the proper term for Comanche, "But she came to live with our family at the time that I went to live with hers. But her parents died of the sickness, and so she has stayed with us."

"Oh." She seemed pleased. "So your sister is a Human Being, like me, and they were not really brother and sister, like you and me, so that would make marriage all right, yes?"

She could have been a great lawyer. I was not quite sure what the question was. "Yes?" I said, in a small voice.

She said nothing more, simply smiled, and rode a little more erect in the saddle, humming a tune.

Fortunately, Horse Dancing chose this moment to ride alongside me. "Daughter," he said sternly, "this is most unseemly. Ride with the other women!"

"Yes, my father," she said meekly, her eyes dancing merrily as she turned her horse away.

"I apologize, my son," Horse Dancing said to me. "These bad manners come from not having a mother to properly instruct her. Although," he said, sadly, "so many young people seem to have bad manners these days." He shook his head in regret. Patting my shoulder, he urged his horse forward to ride again with the elders.

Crossing the river, I had to admit that I now had much more to think about than myself.

We turned north and eventually arrived in the center of the Shoshone country, the wooded valleys sheltered by towering mountains. To the east, a saw-toothed range dominated the sky. A sparkling river chuckled and hissed near the campsite. Others of the People were already here, some living in the brush shelters typical of the western bands of the Shoshone.

After the excitement of the buffalo plains, winter camp seemed rather quiet. The shorter days flowed with a gentle rhythm. Men repaired weapons, made arrows, and went for brief hunts in the mountains for deer and elk. The women prepared jerky and pemmican for the lean days ahead when fresh game would be unavailable, and made new lodge skins and clothing from the hides. Chilsipee made new clothing for her father, brother and me, for which I was grateful. My old clothing had tattered nearly to the point of immodesty.

I traded some elk's teeth for a razor from a Bannock who had acquired it from a British trading post. After a very painful shave in the icy river, Horse Dancing almost did not recognize me. When he did, he laughed and showed me off to his children. I was dressed in my new hide clothing, my hair was long and braided and, without the beard, Horse Dancing declared that I looked, "Like a true Human Being."

Chilsipee reached up and wiped away a drop of

blood left from my ordeal with the razor. "And such a handsome one too."

Her father and brother just shook their heads in exasperation at the outspoken girl.

Ice began to form at the edge of the river and soon the snows began. This was the season of visiting from lodge to lodge and of storytelling in the evening by the old people. Coyote, the trickster, the lazy cousin of the noble wolf, was often the central character of these stories.

It was Coyote who taught the Shoshone the *Naroya* or Ghost Dance. In its original form, it bore little resemblance to the messianic ceremony taught by Wovoka a few years ago. The *Naroya* was intended to drive out the ghosts or evil spirits that brought illness.

It was in December, with the snows piled deep and the moon reflecting full from the icy sheen, that a *Naroya* was announced by the family of a man who had fallen sick. For five nights the People danced around the fire and even I joined in. The men would form a circle and then the women would step between us and we would interlock fingers. With no instrumental accompaniment, the dancers would sing and shuffle their feet sideways to the left, always to the left. At the conclusion, we would shake our robes to drive away the evil ghosts. Finally, on the last day, we danced around a pine tree in the daylight. The ceremony seems mind-numbing in its simplicity but, I must confess that, as the dance continued, I felt a growing sense of unity with the People, as if I was connected to them in some intangible way.

Time seemed as frozen as the land, that winter.

Game was more and more scarce and the hunters and gatherers had to search farther and farther from the camp. This was very dangerous because a winter storm could howl into the valley with incredible speed, as I soon learned.

By late February, we had almost two weeks of snow and nothing to eat but pemmican and jerky. No one expressed their fear, but the faces of the people were tight with concern. Perhaps there would not be enough food to last until spring! What if the storms did not abate? If only the Crows had let us hunt just a little while longer!

Finally, a morning came when no wind tugged at the lodge skins, no snow swirled through the camp, and the sun rose in a sky of liquid turquoise. The blanket of snow was clean and white and unbroken in every direction. We stood at the entrances to our tepees like prisoners released from jail. Smiles were traded and nods exchanged. It was a good day for hunting. Tracking would be easy in the unblemished snow.

Hawk Striking and I strapped on snowshoes and headed north up the valley searching for signs of game. Horse Dancing remained at the lodge, nearly crippled by his cold-inflamed arthritis. We walked in comfortable silence for nearly an hour before seeing any tracks. At last, near the river's edge we discovered two groups of tracks. Apparently a family of deer and a family of elk had come together to drink a short time before. At the sound of our approach, they had left in different directions. Hawk decided to follow the deer while I pursued the elk.

The tracks led me up the valley, but then turned east up a canyon. As the sun rose higher, the trees began to shed their burdens of snow. The silence was profound. My own breathing was nearly the only noise. So intent was I on tracking the animals, that I lost track of time. It must have been midafternoon before I finally spotted the elk—a big male, three females and two yearlings. They stood at the edge of a clearing, nibbling on the lower branches of an aspen while the male kept watch.

The lack of any breeze moving through the still, cold air worked in my favor since my scent would not be carried on the wind to the animals. Ever so slowly, I crept forward, keeping to the shadows of the trees. It took half an hour to cover the hundred feet necessary to get within bow range. I could see the steamy breath from their nostrils and could hear the tearing sound as they grazed on the branches. I nocked my arrow and slowly drew the string, sighting on the largest female. The male flinched as my bowstring hummed. The arrow found its mark. Instantly, all of the elk took flight, my prey leaving a trail of blood.

It had been a clean hit. There was much blood, so I knew that the elk would soon fall. A hundred yards into the trees, I found her. Her eyes had a dreamy, distant look so I knew that she was beyond pain. I could have cut her throat and speeded her death, but instead, I crouched beside her and lay my hand on her soft neck. Briefly, I prayed, thanking God and this creature for the sacrifice that allowed our lives to continue. Sacrifice. As Father Saavedra taught, sacrifice was at the heart of religion. And of life, I thought.

The elk lay still in death, her eyes glassy. Wind moaned through the pine needles around me. Looking up I could see clouds racing swiftly above the tree tops.

I had to move fast. Taking my knife, I quickly cleaned the elk, allowing the blood to drain downhill. I cut pine boughs to form a crude *travois*, lashing the branches together with pieces of the fringe from my shirt.

I could not tell if it was snowing anew or if the snow was simply blowing from the trees. A small knot of fear began to tighten in my stomach. With difficulty, I rolled the elk on to the sled and started downhill, dragging the heavy load. My own tracks were already being obliterated, but I could follow the contours of the valley easily enough. What I could not do was quicken my ponderous pace. It was snowing in earnest now, the trees shaking in the wind and the light was fading rapidly. Like a fool, I had not paid careful enough attention to distances, so I did not know how far I was from camp. I only hoped that Hawk Striking had made it back in time.

It was nearly dark. I had to decide whether to press on for the camp or use the little remaining light to make a shelter. I stopped and lowered the poles of the *travois* from my aching shoulders. Through the wind, I thought I heard my name. There, up ahead, someone was struggling toward me.

"Little Spaniard!" I heard it clearly now. I went forward to meet the floundering figure.

"Chilsipee! What are you doing here?" She fell forward into my arms, her face buried in my shoulder. She was sobbing and choking out an explanation. I was quite unnerved by her distress, so in contrast to her usual self-possession. I could not understand her words, so I interrupted her with a question. "How far are we from camp?" I had to shout to be heard above the wind.

Chilsipee shook her head. "I don't know. Maybe a long ways."

A long ways! It was quite dark now. Chilsipee had no snow shoes. We would never make it. I had to make a shelter. "Come on!" I took off my snowshoes and plowed a path through the snow into the trees on the side of the valley. She struggled in my steps behind me. In the relative shelter of the trees, I sat the exhausted girl down and proceeded to gather and cut branches and boughs. Between two trees, I constructed a small lean-to, its back to the north wind. As the snow drifted against it, it quickly became air tight.

Chilsipee was stiff and drowsy with the cold and her legs felt like ice. I half carried her into the shelter of the lean-to and covered her with my buffalo robe. I had been working at such a frantic pace that I was really quite warm. There was just enough light for me to make out the dark shape of my elk on the valley floor. We might need that, I thought, so I tied on my snowshoes and leaned into the wind. It was a struggle to haul it back but, after twenty minutes of effort, I made it. Chilsipee lay unmoving in the lean-to.

I knelt beside her and tried to wake her. She murmured drowsily but would not open her eyes. She felt so cold! I had flint and steel and some moss for tinder in my *parfleche* but the wind was so strong I was not sure that I could start a fire. I had to try! Stumbling in the dark among the trees, I gathered as much firewood as I could. Scraping the snow back from the entrance, I prepared a fireplace. Hunching my body over the tinder, I tried and tried and tried again to strike a spark that the wind would not steal away. I was nearly mad with desperation.

Finally a brief lull in the wind, a spark, a glow, a flame. "Yes!" I shouted to the freezing night. We had a fire! Carefully I fed it until it crackled bravely against the darkness and cast a dancing, ruddy glow on the face of Chilsipee. I tried again to rouse her without success. She might die! The thought screamed in my brain.

I held her tightly along the whole length of her body, my arms around her. It was like embracing an icicle but I had to transfer some heat from my own body to hers. From time to time, I would reach out and add more wood to the fire.

At first, I could only feel myself growing colder and feared that we would both die but finally, I began to feel some warmth returning to her body. Soon she relaxed into a more natural sleep. Sometime before dawn, with the storm still howling in its strength, I too fell asleep.

Chapter Eleven

The cold woke me. There was some light, but the storm continued. The fire was nearly out. I reached out and fed more wood to the embers. My movement must have awakened Chilsipee. She sat up suddenly, turning wide eyed to look at me.

"Little Spaniard! What . . . ?"

"Hush! Get back under the robe or you will freeze! I will explain."

She hesitated only a moment, shivered violently, then complied, her back to me, her body tense. I adjusted the robe around her shoulders. "You were freezing, I was afraid that you would die." Chilsipee did not reply, but some of the tension went out of her body. "Why did you leave the camp?"

She was silent for so long that I was about to repeat the question. In a barely audible voice, she said, "The storm began so quickly and you were not back. Hawk

Striking came in with a deer just after it began to snow. I stood at the edge of camp to see you return. But as the darkness grew, I moved further and further from camp and I still could not see you." I could feel a tear fall on the back of my hand beside her face. "It was like madness! I was afraid that I would never see you again. The wind was laughing at me and I couldn't bear it. Soon I was running and the snow was so deep and the wind was trying to keep me from you." She covered her face with her hands and her body shook with sobs.

I tried to comfort her. "Shh, don't cry. It's all right, you're safe now." I turned her to face me and held her trembling body close.

"Don't despise me, Little Spaniard! Please don't despise me!" She clutched me fiercely, her face against my shoulder, tears running freely. "I am such a bad person. I talk too much and I don't behave the way my father wants me to and now I have become a fool in your eyes and . . ."

I placed my fingers on her lips to stop the tumbling words. "I don't think that you're a fool and I don't despise you. Quite the contrary, I think that you are an extraordinary young woman and I care about you much more than I should." Without thinking, my hand began to stroke her smooth back, the way one would gentle a frightened colt. Her body relaxed and some discreet sniffling told me that her tears had ceased.

She placed her hand against my cheek and looked up. I felt myself drowning in the depths of her eyes. As if from a great distance, I watched myself kiss her, gently at first, then crushing her to my chest. Her arms went around me with a small kitten sound and there, beside the life-giving fire, while the blizzard raged, we made love.

Later, I lay on my back with her in my arms, her long hair spilling around us. Rising up slightly, she looked into my eyes.

"You have to leave in the spring, don't you?"

I nodded.

In a whisper, her eyes fixed on mine, she asked, "May I go with you and be your wife?"

I did not shift my gaze. The question had occurred to me as well, several times since I had met her. But I had to admit that Chilsipee would probably hate life among the Spanish no matter how hard I tried to make her happy. My countrymen would never completely accept her. Just then and for the first time, I knew how unhappy Amada probably was.

"I want you to . . ." I began, but she stopped me as I had done, with her fingers against my lips.

"I wanted to hear that much," she said, "and see in your eyes that you mean it." She laid her head back down on my chest. Quietly, she spoke. "We Shoshone know that there is another world that lies beneath this one. Once long ago, a brave Shoshone found the hole that connects the two worlds. He came back and told us that there were people very much like us living in that other world. Since then, though, no one has been able to find that hole." She was silent a moment, then she added, "You have found that hole, Little Spaniard, that connects the worlds. But it takes great courage to pass through it. More courage than I possess. So I must be content to lie with you now beside that hole, here in our own world while the storm lasts."

I could not reply. I could only hold her tightly and wish that the storm would never end, knowing that it would.

On the third morning, the storm died before sunrise. Chilsipee and I both took an unnecessarily long time to get ready. We packed and repacked our meat *travois*, and tinkered with the crude snowshoes that we had fashioned for her. Finally, silent and sad, we stood beside the lean-to, now barely visible in the deep snow.

I had to speak. "Chilsipee. I am sorry. I should not have taken you as I did. Because I cannot stay with you, I had no right."

Chilsipee shook her head with the bemused expression her father often gave to her. "Because you cannot stay, I am glad that we shared our love." She nodded at the lean-to. "We have lived a lifetime together here. I wish it could be longer, but I could not wish it sweeter." She placed her hand on my chest above my heart then, to hide a tear, she let her hair fall forward across her face in a gesture so like Amada that my heart broke twice. My breathing felt like a tedious, burdensome labor. I could not speak. I could only cover her hand with mine and close my eyes. The pain I felt would not even allow tears.

We stood like statues, unable to move from our pedestal, like Adam and Eve, unwilling to leave the Garden, until the sound of our names, called from a distance, shattered the crystalline silence and divided us forever.

Hawk Striking, in advance of a small party of men, had spotted us from a hundred yards down the valley. Dragging our *travois*, we went slowly forward to meet our rescuers, feeling more like the condemned going to meet their executioners.

The usually reserved Hawk, embraced both his sister and me, a ringing "*Ah-hi-ee*!" echoing through the snow-shrouded pines. At first light, they had left camp to search with no real hope of finding either of us but the entreaties of Horse Dancing urging them on. We received the prodigal's welcome in the camp, the arthritic father weeping as he hugged his daughter in an open show of affection.

That proved to be the last big storm of the winter. As the sun rose higher in the sky, the spirits of the people kept pace. With snow still on the ground, spring was in the air—but not in the lodge of Horse Dancing. Where once the spritely enthusiasm of Chilsipee had filled the tepee with light and life, she now went about her work with quiet introspection. The long looks and heavy silence we shared did not go unnoticed by her father and brother.

One morning, about a week after our return, Hawk Striking took me aside. He was obviously reluctant to speak. "My father asked me to talk with you, elder brother. He knows . . . we both know . . . that you have strong feelings for my younger sister. And we can see how she feels about you. But my father has decided that Chilsipee should be married now." He cleared his throat, scuffing the toe of his moccasin awkwardly in the grass. He looked off toward the mountain tops.

"You probably did not know that Chilsipee is betrothed," he continued. "She may not have even remembered. It was arranged a long time ago. I have an older sister, you see, who is married to Oapiche, the Big Man.

Well, at the time that marriage was arranged, it was agreed that when Chilsipee came of age, and my father agreed to let her go, then she should go to Oapiche's lodge as his second wife." Hawk Striking seemed almost as unhappy as I. The lot of a second wife was often unenviable, consigned to all the hardest work of the household at the beck and call of the first wife.

As if to cheer us both, Hawk added, "My elder sister is a good person and very fond of Chilsipee." He was silent again for a while. "The bride price has already been paid. Oapiche reminded my father of that just yesterday."

Chilsipee was nearly seventeen years old and her peers were already wives and mothers. Horse Dancing's love for his youngest child had caused him to delay the marriage as long as possible.

I knew Oapiche. In a Shoshone camp, everyone was known to everyone else. Aptly named the Big Man, Oapiche must have been well over six feet tall, broad-shouldered and enormously strong. He seemed to me to be a good man, if a bit simple. Thanks to his strength and plodding manner, he was a good provider, but it was common knowledge that his wife, whom I had not known to be Horse Dancing's daughter, was the true ruler of their lodge. Oapiche did not seem to mind. The only thing lacking from his tepee was children. Umentucken, Mountain Lamb, was thus far barren.

In spite of myself, I was stunned by the news—stunned and jealous. Even though I knew that I could not stay and be her husband—or so I told myself—the thought of Chilsipee in another man's arms was like a knife deep within me. With a sidelong glance, Hawk Striking voiced my inner thoughts. "I suppose you must go back to your people? They have need of you?"

I nodded glumly. "Yes, they need me." *And here I am a thousand miles away.*

That evening, Chilsipee would not even look at me, and I tried not to look at her. Both Hawk Striking and Horse Dancing were trapped in the uncomfortable web of our silence. We all retired early, but I could tell by her restless shifting in her robes across the lodge, that Chilsipee slept as little as I.

The next day, Rattler announced that he would lead a party of warriors to punish the Crow as soon as the mountain passes were open. Many of the younger men eagerly joined his ranks. The elders tried to dissuade them, saying they would be needed to protect the people on the journey to the Camas Prairie, but Rattler was obdurate. That evening Horse Dancing and Hawk Striking came as close to an argument as I had ever seen them. The son pleaded for the father's assent to his joining Rattler's raid.

"There is more honor in the hunt than in the battle," Horse Dancing reasoned. "The one gives life to the People, while the other only brings death."

"But my father, the Crow will not even permit us to hunt. We must fight or the People will be hungry."

His father was silent for a long time before this logic. Finally he said, "I will permit you to go against the Crow, but only if the Little Spaniard agrees to go with you. I will trust his arrows to cover your youth."

Chilsipee had come into the tepee in time to hear her

father. She stood wide-eyed at the entrance, two plates of food in her hands, waiting.

I did not feel equal to the responsibility, but I knew that I had to leave some time, somehow. The time had come. "I will go," I said quietly.

"Ah-hi-ee!" Hawk cried, a broad grin on his young face. The two plates of food clattered to the ground. We all turned to see Chilsipee, in confusion, trying to pick up the spilled food.

"I'm sorry, my father," she said in a choked voice. "I'm so clumsy. I'm sorry." We could not see her face through the veil of her hair.

I made a move as if to go help her, but Horse Dancing restrained me. Looking into his face, I realized that he knew all that had occurred between his daughter and me. I understood then that this was why he had agreed to Chilsipee's marriage and why he required that I leave. "It is all right, my son. My daughter is strong enough to bear the burden alone." He patted my knee, a look of compassion in his eyes. In a moment, Chilsipee ducked outside. It was a long time before she returned with more food.

Two weeks after our return from the snowy woods, it was announced that Rattler would leave with the war party the next day. It was also announced that two days hence, Oapiche would take Chilsipee to his lodge. I lay awake a long time that night. I could tell that Hawk Striking was having trouble sleeping too, but eventually his breathing grew as deep and regular as his father's.

Chilsipee arose quietly, her robe wrapped around her, and stepped outside the tepee. I tried to stay in my bed, but after only a minute, I too stepped outside. The moon, nearly full, poured silver over the world. The trees were dark shadows but the snow beneath them gleamed with lambent light.

She stood with her back to the lodge, looking up toward the moon. I said nothing, but stood a few feet from her looking at the yearning profile of her face. Without looking at me, she asked, "Does the same moon shine on your village, your Santa Fe?" She pronounced each syllable of the Spanish word very precisely.

I stepped close behind her and also looked up at the moon. "Yes, it is the same."

She nodded. "The same moon, the same sun, the same earth, and yet we, our people, are somehow different." She shook her head. "It is so strange."

I could think of no reply. Tentatively, I placed my hands on her shoulders, the first time that we had touched since the storm. Chilsipee did not turn, but she leaned back against me. We stood there in comfortable silence.

"I have a secret," she finally whispered. She turned into my arms, her forehead against my chest, her hands clutching the front of my robe. "I am carrying your child."

My body strained toward heaven. My eyes searched the stars for a glimpse of redemption. I wanted to howl like a coyote in my misery. In a strangled voice, I declared, "I must stay now."

"No," she replied calmly. "You must go. There are others who need you. I will serve the lodge of Oapiche, and he will provide for me. I will raise our child so that you would be proud." Chilsipee looked up into my face, a slight smile on her lips. "I was selfish. I wanted you with me always. And now you will be—in my heart and in our son." So saying, she pressed my hand against her flat abdomen.

We kissed once, lightly, then she rested her forehead against my chin. In the distance, a wolf called mournfully to the moon. Chilsipee stepped back from my arms. "He who created the earth is calling you," she said, with a wan smile. "He will preserve you on your trail." With that she stepped back into the lodge.

The camp rose early. Rattler and his party were eager for an early start. Though I looked for her, I did not see Chilsipee and I dared not ask for her. As the sun cleared the mountains, Horse Dancing embraced both Hawk and me. I saw courage and loneliness in his eyes as he bid farewell to his son. We rode from camp with cheers and brave words, but I, the last to leave, was silent.

Where the valley curved, I looked back one last time. There, at the edge of the camp stood Chilsipee, alone. I stopped my horse. As I watched, she crossed her hands at the wrist and pressed them to her heart. I too made the sign for love, then watched as she walked back into the camp. I turned my horse and spurred him to catch up to the others.

Chapter Twelve

Each day we turned our faces toward the rising sun. Once through the great pass, we turned north from the Sweetwater to follow the Bighorn Valley into the heart of the Absaroka country. We camped without fires, though the nights were still bitterly cold. Our greatest ally would be surprise. The Crow would not expect raiders so early in the spring. Surprise would have to offset the rifles of the Sparrowhawks.

We located a village just before sunset. Rattler claimed that the warriors who had attacked us the previous fall had come from this village. I wondered how he could divine that but, since I seemed the only one inclined to dispute it, I kept my counsel. I resolved to protect Hawk Striking and look for Jake, but I refused to inflict any unnecessary harm on what might be an innocent camp.

As if reading my thoughts, Rattler spoke to me later, apart from the others. "They are not so innocent as you suppose," he said, waving his rifle in the direction of the Crow camp. "They approve of the attacks against our People and they benefit from them." Saying no more, he walked away. Nor was I so innocent, I thought. The rifle which Rattler carried into battle was the one which I had given him.

We assembled before dawn. In battle, Indians rarely adhere to any complex strategy. Rather, each man is intent on his own honor and plunder, relying on his own medicine for protection. But Rattler convinced the others to conform to a rough plan calling for a split attack on the large horse herd and the sleeping camp. The horses would come first, then the camp.

The battle was brief but successful. We took most of the herd, nearly a hundred horses. Those attacking the camp came back with a good number of rifles and ammunition and a few women captives. Hawk Striking and I had been in the horse raiding party and he was exhilarated and unharmed. I was relieved. Rattler had led the attack on the village and, afterward, called me over to where he stood with the captives. The women all sat upon the ground, blankets pulled up over their heads, waiting to die.

"There was little resistance," I commented as I approached Rattler.

He nodded. "Most of their warriors seem to be gone." With his toe, he nudged two of the women at his feet. "These should interest you, Little Spaniard. They are the wives of the Straw Beard."

I looked at the two. They were young and plump and

pleasant looking. By their likeness, I assumed that they were sisters. Now they sat in tear-stained dejection, leaning against each other for comfort.

"Jake!" I said out loud. They both looked up at me. In sign language, I asked if they were the wives of that man. They looked at one another, shrugged and nodded. Next, I asked where their man had gone. One pointed toward the east and moved her pointing hand in the sign for river.

In the Absaroka tongue, another of the women, older, said something harsh to my informant, causing her to fold her hands in her lap, her eyes cast down. With his foot, one of the Shoshone guards pushed the older woman onto her back, snarling at her to be silent. I laid my hand on the man's arm to restrain him and signed to the woman the same question, Where had the men gone?

With a hateful look, she said in broken Shoshone, "Men go north, river go. Take them east to Hidatsa." She then lapsed into sullen silence.

Turning to Rattler, I asked, "Is there a river to the north?"

He nodded. "This Bighorn River flows into the river of yellow stones and then that flows to a big river in the north. They say that the big river goes by the villages of the Hidatsa to the east."

I considered this information, then asked the older woman why the men were going to the Hidatsa.

"Trade furs," was all she said.

The raid was very successful in everyone's eyes—everyone's but Rattler. He wanted to move on to strike other Crow villages, but the rest felt that their honor was adequately vindicated by the horses and guns. Though he later became a man of peace, there was a fire in the young Rattler that was not easily quenched. Since the idea of unquestioned authority was alien to the People, the men prepared to return to the homeland. Rattler rode off angrily on his own to inflict more pain on the enemies of his people.

While I did not altogether trust my informant, I knew that I had to follow Jake and bring to a close this quixotic chapter of my life. My family was waiting. I bid a reluctant farewell to my dear younger brother, Hawk Striking. We embraced and held each other at arm's length for a long time.

"Watch over her," I whispered. He nodded, understanding my meaning, then turned away with a smile. I sat on my horse and watched my friends ride away with their spoils, then turned my mount north, to follow the river and Jake.

I should not have trusted the woman. Jake and the others probably had followed the Yellowstone for a way but, to avoid an encounter with the Blackfeet, they had turned east before striking the big river, which turned out to be the Missouri River. Traveling across the plains, they would meet the Knife River and follow it to the Hidatsa. I did not see the signs of their turning because, as usual, I was not looking for them. My thoughts were elsewhere.

I did keep my eyes on the sky, though. Early spring can be a dangerous time on the northern plains. The weather can change from idyllic spring sunshine to deadly winter storm in little more than an instant.

Crossing over to the north side of the Yellowstone, I followed the river to its confluence with the Missouri.

Camping on a bluff overlooking the two rivers, I could hear the crack and boom of breaking ice all night. In the morning, I surveyed the rivers and realized that I would have great difficulty crossing the spring-flooded streams. I rode west for a few miles to look for a possible crossing. What I found instead, were Blackfeet.

Actually, they found me. My eyes were on the river when, below me, from the trees along the bank, a dozen painted riders burst forth like a startled covey of quail. I did not pause for a second look. Spurring my horse, we pounded up the embankment and headed south across the open ground. Behind me, the Blackfeet were screaming in delight at such sport. Mine was a strong, long-legged stallion who had proven himself many times in the past several months, but even he was not invincible.

I heard the excited chirping of the sentinel, but not in time. At a full run, we entered the prairie dog town. The furry inhabitants dove into their burrows all around us. Before I could rein him in though, my horse's right fore foot sank into a hole, breaking the leg across the pastern as we pitched forward. I must have been knocked briefly unconscious by the fall. When I awoke I heard the awful screaming of my fine stallion cut short by a gunshot, and I saw a horribly painted face staring down at me along the barrel of a rifle.

Jerking me to my feet, my captors quickly disarmed me, prodding me with their weapons and commenting, I assumed, on my Shoshone attire. Searching through my *parfleches*, they found little of value beyond some jerky and pemmican, quickly devoured. After a short conference, it was apparently decided that I should become the principal participant in what must have been the national pastime of the Blackfoot nation. Since at least the time of John Colter, several mountain men had experienced the sport and now it was my turn.

The game began by stripping me naked. By signs, the warriors indicated that I was to be given a head start before they would pursue me. I could run in any direction I chose. With grins of anticipation, they explained that, if they caught me, I would die a horrible, tortured death. If I evaded them, I would earn the privilege of wandering naked and unarmed in a hostile wilderness. I was not encouraged.

I knew that, despite the incentive of survival, my short legs could not outrace the Blackfeet over any great distance. Therefore, when the signal was given, I sprinted back toward the Missouri River. Behind me, the warriors howled with glee, convinced that I was running into a trap. I did not bother looking back until I had reached the edge of the bluffs overlooking the river. There were three Indians in pursuit, the nearest a scant fifty yards behind. I considered and rejected the idea of making a stand. Instead, I rushed down the slope, barely keeping from falling and tumbling.

After the first dozen steps, I had ignored the pain in my bare feet. Crashing through the branches and brush along the river, I also tried to ignore the scratching on my body. No doubt to the surprise of the warriors, I ran directly out into the river. Actually, it would be more accurate to say onto the river. At that season, the Missouri was a roiling mass of ice floes crashing and crushing themselves together as the river carried them along on its torrent.

By the mercies of God, I managed to keep my footing as I leaped from floe to floe toward the center of the river. It was like walking the back of an angry dragon. On the shore, I caught a glimpse of my astonished opponents, trying to keep pace with my progress and calling for their armed and mounted brethren. I could see the mounted Blackfeet pointing my way from the bluffs. One paused to fire his rifle. I saw the puff of smoke but, at that range, accuracy was impossible.

The river was moving at tremendous speed. The warriors on foot were quickly left behind and, when the riders reached the confluence of the Yellowstone, they too were forced to stop. The ice pitched and bucked like an unbroken mustang, and I was obliged to shift and jump constantly to maintain my balance. The inflow of the Yellowstone caused such turbulence that I very nearly fell between the grinding blocks of ice.

My feet were frozen and bloody and the spray from the river had me shivering uncontrollably. Past the Yellowstone, another creek flowed in from the north and finally succeeded in upsetting me. I skidded to my hip and slid toward the turbulent water. My fingers scrabbled frantically on the rough ice for a grip, but not before a neighboring floe had smashed against my leg. The pain was excruciating. Before I knew it, I was in the frigid water. As I sank, the ice closed above me and I flailed in panic against my frozen tomb.

Then my hand felt something different, something softer. In desperation, I gripped and pulled myself toward the light. With a gasp I cleared the surface and saw before me brown fur. Using both hands, I hauled myself up and found that I was clinging to the bloated carcass of a buffalo. In the spring, buffalo would often walk out onto the frozen surface of rivers, only to have the ice break and plunge them to their death. Hundreds, perhaps thousands, of the creatures were drowned in this way every year. Now, exhausted, I lay upon my grisly raft and sank into unconsciousness.

I do not know how long I drifted. The blow I sustained at the prairie dog town must have been quite severe, for most of the time I was in merciful blackness. Dimly, I was aware of the swaying of the river then, like a riverine Ulysses, the song of sirens invaded my darkness.

Rough hands were on me, lifting and turning. Strange voices murmured around me and, above it all, the delicate sound of young women singing. Pain in my leg drove me up into full awareness. I was lying on the ground looking up at a circle of strange men. Many wore their hair parted across the head rather than down the center. The bangs created were chopped off above the eyes and curled outward. Lank strands framed the faces to the shoulders and were adorned with every kind of bauble, while the rest of the hair streamed down their backs to the waist.

When my eyes opened, they leaned back and exchanged looks and comments. The strange singing persisted, so I assumed that I was experiencing a delirium that would soon pass, but then another face was thrust into the circle, a face with a straw-colored beard.

"Damned if you ain't worse than a burr on my hide,

Spaniard!" Jake spate into the dust beside my head. "You picked a mighty poor mount to ride in on though, I'll say." He said something to the Indians and two of them lifted me up by my arms.

Upright, I could see that I was on the west bank of the river. The buffalo carcass had also been dragged ashore. These river Indians, it seems, considered such flotsam a special treat and regularly harvested the floating carrion. So outnumbered were they by the armed and mounted tribes of the plains, like the Sioux, that they rarely dared to leave their palisaded villages to hunt.

My leg was very painful and, I feared, broken—a large and livid bruise visible on my thigh. Supported by the two men, I was carried into the village past the community's gardens. The singing, it seems, came from young girls who camped on platforms in the fields to scare the birds away and sing to the growing corn.

The village was on a bluff overlooking the river but below the level of the surrounding plains. A wooden wall formed a protective stockade. Inside the wall, the houses were formed by piling dirt over a circular frame structure. The result looked very much like ant hills, spanning anywhere from forty to eighty feet in diameter. Aside from an open central plaza, the buildings were scattered in a random way throughout the town. I never had a clear view of the whole, but my impression was that there were forty or more buildings in the village.

I was taken to one of the houses near the wall. After being dragged through the entrance chamber, I was dumped roughly onto the floor near the central fire pit. The house appeared to be empty.

Jake thrust forward once more through the men. One or two Crow warriors were with him, as well as a man I took to be a European with a scarred and disfigured face. Jake referred to him as Rose. Squatting down before me, he spat again, commenting, "You are one sorry lookin' greaser!" His eyes scanned my bruised and naked body and he nodded as if in agreement with his own assessment. "Now suppose you tell me why yore so het up to git yore hands on ole Jake. I don't know you, no wise!"

My voice was cracked and raw from thirst and lack of use, but I rasped out, "Brother . . . you killed . . . brother!"

Jake's eyes widened and he sat back on his heels. "Seems like you come a long ways fer nothin' Spaniard. Twarn't me what done fer yore brother. It was the woman." Pushing up with his hands on his knees, he stood to his feet. "Makes no never mind, though. I aim to kill ya anyway. Seems like the only way to scrape you off my moccasins." He said something to his companions and the crowd began to leave.

" 'Cept that particular pleasure is gonna have to wait 'til mornin'. I got other pleasures in mind for tonight." He smacked his lips and leered. "Them Mandans down the river is mighty generous with their women." He walked to the doorway, turned and smiled coldly back at me. "I leave you to think on yore sins tonight. I'll lift yore hair in the mornin'." He was gone.

My past sins—though many—were not foremost on my mind. My present circumstances were. And those circumstances were none too pleasant to contemplate.

Looking around me, it appeared that the building had only two openings—the entranceway and the smoke hole.

By the light filtering down from that hole, I could see that the building's main structural support came from four large posts set up to form the corners of a square about ten feet apart. These extended upward some fifteen feet. Shorter posts, about six feet high, formed the uprights of the outer walls. Beams were laid across the tops of the uprights and rafters extended from the inner to the outer beams. Lighter poles, like the *latillas* which support the roofs of our homes in New Mexico, were laid across these, then willow boughs, grasses and two to three feet of dirt were piled on top of the whole. Clearly, digging through those sun-baked, earthen walls, was out of the question.

Having thoroughly surveyed my prison, I then assessed my body with equally discouraging conclusions. There was an unnatural protrusion on my left thigh which, along with the pain and swelling, seemed to indicate a broken bone. I was hungry and weak and scratched from head to toe from my race with the Blackfeet. Laying back beside the stone-lined firepit, I decided that I could at least rest. But my thoughts would not allow even that.

"It was the woman," Jake had said. My mind prodded at the statement the way you would prod a snake you only hoped was dead. It was possible, I thought, that Jake was lying in order to make me think he was blameless. But with me at his mercy, and scheduled to die at his hand in a few hours, my opinion could be of no consequence to him. Which must mean he was telling the truth. Closing my eyes, I tried to visualize Amada's room as I had found it.

I had to concede that, while I had found signs of Jake outside the window, I really had no evidence of him within the room. The vague traces I had found on the floor indicated only two sets of footprints—a man's, no doubt my brother's, and a woman's, a small woman.

I sat up. Lupita was a small woman! I could see her now, sullen and suspicious, hovering over Amada like a puppeteer. Now I remembered that it was Lupita who had said that a man had come in and killed Esteban, though she claimed to have not seen him. I berated myself for not seeing that contradiction sooner. And it had been Lupita who had hastened to confirm the *capitán's* statement that the mountain man had killed Esteban, when my brother came to Amada's defense.

Of course! I slapped my forehead. As a Yaqui, Lupita must have been weaned on hatred for the Spanish and, given my brother's overbearing manner, she must have seethed with hatred for him. Perhaps the thought of Amada, who was Indian like her, being wed to the hated Spaniard, was more than she could tolerate. Given the merest provocation, she could easily have struck the blow that killed him.

Further, I thought, Jake would hardly have chosen a candlestick as a weapon, not with a knife at his belt. What a fool I had been! But then another, more disturbing thought occurred to me. Amada knew who killed Esteban and yet allowed the accusations to fall on Jake. *My poor Amada. Out of what misguided sense of loyalty, or fear, or confusion did you act?*

My thoughts were interrupted by the swish of the hide entrance cover. Someone had entered and was standing in the gloom watching me. It was evening now and the dim light through the roof was growing fainter. I could do no more than lie there, aware of eyes that I could not see. After a while, the person walked forward into the light. It was a man, but dressed, painted and coifed like a woman. I stared at him in astonishment. Yes, it was indeed a man and, aside from the attire, an otherwise handsome and rugged looking fellow. He continued to look at me and I grew increasingly conscious of my nakedness. Finally, he spoke. His voice was very low and I could not understand the words, but he accompanied them with sign language.

"I saw you last night," he signed. I thought this odd, since I had only arrived in the village that afternoon.

"I am *berdache*," he added. This explained much. The *berdache* were men who dressed as women and did women's work in obedience to visions experienced after fasting. Among Indians, such men were reputed to have great supernatural powers and certainly, there was a strange, ethereal quality about this one.

"I have come to set you free," he said.

I sat up at that news. "How?" I asked, looking toward the entrance.

"There is a Black Mouth at the door," the man stated following my look. The Black Mouths were a society among both the Hidatsa and Mandan that exercised police functions in their villages. "In my dream, you were smoke, ascending to the stars." His hands and gaze floated up toward the smoke hole.

I realized that this *berdache* had had some kind of

premonitory dream about me. I too looked up at the smoke hole nearly twenty feet above my head. "It is very high," I indicated.

His heretofore impassive face, lit up with a smile of satisfaction. "You will fly like the sparks," was his explanation. "But not yet." He dropped a *parfleche* on the ground and knelt beside me. Running his hand gently over my injured leg he concluded, "Broken, and badly set." With his two fingers he indicated that the broken ends of the bone must be realigned. That was not welcome news, for I understood how dangerous a break could be. My own father, after all, had died from gangrene after such an injury.

The *berdache* was looking at me, awaiting my decision. I nodded. The man gave me a strip of rawhide which I wrapped around both hands. The length between my hands, I clamped between my teeth. Laying my leg flat, the man placed both hands over the break. With hands and teeth, I clenched the rawhide and nodded my assent. There was a crunching sound and a burst of terrible pain as the *berdache* brought his weight firmly down. My eyes bulged and sweat broke out on my face but, nearly as quickly as it had come, the pain subsided to a dull, throbbing ache. The swelling remained, and the bruise, but the unnatural lump had gone from my thigh.

Herbs were rubbed over my leg, then a deer bone splint was wrapped tightly against the break with thongs of buckskin. Next, the *berdache* took clothing—men's clothing, to my relief—from his bag and helped me dress. By now I felt exhausted and my head was pounding with pain. The man indicated that I should sleep, which I did, while he sat in silence, his eyes on some distant object which only he could see.

When he woke me, it was dark. Through the smoke hole I could see a profusion of stars. With his hands close to my face he explained that the time had come to fly. Once free of the building, I should walk down to the river where he would be waiting with a boat.

There is a saying that the Lord works in mysterious ways, but this was almost more mystery than I could bear. With my hands, I asked him why he, a Hidatsa, was helping me.

With a look of terrible sadness in his eyes, he said, simply, "I must obey the vision." I nodded.

He helped me to my feet and stepped into the fire pit. By gestures, he indicated that I should step into his hands and fly out of the smoke hole. I had some reservations about this plan. Even if he could toss me that high, it seemed as likely that I would hit the ceiling as the hole. But, since I could think of no alternative to his plan, I could only agree.

Softly, he began to sing, standing in the starlight, his arms raised. I assure you that I prayed as well. After a few minutes, he crouched, his fingers webbed together to form a stirrup. Because of my broken leg, I could provide little help, but thanks to his strength, my undernourished state, and a merciful God, when I stepped into his hands he launched me upward with tremendous force. As in his vision, I fairly flew, my arms extended like a diver's above my head.

My trajectory was only high enough to permit me to

grab the edge of the smoke hole. I dangled there above the room, imagining a second broken leg or worse should I fall, and struggled to pull myself up to freedom. First my head, then my shoulders, my whole body quivering with exertion, I inched into the night. At last, I was able to get my right foot onto the end of a *viga* and, finally, I was free, lying on my side, panting on the roof of the lodge.

The moon was dark, but the myriad of stars showed the shapes of buildings and sparkled on the surface of the river. I looked back down into my prison but could see nothing. As carefully and quietly as I could, I eased myself down the rounded sides of the building, away from the entrance. Despite my caution, a steady sprinkling of dislodged dirt preceded my descent. Once on the ground, I crouched and listened, but no sounds of alarm arose.

It was late and there appeared to be no one abroad in the village. Stealthily, I crept around the palisade. I felt that I could evade any sentries, but I was worried about the dogs. Near the entrance to the village, I spotted two of the Black Mouths apparently assigned to guard duty. Unfortunately, they seemed to be awake and conversing in low tones.

I crouched and considered what to do. It was possible that I could bluff my way past, dressed as I was in Hidatsa clothing, but I would undoubtedly be called upon to say something and I knew not a word of the Hidatsa tongue. I saw movement out of the corner of my eye and flattened myself on the ground. It was a dog.

Ordinarily, camp dogs are kept for utilitarian rather

than sentimental reasons. Before the Spanish brought the horse, dogs served as diminutive pack animals and, at all times, they were useful in cleaning up any scraps around the camp. In hard times, the dogs might even wind up in the cooking pot. But they were particularly good at warning the camp of any threatening activity, by their barking. It was this latter function that concerned me now.

The dog was a mangy, skinny specimen who seemed to be following his nose along the ground in search of edibles. About ten feet from me, the beast raised his head and stared. Now, I thought, now he will bark, they will find me and that will be the end. As the mountain men would say, I was gone beaver. But this dog did not bark. His nose twitched as he sampled the night air. I realized then that the poor creature was nearly blind. Stiff-legged, he approached a little closer. Another sniff and he seemed convinced that a human was near. Softly, a growl rose in his throat.

As slowly as I could, I reached down and removed my right moccasin. The growl stopped as I stretched the moccasin out toward him. Another painful step and he stretched out his scrawny neck in an attempt to smell the offering from a safe distance. I could see the grey hairs on his aged muzzle. Inch by arthritic inch, the old dog advanced on the moccasin. One last sniff at close range produced a half-hearted wag of the tail. Tentatively, his mouth closed on the moccasin's toe. I released my grip and the dog turned and ran awkwardly toward the entrance, his prize clenched victoriously in his mouth.

The two guards watched as the dog hobbled by and they began to laugh. Both moved down the path a ways to watch the pathetic animal. One picked up a rock and hurled it after. Their backs were to me and, in a moment, I was around the corner and swallowed by the night.

I felt as much as saw the path to the river. The rushing water hissed in the dark. The *berdache* was waiting. He led me to a round, buffalo hide bullboat and helped me climb painfully over the gunwale and get settled. "You will drift safely past the Mandan, but you must beware of the Arikara. It will be daylight by then." He seemed so certain, I knew that he was speaking from his vision.

"What will happen at the Arikara village?" I asked.

Handing me a paddle, he straightened up. Striking his right hand down past his left fingertips, he said, "The vision ends."

With that, I lost sight of him as the current caught the bullboat and pulled me once again into the river's embrace.

Chapter Thirteen

A bullboat is an awful thing to navigate. Consisting of two buffalo hides sewn together and stretched over a willow frame, it lacks a keel. As a result, it requires great skill to both advance the craft in the desired direction and prevent it from spinning like a leaf on the current. I lacked such skill, so I had to content myself with letting the current carry me as I tried to fend off snags and shallows, all the while careening dizzily.

The night air was cold and clear and the sky was bejewelled with an infinity of bright stars. The moist aroma of the river was an exotic perfume to my New Mexican senses. The stream flowed east and then south. Before dawn, I glided past the Mandan villages undetected. There were still some fires burning, so I assumed Jake's revelry was continuing. Perhaps there were other mountain men there as well.

The sunrise was golden and beautiful on that morning, but I suppose all released prisoners must think that. As the river wended southward, the trees grew sparser along the bank. For more than a mile, I drifted past the edges of a herd of buffalo watering. Late in the morning, I spotted a village. I was able to see it at a great distance. With difficulty, I paddled the bullboat to the river bank.

I was on the east bank and the village was on the west side of the river. My leg was throbbing from the hours crouched in the boat, so it was with great discomfort that I hid the boat and dragged myself into the shelter of the chokecherry bushes. Gratefully, I stretched out on the ground. The *berdache* had warned me to beware of the Arikara. I could see activity in the village, but it did not appear that anyone had noticed me.

The Arikara, like the other river tribes, were a hard-pressed people. Not too many years earlier, they had led prosperous lives mixing abundant agriculture in the flood plain with buffalo hunting on the surrounding prairies. Even after the coming of the white traders they had managed to capitalize on their position, growing prosperous as middlemen in the trade between Indians and whites. But now, the whites were dealing directly with the horse Indians. Those horse tribes were receiving plentiful arsenals of firearms in return. The Arikara particularly, hard hit by diseases introduced from the whites, had grown bitter and unpredictable.

I would have to walk around the village rather than risk floating by so closely, even at night. The *berdache* had supplied me with a *parfleche* of pemmican, so I ate a few handfuls and fell into a fitful sleep as the sun warmed the earth around me. Toward mid-afternoon, the buzzing harassment of flies woke me. My head ached and my mouth was parched. Hoping to be able to creep undetected back to the river for a drink, I peered cautiously from my brushy shelter.

There was little activity toward the village, but when I looked to the north, I saw a boat coming downstream. I crouched back down to wait. It appeared to be a wooden, canoe-like boat of the type the French call a *pirogue.* It was piled high with packs of furs and trailed a fully laden bullboat by a painter. One man was paddling the craft and, when he drew opposite my position, I saw that the man was Absaroka Jake.

Jake seemed to have no qualms about paddling openly by the Arikara village. Shortly after he passed my hiding place, someone in the village spotted him. A small crowd of people formed on the river bank, one or two men even wading into the water. Although the river was running strongly, Jake managed to slow his *pirogue* in order to consider the Arikara proposals. I was too far away to hear anything, but it was clear by their gestures that they wanted Jake to land and spend the night.

Jake seemed disinclined until someone, with inadvertent brilliance, brought forward a couple of young women. They indicated that the women would be at his disposal if he would spend the night with his Arikara brothers. They had found Jake's price, because he immediately turned his *pirogue* in toward the shore. But, if women were Jake's weakness, impatience was the Arikara's.

Jake had barely reached the shallows, when two of the men lunged to grab the *pirogue*. Sensing a trap, Jake began to furiously back paddle but, before he could get far, there was a puff of smoke and Jake pitched over the side. It was another moment before the sound of the rifle shot reached me. The Arikara made heroic attempts to reach the *pirogue* and bullboat but the current was too swift and the vessels too far out. I could not see Jake's body, but I assumed it was not far behind the two boats as they flashed down the river, a dozen young men on the shore futilely trying to keep pace.

I lowered my head on my arms. For more than half a year I had clumsily pursued Jake on a misguided mission of justice and now, almost casually, he was dead for no particular crime beyond the evil intersection of time and place. I was very tired. I wanted to go home.

After sundown, the river was in shadows, so I crept out and drank my fill of the cold, muddy water. A long night lay before me. Gingerly, I climbed up from the river onto the plains. Again the night was star bright with just a sliver of moon to light my way. All night long I walked, with frequent stops to rest my aching leg. A driftwood branch served as a crutch.

By dawn I was thoroughly exhausted. I doubt if I had covered more than three or four miles in all those painful night-time hours. I let the sun chase me back to the shelter of the trees along the river. It would be folly to be caught out in the open by the Sioux or Cheyenne. In my condition, running away was clearly not possible.

My discouragement bordered on despair as I stumbled back down to the river to drink. My plan, if it could be called such, involved following the river down to the American settlements and then finding some way to get back to Santa Fe. Physically, I was quite incapable of stealing a horse and riding, and it now appeared that I was equally incapable of walking. I regretted not trying to float by the Arikara village and now considered walking back upstream in the hopes that my bullboat was still there.

But as I considered my gloomy possibilities, something in the river caught my eye. In some past flood, a tree had been undercut by the waters and now tilted sideways, its branches reaching down into the river. Driftwood and debris were tangled in those branches and, miraculously, so was something else.

Carefully, I limped my way out along the trunk of the tree and looked down on the boiling waters. There below me, pinned sideways to the branches of the old cottonwood, was Jake's *pirogue*, its bullboat companion still tied to it, bobbing in the churning river alongside.

I hated to quibble with answered prayer, but the situation posed something of a dilemma. I could conceive of no way to retrieve the boats. If I dislodged them with a branch, the river's current would snatch them from my grasp. I could think of only one course of action and that, as usual, involved risks.

My position was about ten feet above the *pirogue*. It was possible that I could climb down the branches that pinioned the boat, get in, and work it back to shore along the horizontal ladder formed by the fallen tree's branches. That was possible, but what seemed more likely was that my splinted leg would cause me to tumble into the cold, swift waters and be drowned. Still, it seemed more promising than walking or waiting to be discovered.

I lay down on the tree trunk and swung my legs over the side, searching for a foothold among the branches.

My right foot finally lodged on a firm feeling place. I shifted my weight and lowered myself. Fortunately, I had not yet let go of my grasp on the trunk. The branch beneath my foot snapped and there I hung, by my fingertips, swinging above the rushing river.

Looking down, I could see that I was right above the *pirogue*. My fingers, hands, wrists and arms quivered with the strain as my foot flailed blindly for a sanctuary. I must have maintained this ludicrous posture for over a minute when my grip finally broke and I fell. Landing on the cushion of furs, I slid into the open area at the rear of the craft. However, the impact of my fall, plus my added weight, proved to be more than the restraining branches could bear. With a sharp report like a gun, the branches broke and away I twirled down the river, seated backward in the bobbing *pirogue*.

I had no paddle, so I could be little more than a spectator as the boat ran its course. In no time at all, I had covered more distance than all my previous night's exertions had attained. Out of the debris still clinging to the side of the *pirogue* I extracted a strong pole which I used to combat snags and other floating hazards.

All day long I skimmed along on the current. The river twisted and turned like a snake. A thin fringe of trees and brush clung to the water's edge while beyond, the hills rolled away into the distance like mighty ocean swells. The usually tawny grasses were a bright, springtime green, dotted with occasional herds of buffalo and antelope. Above me the sky was a bright and polished blue.

In contrast to my morning mood, I passed the rest of the day in a state as sunny and hopeful as the climate.

Tucked within the folds of the furs, I had found Jake's rifle and shot bag, along with a *parfleche* of jerky and pemmican. All things considered, I was quite content to float along and wait for what God had planned for me next.

Just at sunset, I spied something ahead on the east bank of the river. It appeared to be a wooden tower. Below it a stockade wall was under construction. The design did not look like anything I had heard of Indians building so, surely, those must be Americans ahead! I was jubilant, but only briefly. I realized that, without a paddle, I was a prisoner of the river, able to do no more than wave as I floated past.

With my pole, I tried to touch the river bottom, but with no success. I had no idea how far it might be to the next outpost, therefore I had to do something to reach that stockade. There were people moving on the bluff so, as carefully as I could, I rose to my feet. I was able to give a shout and one wave of my arms before I lost my balance and plunged over the side. With one hand clutching the side of the *pirogue*, I thrashed and spluttered in the muddy water. With one arm and one leg, I tried to swim with my boats toward shore.

I would have drowned had I not been spotted. Men ran down the bluff to the river's edge. Two of them quickly cast off in a canoe and paddled across the current to try to intersect my course. The men clearly knew what they were doing. Even though we drifted swiftly below the buildings on the shore, they managed to catch me. The man in front grabbed hold of the *pirogue* on the side opposite from where I clung.

"Just hang on!" the man shouted. I could not reply so I just did as he directed. Skillfully, the paddler in the stern angled us in to the muddy bank. There in the shallows, I could not even rise to my feet. The man from the bow stepped out of his canoe and slogged through the muck to where I lay.

"What's the matter with you? Got a broken leg?" He gave a short laugh.

Wearily, hair and water streaming over my face, I cocked my head to look up at him. "Yes," I replied simply. At that, his expression grew concerned and he leaned down to help me to my feet. "Thank you," I gasped, as I sank onto the furs in the *pirogue.* "I did not have a paddle, so I could not control my boat." I tried to smile at the absurdity of my situation, but I am sure that my expression was more of a grimace.

He and his companion stood looking at me as I tried to control my labored breathing. Others from their party were arriving now on horseback. By the expression on their faces, I knew that I must have presented a curious spectacle. Wet and muddy, dressed in castoff Hidatsa clothing, my black hair long and bedraggled, they probably were not sure if I was Indian or European.

I had so much to explain, I did not know where to begin, and my rescuers had so many questions they were equally at a loss, until finally the man who had helped me to my feet, stepped forward.

"My name is Charles Bent," he said. "We're the Missouri Fur Company, building a fort here." He nodded toward the big man who had paddled their canoe. "This here's Moses Carson."

I nodded and, as my breathing grew more normal, I started to introduce myself. "My name is . . ." I had to pause. For so many months I had been the Little Spaniard of the Shoshone that I had to consciously think of my other identity. "I am Jose Garcia," I said, shortening my name for their American ears. "I am from Santa Fe in the Province of New Mexico."

Their eyes grew wide. "You're a long ways from home!" Bent exclaimed.

"Yes, I truly am." Other explanations would have to wait.

On horseback, they brought me back to their camp. Dry clothing, buffalo stew and hot coffee had me quite revived, so I was able to give a brief narration of my recent experiences. When I told of the death of Jake and my fortuitous recovery of his boats, I could see looks of skepticism exchanged by some of the men. They obviously thought it more likely that this piratical looking Spaniard had murdered Jake and stolen his pelts.

Big Moses Carson, however, declared his faith in my words by saying, "I knew Absaroka Jake." He nodded, his lips tight in his bearded face. "Ain't nobody likely to mourn that varmint!"

Another man, Robert Jones, leaned forward into the firelight. "I took a look at the pelts in your boats. They're rich, I'll say! Real prime fur! Where abouts do you suppose this Jake was setting traps?"

"Well, he was on very friendly terms with the Crow, so I imagine that he did not stray too far from their territory. Actually, I saw signs of many beaver all along the Yellowstone country. The Crow have a reputation for being pretty tolerant of whites, but the Blackfeet to the north, I cannot say the same about." The men all laughed at my understatement.

I spent that night and all the next day with the fur men. That was the beginning of my long friendship with Charles Bent and his family. He was an intelligent, educated man, only a year or two older than I and of approximately the same physical stature. Though he came from a prominent St. Louis family, the lure of the open lands drew him west into the fur trade. I recall standing on a bluff above the river with him, watching the sunset. The land grew softer as the shadows lengthened.

"It's like velvet," he said, a look of rapture on his face. He was a true plainsman, in love with the endless space and limitless sky.

On the next morning, I took my leave. I now possessed a paddle for my *pirogue* as well as directions, supplies and messages for friends and relatives down the river. Charles insisted that I stay with his family in St. Louis and even penned a note of introduction for me. Moses Carson, as he helped shove my boats out into the river said, "I'd appreciate it if you'd look in on my people in the Boone's Lick country, around Franklin. Let'm know I'm still above ground. I got a brother, William, who'd be proud to put you up for a spell."

"All right," I shouted back as the current drew me away. "Thank you all! Go with God!"

I saw their waves, then turned my attention away from their Fort Recovery, as they named it, and back to the river and home.

Chapter Fourteen

From what the fur men had told me, I knew that I was not yet out of danger from some of the surrounding tribes, but I saw nothing more than an occasional distant rider during my travel. I stopped briefly at Fort Atkinson near the Council Bluffs and then paddled down to the Missouri Territory.

This was well-watered woodland country, more like the land around Washington City than New Mexico. Numerous small creeks emerged from the forests to contribute to the muddy river. I stopped for a night at Fort Osage where the New Harmony Mission sought to win the Osage to the Christian faith. Among those missionaries was a tall, gaunt, stoop-shouldered, red-haired preacher by the name of William Shirley Williams, who would become known as the legendary mountain man, Bill Williams.

From Fort Osage, I paddled on to the Mississippi River and St. Louis, drawing alongside one of its stone levees on a misty spring morning with the eastern sky tinged in pastel colors. The city lay between the river and the bluffs. Three main streets running north and south formed the tiered center of St. Louis. Only a few years earlier, those thoroughfares had borne the names of Rue Royale near the levees, Rue de l'Eglise before the Cathedral and, on the higher ground the Rue des Granges. But as the character of the town had changed from French to Anglo-Saxon, so the streets had been transformed into Main, Second and Third.

Near the waterfront, the taverns and billiard parlors were thronged with every type of humanity—Canadian trappers and American hunters, Spaniards and Frenchmen, Indians and negroes, ill-clad brothers of the bottle and black-clad Sisters of Charity. I was uneasy about leaving my furs unattended while I searched for a buyer, but this problem was taken care of by a black-haired, round-faced young man named Ceran St. Vrain, whose job, at that time, was to prowl the waterfront enticing trappers into his employers' warehouse.

So it was that I obtained nearly a thousand dollars for Jake's pelts from Pratte, Cabanne and Company. I bid good-bye to young St. Vrain, who would also later come to New Mexico, and went in search of the family home of my new friend Charles Bent.

St. Louis was a tangle of muddy, rutted streets during this season. Nearly six thousand people made up the permanent population with, it seemed, at least that many in transit at any time—mountain men, keel boaters, settlers, soldiers and land swindlers. Most of the houses were of wood, single-storied with porches built on to them, providing a place to catch the evening breeze during blazing hot summers. But many of the increasingly prosperous citizens had built fine two-story homes of stone or brick surrounded by spacious verandas. The streets, though unpaved, were pleasantly shaded by the city's many locust trees.

At this time, Silas Bent, Charles' father, was a judge of the Supreme Court of the Missouri Territory. The United States Congress in that year of 1821 was vigorously debating whether to admit Missouri as a state. The Bent family had most of their eleven children housed in a solid home near the old French residences with their deep green lawns and fragrant fruit trees.

I spent a pleasant few days with the Bents, where eleven-year-old William hung on my every word as I related some of my experiences in the mountains and plains and described our New Mexico homeland. In my last evening, I shared coffee with Judge Bent while the fireflies flickered and the moon reflected from the Mississippi River wide beneath us.

"Don Jose," he said in his courtly way, "I have spoken with the Spanish consul here in St. Louis and he is frankly pessimistic about your plans for traveling to New Orleans and booking passage to Vera Cruz. His information is rather scant, but it would appear that New Spain is very chaotic right now. The insurrection is widespread and he feels that the Spanish will very shortly withdraw from Mexico. Transportation is likely to be difficult for some time to come."

I frowned into my cup. "Did His Excellency, the consul, have anything to suggest?" I asked.

The Judge smiled. "He suggested that an educated young man, such as yourself, could do well in business right here in St. Louis. I would be pleased to introduce you to some of my acquaintances."

"Thank you, very much, sir. You are most generous. But I must return to my family as quickly as possible."

My host remained silent for quite a while as he pondered my situation. Then he looked at me and smiled. "You've proven yourself to be most resourceful, thus far. Perhaps you could obtain horses in the western part of the territory and from there, make your way to the Spanish settlements in Texas? It could be dangerous, but you are obviously not a man dissuaded by danger."

I thought about his suggestion long after I retired that night, and the next day announced that I would indeed be leaving for the western frontier again in the hope of finding some means of reaching New Mexico. The Bent family was obviously disappointed that I had not decided to settle down in St. Louis, but extended every kindness to aid me on my way.

Arrangements were made and, the next morning, I was taken in the Bent carriage to the landing where I embarked for my first steamboat journey. It was noisy and sooty, with sparks and glowing cinders scattered everywhere. I was quite caught up in the excitement of the departure until my attention was arrested by a gang of negro slaves being led up the gangway in chains.

I kept to my cabin for most of the journey until we landed at the town of Franklin. This western river town had been organized only a few years before, but already it boasted over a hundred and twenty log houses, a dozen stores and businesses, a courthouse, post office and log jail. New settlers were arriving every day. The area had originally grown up around the salt works developed by the two sons of Daniel Boone—from which it derived the name Boone's Lick—but farmers and craftsmen were now in the majority.

My first stop was at the office of the region's newspaper, *The Missouri-Intelligencer*, where I asked for news of the Carson family. I was given directions to both the farm of William Carson and that of his stepmother and neighbor, the widow Rebecca. But, I was told, I was as likely to find William down at the blacksmith's shop, since he often brought tools in for repair on Saturdays.

A small group of men stood, sat, and leaned against the walls inside the smithy, talking and loafing, as the blacksmith's anvil rang. I spotted a strongly built man who resembled Moses Carson and introduced myself.

"I met your brother just a few weeks ago on the river above Fort Atkinson," I said. "He asked me to stop by and let you know that he is well."

William shook my hand. "Well, I do appreciate the news, mister. It's real hard to keep track of ole Mose, so it's nice to know he's still kickin'."

We talked a little longer about Moses and about me, until the blacksmith called William's name to tell him that his work was finished—a new iron rim had been fitted to a wagon wheel.

"Why don't you come on out to the place for a while, til you get your plans set?" Carson asked me. "The folks would be real tickled to meet you and hear somethin' new."

I accepted the invitation gladly, feeling slightly guilty that I had been hoping that he would invite me.

My leg needed time to heal and my mind time to think of a way to get home. From the blacksmith's, we drove the wagon to one of the mills where William had earlier left some grain. I helped load and then we rattled off down a badly rutted, tree-lined road to the Carson farm.

At dinner I met his wife Cassandra, a strong, quiet woman, and his delightful daughter, Adaline. After dinner, we walked across the fields to his stepmother's farm.

"Since my pa died, I try to help out over there as much as I can," William explained. "It ain't easy on Rebecca, a woman alone with half a dozen kids to raise." William's father, Lindsey, had been killed three years earlier by a falling branch while clearing trees from a field. Now the widow struggled with the help of her three oldest sons, Robert, seventeen, Hamilton, thirteen and Christopher, known as Kit, eleven.

The evening was pleasant. It was May by now and the air was warm and thick. A small smudge fire was kindled to keep the mosquitoes at bay as we sat on the porch. As the guest, I did most of the talking, bringing news of Moses and describing some of what I'd seen of the world. I entertained the family for several evenings in this way, with young Kit particularly, hanging on my every word. By then, the formality of 'Mr. Garcia' had passed, and I was being referred to as Josey, since the proper pronunciation of Jose seemed to evade them.

During the days, despite a certain amount of pain I still felt in my leg, I would help out as much as I could with the chores and labor for both William and Rebecca, with the result that I spent quite a bit of time with Kit. When Kit ran away some years later to become the legendary Kit Carson, I understand that his mother assigned some of the blame to me for filling his head with stories of adventures among strange peoples.

Chapter Fifteen

Although a strong French influence in economic and cultural affairs endured in St. Louis, I should point out to you, my grandson, that Spain had been the actual ruler of that vast area west of the Mississippi River for virtually all of the forty years prior to the Americans' purchase of Louisiana from Emperor Napoleon. While complaints about the stern, even despotic, rule of the Spanish authorities were justifiable, there were many in Missouri who regretted its passing. The Louisiana Purchase did extend the boundaries of the United States, but the authority of the government back in Washington had little force in this vast territory for many years. Unfortunately, the rich Missouri bottomlands attracted not just hard working farmers like the Carsons and civic-minded professionals like the Bents but people who held the rule of law—any law—in contempt.

With the immigration of Americans came fugitives

and malcontents of much the same caliber as Absaroka Jake. These rabble created turmoil and disorder, preying on the livestock of the settlers and abusing the heretofore tolerant native peoples, the Sac and Fox, Kansa, and Osage.

This blatant criminality was compounded by the arrogant evil of the wealthy slave owners who came to the territory. As is all too often the case, those of power and affluence assume that their selfish interests were equivalent to their notion of the public interest. Because of the power of their money, they are able to control the newspapers and the offices of governance and so mislead the vast majority of ordinary people into thinking that patriotism and righteousness are synonymous with the interests of the elite.

Despite their democratic rhetoric, this elite did not even deign to submit their proposed state constitution to a popular vote in Missouri. The irony of this hypocrisy, however, seems to have been lost on the majority of Missourians though, as they rallied to defend the 'sacred' right of 'free' people to enslave other human beings. In what is now known as the Missouri Compromise, the Congress of the United States chose to evade the moral issue of slavery and settled on a political compromise to permit entry of Missouri as a state, thus postponing and aggravating the terrible resolution until the Civil War forty years later.

Adding to the general turmoil of Missouri in 1821, was the economic situation. Much of the territory's earlier growth had been generated by a massive reliance on credit. The so-called Panic of 1819, however, had led to a collapse of this gossamer financial basis and left many people in dire circumstances, harried by creditors like a wounded buffalo surrounded by wolves.

One evening a few days after my arrival, I found my host, William, hunched in introspection at the family's plank table. I overcame my usual reticence and said, "You seem troubled, Will. May I be of assistance?"

He smiled wearily. "Not unless you got a gold mine in your possibles! But I appreciate the offer."

I sat down opposite him at the table. Evening light cast a pale illumination through the cabin's open door. "You have money troubles, yes?"

"Oh, yes! Me and everybody else I know." He ran his hand absentmindedly through his hair. "Most of what we need we can do for ourselves with just a little hard work farmin' and huntin'. But there's some things you just need cash money for and there ain't none around, 'cept in those banks back east. They're like spiders and there's plenty of us flies caught in their web."

I nodded. "It is the same for us in New Mexico. The viceroy controls what comes in and out of the province, and what price we will pay, so we are reduced to bartering goods and services among ourselves because there is no money. Like you, we are the frontier, so we must pay dearly for what we need."

"We're not as bad as some, neither," Will conceded. "What set me to thinkin' so down was that a neighbor of ours got himself arrested today, 'cause he couldn't pay his debts. Now his family can't even post his bond." Sadly he shook his head.

"Have I met this man?"

"Don't believe so. He's a good man, if a trifle hot-tempered at times. William Becknell's his name. He's about my age. He come out here from Virginia around the same time we come out from Kentucky. He spent three years with the Boone boys in the Rangers back during the war. He's done this and that since then, but now the damn bankers got him so tied up I can't see how he'll ever get shed of 'em."

We talked a little while longer, as the light faded, then I bade him goodnight. But I did not have a restful night. Rather, I tossed and turned, my mind juggling thoughts like a circus performer. By dawn, an idea had taken shape that I presented to Will even before we had eaten breakfast.

Carson frowned at the intensity of my expression. "You feelin' all right, Josey? You look a might feverish. Your leg ain't turnin' on you, is it?"

"No, no, I am fine. I was thinking about our discussion last night and I have an idea . . . a theory . . . I would like you to consider."

He sat down on the tree stump used to split firewood. "Fire away, friend!"

"In my country, we get very little rain. The ground is rich and fertile, but it lacks moisture. So we build *acequias*, irrigation ditches, to carry water from the river to the fields. But even then, the far edges of the field are often still dry. But the *acequia* itself! It gets so much water, that we have to constantly cut back the weeds that flourish there and threaten to soak up the water." I was pacing restlessly back and forth before him. "Now, Missouri and New Mexico, we are like the far edges of the field. We are frontiers and only a very little moisture makes its way out to us. But if we could instead become *acequias*, we would be able to flourish like the weeds." I clapped my hands, beaming in triumph.

Will gave me a quizzical look. "Now it may be we got a little language problem here, Josey, or maybe you just didn't sleep too good, but I don't see what you're gettin' at."

I tried to be more clear. "Right now we are beggars for scraps, standing outside. But if we put ourselves in the middle . . . ?" My mind searched for a better example. "When I was in St. Louis, I saw some very wealthy homes. And why? Because the people who built them are successful in the fur trade with the Indians. They take the manufactured goods from the United States and take it out to the Indians in return for the furs and pelts that they have access to. The Indians want the manufactured goods and the Americans want the furs. And who makes money? The middleman—the fur trader."

I squatted down and drew a map in the dirt. "Now there are several ways this could succeed. First of all, there are many tribes between here and New Mexico, such as the Comanche, with access to a wealth of buffalo. These tribes are generally beyond the reach of the Missouri river traders so far to the north." I stabbed the top of my dusty map for emphasis. "Then there are the goods of my own country—buffalo and beaver, sheep, salt, blankets, leather, copper goods. And in return, New Mexico too needs manufactured goods. And Missouri is about the same distance from Santa Fe as Chihuahua. And, finally, goods brought into New Mexico can then be traded down to Mexico in return for other goods, silver and gold." I stood up, my palms held out in supplication, begging him to see the logic of my idea.

Will only nodded. "I can see where there's some money to be made in all that, but there's still a problem. Your government don't care much for outsiders comin' in. I recall a dozen men or more who've tried what you're suggestin' and wound up in a prison cell in New Spain for their trouble."

"That's true. But right now, Spain is withdrawing. There is rebellion in Mexico. That means that the viceroy's grip will be loosened. Now is the time to establish the trade before someone in the new government can again impose a monopoly. And, even if we find New Mexico still closed to Americans, I may be able to help establish profitable ties with the Comanche. I speak their language and they have no quarrel with the Americans."

He sat in serious contemplation, his eyes on my tracings in the dirt. "It makes sense," he finally conceded. "Darned if it don't! But it'll take some cash to get some trade goods together and, like I said, cash is about as scarce as teats on a bull right now."

I cleared my throat, feeling embarrassed and slightly guilty. "I have some money." In explanation, I added, "I had some furs when I came down the river."

Carson slapped his knee and stood, glowing with excitement, finally. "Well, who says the sun don't rise in the west? Why, I've a mind to go with you, if'n you'll have me."

"Of course!" I extended my hand. "We will need quite a few men to ensure a safe passage."

Will waved his hand. "That shouldn't be a problem. I can think of a couple right now who'd be fair company." A frown clouded his expression. "In fact, the best man I could think of to put something like this together is the fella I told you about last night, Becknell. 'Cept he's in jail."

I shrugged. "Perhaps we should go to the jail and see what is required to get him out?"

With that, we went in to breakfast. My appetite was excellent. In my heart, I knew that I was going home.

Four hundred dollars bond set Becknell at liberty. I found him a man of intelligence and energy and, at that moment, anger.

"Leeches!" he described his creditors. "Win, lose, or draw, they'll get their money and let somebody else do all the work and take all the chances."

We stood outside the log jail. As the sun rose, the day began to turn sultry. "I'm obliged, sir." Becknell shook my hand.

"Josey's got an idea," Will volunteered, "could dig us all out of debt."

"Now that," Becknell said, with emphasis, "would interest me."

We moved away from the glaring sunlight beating down on the street to the shade of a hickory tree. When I had explained my plan, Becknell said, "But there's no river. The Missouri flows too far north." Historically, American expansion had always followed watercourses and American eyes continued to seek out rivers as the roads to progress.

"The Indians travel a thousand miles in any direction they please," I countered. "To a man on horseback, the plains are no more of an obstacle than the ocean is to a ship, provided he can find water to drink. Once you strike the Arkansas River—which you can drink even if you cannot navigate it—you can follow it all the way to the mountains, then turn south into New Mexico."

"So you really think a mule train could make it?" he asked.

"Yes, I do."

He was silent, his hand stroking his chin as he thought. "Yes," he decided. "I can see where it would work. Certainly I've no better means at hand to shake the leeches of me. I'll take the gamble."

And so he did. With my money from Jake's furs as a down payment, Becknell was able to obtain merchandise and mules on credit. An advertisement in the *Missouri-Intelligencer* issued a call for seventy men to join us for the purpose of trading horses and mules and "catching wild animals of every description" in the west. To protect our commercial advantage, we thought it best not to mention New Mexico as a possible destination.

Seventy men seemed like a good company of men in order to be protected from hostile Indians but, as it turned out, far fewer than seventy men accompanied us. In addition to Captain Becknell, William Carson and myself, we were joined by Ewing Young of Tennessee, who would later perform prodigious feats of exploration on his own. I am afraid my memory is weak as to the names of our other intrepid companions, but I think they were Marshall and McLaughlin.

Throughout the summer, we made our preparations. Horses and mules, tack and saddles, trade goods, powder and lead all had to be acquired. My leg was nearly healed now, strong enough to lift me into the saddle, even if I did continue to limp. Becknell proved to be a good choice for leader. Disciplined and organized, he could direct his energy with great concentration and inspire followers without resorting to harshness.

I remember the summer of 1821 as a buzz of activity, anticipation, flies and mosquitoes for I have to admit the Missouri climate was not so agreeable to me. However, before dawn on September first we were ready. I shook hands with all my rough hewn American friends, thanking them for their great kindness and hospitality. The women and children left behind were remarkably stoic, even though they could well imagine the perils that lay before their departing men. Having endured so much in their frontier life, endurance had become a habit.

We left Franklin just at sunrise. I never saw it again. A few years later, the river flooded and washed nearly the entire town off its ill-chosen site. We proceeded along the north bank quietly, each man immersed in his own thoughts, crossing the river by ferry at Arrow Rock. Heading west, away from the winding river, we continued another five or six miles before camping for the night.

In the morning, we rode along an old Indian trail, known as the Osage Trace, that took us some thirty miles across the Little Osage Plain. The fourth day brought us to Fort Osage, where I renewed my acquaintance with Bill Williams and introduced him to my companions. I noted a certain wistfulness in his expression as he heard of our vague plans to head west in search of profit. His restless temperament yearned for something more adventurous than the commendable work of interpreting for the Mission.

Finally, on the fifth day, we left the Missouri Territory. Riding down from the wooded bluffs, we embarked on a sea of grass. Later settlers would call this region the Blue Country, in part because it lies between the Little Blue and Big Blue rivers and, in part, because of the beautiful indigo haze that tinges the evening air along the rich bottomlands. The dense stands of timber that characterized Missouri gave way to groves of oak, hickory, dogwood and willow along the creeks and rivers, but grasslands were the dominant feature of this part of the country.

And such grasses! Standing green or golden in season, the grasses would grow tall enough to brush our stirrups or tickle our horses' bellies in spots. From every side came a symphony of birdsong while winged clouds darkened the sky above us. Though we carried some supplies, our party was small enough to subsist quite well on the abundance of game provided by this beautiful country. And, for now, water was not a concern because many shallow streams laced our path.

Of greater concern were Indians. Osage and Kaw Indians called this region home and, though generally peaceful, increasing pressure from settlers were trying the ability of the elders—'the Little Old Men' or *No'n-Ho'n-Shinkah* as the Osage called them—to control their outraged youth. We rotated guard duty throughout the nights, alert for any restlessness in the livestock that might signal a stealthy Indian approach.

Over the years, I have had only slight dealings with the Osage but I have found them an appealing people. These Children of the Middle Waters, as they were known, called themselves the Little Ones in all humility. Believing themselves to be descended from the stars, they assumed a responsibility from *Wah'Kon-Tah* to care for the Sacred One—the earth—after a heavenly model. Their taking on this sacred task reminded me of the admonition given by God to Adam to tend and to keep Eden. I have felt a certain kinship and affection for the Osage ever since.

Our path lay roughly southwest and, for several days, was a rather pleasant, uneventful ride through golden meadows of late summer. The spirits of our party were high as we dined on fresh game, fish and wild strawberries while our animals stayed fat on the luxuriant pasturage. When we reached the Neosho River, we spent the night beneath a canopy of branches from a grove of oaks, elms and hickories.

With the crossing of the Neosho, we seemed to cross an invisible boundary. The prairies of tall waving grass soon yielded to the short, tawny buffalo grass and the moisture fled from both ground and air. We also passed from the region of the Kaw and Osage into that of the Comanche, Kiowa and Pawnee. Our vigilance increased by day and night. Every distant herd of buffalo and each bounding antelope had us reaching for our guns for fear that they might be warriors.

Two days after passing the Neosho, I was keeping

the watch over our sleeping camp for those dark hours before dawn. I was quite alert, my mind grappling with a number of thoughts, when my attention was caught by a faint glow on the horizon. At first I was pleased, thinking the time had passed quickly and the sunrise was at hand. But then I heard or sensed a stirring in the night. I cocked my rifle, raising it to my shoulder, and nearly fired as an antelope bounded into the campfire light, its eyes wide with fright. After it had blundered out of sight again, I smelled it—smoke.

"Wake up!" I shouted. "Everyone up! Fire!"

My companions bolted from their blankets, full of sleep and questions. Half-dressed, Becknell ran to my side, a pistol in his hand. "What is it, Josey?"

"Fire," I repeated, pointing toward the eastern horizon. "It's still too early and that light is too far north to be the dawn."

The others joined us.

"Yep," Ewing Young agreed. "I can smell it now."

Becknell frowned. "It looks pretty far away. Should it concern us?"

I nodded. "You have seen how dry this country is. Out here, fire can travel as fast as a horseman, sometimes faster." I paused, then added, "Indians will sometimes light fires to drive animals—or enemies."

That decided it. "Let's load up!" Becknell ordered.

The men worked quickly and efficiently, without panic. Horses and mules were nervous and balky, but we were mounted within a quarter of an hour. More wildlife was racing by us now, fleeing the fire. Rabbits, deer, quail, and even mice were on the run. The predawn breeze brought the sting of smoke to our eyes.

For once, the mules needed no extra urging to keep up as we loped through the grey light.

Looking back, I could see the flames now. The fire was gaining on us. The others had seen it too. Without a word, we spurred to a gallop. Our only hope was to reach some kind of sanctuary since the fire was too wide and showed no sign of slowing. It extended over such a great distance and was moving so fast that we could see no way to get around it; we needed to stay ahead of it until we found some place of refuge—if we could.

Just as the sun broke over the horizon, we reached a ravine. From a hundred yards, we could not see if any water was flowing but without slowing, we scrambled over the crumbling bank and plunged down the slope. I was at the rear of our little train, so I could hear whoops of joy before I saw the splashing. In the creek bed, we turned south and trotted a short distance to a more gradual incline made by animals coming to drink. There we climbed up the western edge and stopped along the rim.

The fire was very near now, roaring like a dragon. We could see the plain before it alive with fleeing creatures and could hear the screaming of those that were too slow. Coyotes and rabbits, wolves and antelope, hunter and hunted were united in despair and death.

"It's sure moving fast!" Will Carson observed.

"It could jump this creek, I think!" I added.

Becknell nodded, his mouth a grim line. "Back down in the water!" he snapped.

No one questioned the decision. We drove our animals back into the shallow creek. The risen sun was hidden behind a curtain of smoke on our left. Snakes were slithering down the slope, oblivious to all except escape from the fiery foe. The heat was growing and stealing the breath from our lungs.

"Dismount!" Captain Becknell yelled.

Choking from the smoke, we stood with one hand gripping the halters of our terrified animals while, with the other, we used our hats to douse ourselves, the horses, mules, packs and each other with water. The noise and heat increased. Marshall's horse reared in terror, practically lifting the young man off his feet. Our eyes, throats and nostrils were seared and all we could do was crouch with heads bowed. Above us, the flames danced in triumph until we were sure that hell had come to earth. Then, suddenly, it was over.

In less than a minute, the flames consumed themselves and the heat subsided, as if the door of an oven had been closed. Smoke and ashes continued to drift and choke us, but there were smiles on our burned and blackened faces. There were patches of grass smoldering and flaring to the west but the momentum of the conflagration had been halted by that nameless stream.

We checked the packs for embers and the animals for burns, then washed our faces, drank our fill and rode slowly up onto the western bank. The journey resumed.

Later that same morning, we were hailed by a band of riders who approached us from the north. We grouped together, every gun primed and cocked. When they were within shouting distance, two of the dozen Indians rode forward a few yards closer to us. Captain Becknell nodded at me and we rode forward to within a short distance of the men. The larger of the two Indians called something to us in a language I did not know.

Standing in the stirrups, I signed with broad gestures,

visible at a distance, that we were Americans, coming in peace for the purpose of trade.

The shorter man, acting as interpreter for the big man, called back in English, "We are Pawnee. Maybe we will trade with you." The big man smiled at this, and shoved his rifle into a beaded scabbard beside his saddle.

Quietly, Becknell asked me, "Do you think we can trust them?"

I shrugged. "I have never dealt with the Pawnee before. If our men are careful to keep their weapons near and show no fear, they may really want to trade."

Uneasily, we spread several blankets and displayed some of our wares. Most of our goods remained packed on the mules. This seemed to offend the Pawnee, but I explained that our packs contained mere duplicates of what was there for them to see and did not have any hidden treasures. This seemed to satisfy them and, for nearly an hour, they eyed, hefted, and considered every item several times. Clearly, they had no intention of trading.

Finally, Becknell took me aside and whispered. "What's their game do you suppose, Josey?"

I shook my head. "These may be the men who set that fire and had hoped to find our goods scattered all over the country waiting for them to just pick up. Right now, they may be stalling for time. Either more Pawnee are on the way or they are trying to figure out a new scheme."

The captain nodded. To the interpreter, he said, "We must continue our journey. Nothing seems to strike your fancy anyway." He signaled for us to begin repacking the goods, as the information was translated into Pawnee. This brought frowns and murmurs of discontent.

"You have no rifles, gunpowder, shot to trade?" the interpreter asked. Becknell shook his head. The leader then placed his foot on the blanket that I was trying to fold. Through the interpreter, he growled, "We are still wanting to trade. Why are you so hurried to leave?"

On an inspiration, I straightened up and addressed the Pawnee in sign language. There was a grunt of dismay, and a hurried consultation among the Indians.

"What the hell did you tell 'em?" Ewing Young asked.

With my back to the Pawnee, I smiled and explained. "I told them that we had to get to the Arkansas River where the whole Comanche nation was waiting to trade with us."

Young's mouth dropped and Becknell tried to suppress a smile. "I reckon they don't fancy meetin' up with no Comanche, huh?" Will Carson drawled.

The Pawnee had reached a decision. The interpreter said, "We will ride with you a while."

This was not the answer we had hoped for. Glumly, we bundled our goods and packed the mules. Throughout the day, we rode in grim silence. The Pawnee rode parallel to us at about a hundred yards to the north. I was still at the rear of our train, leading a string of mules.

After several plodding miles, the Pawnee interpreter rode alongside me. "Where did you learn sign language?" he asked.

"From my brothers, the Comanche," I explained, hoping that the invocation of the name might add slightly to the Pawnees' discomfort. It had no visible impact on my listener, however.

"What is your name?" he asked.

Tapping my breast after the manner of the Indians, I introduced myself.

The Pawnee's eyes widened slightly. "You are not an American?"

"No, I am a Spaniard, from New Mexico." I saw a cloud pass over his expression but he made no response. "What is your name?"

"Shereterik. I am also called Baptiste Bayhylle."

We rode without speaking for a while. Something was troubling him. "You speak English well," I commented.

"So do you," he said and smiled faintly.

"You have two names?"

He nodded, squinting ahead at the horizon. "I have two hearts," he explained. "My mother is Pawnee, but my father was a Spaniard like you, from New Mexico."

There was no warmth in the statement. In times past, Apache and later Comanche raiding parties brought Pawnee captives to Taos to sell. The Spanish King had a special fund to ransom captives which, while well intentioned, in practice had the opposite effect. The ransom only served as an incentive to take more captives. The law required that the ransomed captives be returned to their own people as soon as practicable, but this was often none too soon. In the interval, the captive Indians were often placed in Spanish households as 'gentiles'—or *criados*—to be instructed in the Christian faith in return for their labor. Again, something well intentioned often resulted in something evilly practiced. Baptiste's mother may have been just such a gentile who received a baser form of instruction from her Spanish 'godparent.'

I rode alongside Baptiste, or Bat as he was later called by the Americans, for the remainder of the afternoon. He was a serious young man, barely into his teens I would estimate, but with quiet courage and sly humor hidden beneath his sad-eyed countenance.

That evening when we camped, our party said little until the last Pawnee had withdrawn to their separate cooking fire. Captain Becknell voiced everyone's concern when he asked, "How far do you reckon we are from the Arkansas, Josey?"

I shook my head. "This is new country for me as well, Captain. I do not know how far."

"More important," Young said, "what's gonna happen when there ain't no Comanche settin' there to greet us?"

None of us had an answer to that. We sat gloomily staring into the fire, too morose to bother cooking a meal. I still remember the way the sun set on that day. The vast western sky was aglow with colors splashed across a thousand-mile canvas—purple and gold, scarlet and indigo, like the flowing life blood of a million rainbows.

The beauty of that sunset had filled me with a sense of peace that had no relation to our actual circumstances. While the others settled into their blankets for a night of restless worry about the morrow, I confess that I had an excellent night's sleep. As a precaution we had doubled our guard on the livestock. Shortly before dawn I was awakened by a hand on my shoulder.

Becknell smiled at me. "They're gone."

I sat up. "Are you sure?"

The captain nodded. "They were real quiet, I'll have to say that, but they slipped none the less."

The sunrise confirmed it. Where the Pawnee camp had been, nothing remained but the charred pieces of their fire. We could only speculate as to the reason for their departure. Perhaps they decided it expedient not to test our story about meeting with the Comanche, although the Pawnee entered into a peace agreement with the Comanche shortly afterward. Just as likely, the Pawnee simply found nothing of real interest in our packs and had grown bored with our company.

Whatever the reason, we rode unhindered to the banks of the Arkansas River that same day. It was a Monday, the twenty-fourth day of September. There were no Comanche there to meet us, not surprisingly.

We continued along the north bank of the river, thus technically staying in the United States' rather than Spanish territory. My companions had never been this far west before and found much of what they saw strange and unprecedented. The day after reaching the Arkansas, my American friends saw, for the first time, two marvels of the plains. They had their first glimpse of a jackrabbit—to them a fantastic, distorted creature—and they marveled at a prairie dog town that must have covered at least ten acres. This latter sight stirred some rather unpleasant memories for me, I must confess. We were now in the region Coronado knew as his disappointing Quivara.

By the twenty-eighth of September, we were passing the sand hills. As the river curved toward the southwest, we came across the first of the really big buffalo herds.

We climbed up the base of that deep reddish brown monolith known as Pawnee Rock and the Americans were speechless at the sight of tens of thousands of brown, shaggy buffalo grazing nearly from horizon to horizon. We remained vigilant, but there were no Indians hunting near the herd.

In fact, we saw no Indians at all as we trailed beside the river through the warm days of early autumn. I could see the plains beginning to cast their spell over the Americans. The openness of the land, the immensity of the sky, the dry clarity of the vision in every direction either terrified or exalted men. For some, it was so overwhelming that they retreated to the familiar limits of the eastern woodlands, while for others, such as my companions, it drew something from their souls that would remain forever changed and forever longing.

By the middle of October, the breezes from the north were beginning to chill and we hastened to draw near the shelter of the mountains. In the distance, we could see the blue and white line of the shining mountains from every rise of the land. We camped one night beneath the golden leaves of huge old cottonwoods that stretched along the river's flood plain for some twenty miles. In the morning, we had two surprises—frost on our blankets and Indians at our camp.

The previous evening, we had thought our position was well-screened, but the next morning found a half-dozen men on horseback calmly watching us while we slept. I was the first to rise, a custom I have had since my time with Red Hand. Indians habitually rise to greet the sun with morning prayer.

Our sentinel was to the north with our animals, so he was unaware of the Indians across the river. With movements that I hoped appeared casual, I rose and stretched. Rather than alarm the others, I walked down to the gravel edge of the river and greeted the onlookers. There was a tremble of excitement in me as I recognized the men as Comanche.

"You speak Nerm well, *Americano*," one of the men observed. Comanche at that time referred to Americans by the Spanish term, having had more contact with Spaniards than Americans. By my dress, I appeared American.

"I was taught well, by one of the People who is no more." Comanche were reticent to speak the name of one dead for fear that his spirit might mistake it for a summons. Even though I was not Comanche, I did not wish to offend. "Do the People still hunt this far north?" I asked, intending an observation on the lateness of the season.

The group's spokesman smiled and replied with typical arrogance, "We are Nermernuh, we hunt wherever we please." His companions laughed, appreciating his boast.

I too smiled, more at the memories his language evoked than at his wit. Behind me, the Americans were rising, awakened by our voices. The men had the good sense to remain calm and outwardly unconcerned. Captain Becknell came to stand beside me, raising his palm in the universal sign for peace.

"I heard laughter. Friends of yours, Josey?" he asked.

I nodded. "They're Comanche, though I have never

met them. By their accent I would say that they are Yanpareekuh, rather than Kwahadi." To the Comanche, I called, "This man"—I indicated Becknell—"leads our band. We travel to New Mexico to trade. He bids you come and eat with us." Aside to the captain, I said, "I have just invited them to breakfast."

He nodded, his expression serious. "Sure." The corner of his mouth twitched slightly. "It's your turn to cook, anyway."

After a brief exchange, the Comanche waded their horses across the shallow waters of the river. Picketing their horses between the camp and the river, they came and squatted near the fire, ignoring the other men. I tried to make small talk about travels and hunting while I prepared food. We still had some fresh buffalo meat which I carved and spitted. The men would simply lean forward to carve a piece off with knife and fingers.

Although their appetite was unaffected, I could see that the Comanche were a little uneasy at the Americans standing behind them while they ate. "I think you men should come around the fire and sit where they can see you," I told my companions. "You are making them nervous, as I am sure you would be under similar circumstances." The men did as I asked, leaning their backs against the trees and fussing nonchalantly with their tack.

I had saved the best part of the meal for last. I poured six cups of strong coffee, sweetened nearly to a syrup. Murmurs of appreciation came from the warriors as they sipped the liquid treat as quickly as its heat would permit. One of the younger men, even ran his finger around the inside of the cup to get every drop.

Our visitors were more relaxed as I brewed a second pot of coffee. I decided to broach the delicate question that was burning within me. "I must speak of those now dead," I warned. "When I was a boy, I lived for several seasons as a son in the lodge of Red Hand, the son of Four Bears, of the Antelope People. I was called the Little Spaniard. Have you heard of these men?"

Only one of the Comanche nodded at the names. He was a man several years older than I. "I have heard of those men," he acknowledged. "I have heard that they were all killed by the sickness."

"Yes," I said, a lump forming in my throat in spite of the years. "Do you know if any from that band survived?"

The man was silent, remembering. "Maybe some," he said, thoughtfully. "Someone must have lived to bring the news out of that camp."

Maybe, I thought. Or perhaps someone just found their bones and tattered lodges blowing in the springtime winds.

Will Carson saw my downcast expression. "Bad news, Josey?" he asked, concerned.

"Yes, but old news."

To be polite, our visitors looked over some of our trade goods, but did not seem too interested when they learned that we were not trading firearms. Good manners prevailed, though. "When you come back, you will stay with us," they invited. Gripping each man by the forearms, they bid good-bye to each of us before mounting and riding back across the river.

We packed our mules and headed upstream. The visit from the Comanches had stirred many thoughts in my memory, leaving me melancholy. My companions, sensing my mood, left me to myself after their attempts at conversation received only desultory responses. I had made many new friends in the past year but now, upper most in my mind was my home, my family, and Amada.

Chapter Sixteen

That night we camped in a beautiful location. The Cuartalejo Apache had once called it home before the Comanche drove them away. Tall cottonwoods still shaded the lush grass and reeds. Plum and wild grape thickets provided shelter for wild turkeys. Deer browsed on sunflowers and bears shambled through the chokecherry bushes. Such was the garden that God had planted where the Arkansas River received the sweet waters of a creek that flowed in from the southwest.

As in the beginning, however, the garden provided a mere stage upon which man acted out his tragedies. Before Santa Fe had even been founded, a Spanish expedition disobeyed its orders and went in search of plunder. After a quarrel, one of the leaders, Juan de Humana, killed his partner, Leiva Bonilla. Pushing on up this very creek, they slept in the tall green grass. Before morning, all but two were dead, as Indians set fire to the camp. The name given to the stream remained, *El Rio de las Animas Perdidas en Purgatorio.* Now we camped at the mouth of this same River of the Souls Lost in Purgatory, and nearly reaffirmed the name in the days ahead.

From the bluffs of the river we could see the Spanish Peaks rising in the distance. It was time to change our course and seek out the pass through the Raton Mountains. I had never been in that place before, but from what I had heard, I thought that we should press on for a few more miles where another, smaller creek was supposed to enter at the same angle. Though the waters were bitter, the Timpas Creek would provide us with an easier trail. I was, however, a minority of one among our party. The others were seduced by the beautiful portals of the valley and voted to follow the purling waters of the Purgatory to its source in the Ratones. They dismissed my objections as mere rationalizations to cover my superstitious Catholic fears.

So, on October the twenty-first, we left the Arkansas and embarked on the most physically harrowing part of our journey. The valley was gentle and wide and the morning crisp and clear as we began, but by evening the land around us began to rise and our path became increasingly rocky. Day by day the trail grew worse until, by the fifth day, rocky cliffs towered above us and rugged ledges and immense boulders blocked our path.

For half a day we had labored, pushing and pulling our rebellious mules, and we had advanced no more than a mile. To his credit, Captain Becknell was willing to admit his error. Though the air was cool in the shade of the cliffs, we were perspiring freely from our toils.

Becknell mopped his brow on his sleeve and looked wearily at me. "Let me say it first, Josey. You were right." He craned his neck to study the rock walls above us. "We've got to get out of here."

Ewing Young came forward from his mule string, stumbling over the rocks. "It took us five days to get this far." He too gazed at the steep cliff. "Ya think we can climb out without going all the way back?"

"I hope so," Becknell said. "We've wasted enough time on this trail." He sighed. "Might as well unpack the mules. We'll scout this on foot."

With relief for men and beasts, we unsaddled our horses and unloaded the mules. It was agreed that Becknell and Young would try to find a way out while the rest of us tended the animals. Although unspoken, it was understood that my leg made me unfit for such exploration. My limp was pronounced, even though I tried to compensate for it.

Evening came early to that shadowy canyon. It was nearly dark before the two men returned. We had managed to kindle a fire from pieces of wood left behind by a flash flood that had swept the rocky chasm the previous spring.

They sat down wearily on a boulder, grateful for the cups of coffee we presented. "It doesn't look good," the captain confessed. "But there's kind of a sloping ledge we can follow if we move a few rocks."

"A few!" Ewing snorted.

Becknell ignored the comment. "Then there's a series of rocky ledges, like stair steps, that shouldn't be too bad, and then there's that last fifty feet or so that's pretty much a sheer wall."

This did not sound promising. We sat and looked at the captain in silence as he sipped his coffee. "There is a break in the wall and a lot of broken scree that might hold the animals and get us out of here." He looked at each of us. "Do you want to try it or do you want to turn back?"

We knew how bad it was behind us and wilted at the thought of struggling through it again. Being young men, we were naturally optimistic and, assuming the future must be better than the past, we voted to try climbing out.

The next day was an agony of backbreaking labor, pushing and tugging at rocks the size of wagons. By evening, we had gotten to the stair step ledges and looked forward to an easier time on the morrow. But the next day brought new obstacles. Our exhausted animals balked at the slippery footing created by small pebbles spread over the smooth bedrock shelves.

Finally, by early afternoon, we arrived at the break in the canyon wall. A jumble of broken rock formed a ramp to the plains above. It looked like an easy climb of perhaps a hundred feet. But the scree was unstable and the animals frightened.

Becknell went first, urging his string up the slope with yells and curses. He made it. From the top he tethered a rope around a large boulder and, one by one, the men led their horses and mule strings up to the freedom of the plain. Unfortunately, with each footstep, the rocks shifted and became less secure. The Marshall boy was ahead of me and his ascent sent a shower of sharp rocks raining down on me.

I was the last. Will Carson called encouragement back to me. “Come on, Josey! It feels mighty good up here, by God!” His last word echoed and bounced off the rocky walls of the Purgatory.

I considered the slope. “I’m going to send the mules up first,” I yelled. Pulling them forward on foot, I tied the guide rope to the lead mule’s halter.

Becknell was scowling down at me. “You know what you’re doing, Spaniard? Those mules might make it and kill you doing it!”

I simply waved, struggling to keep my balance as I limped back to my horse. Once in the saddle, I patted my horse’s neck. The animal was not deceived by my false assurances. Tossing its head, it nickered in fear at the steady hail of rocks set off by the shifting, braying mules above.

“Pull away!” I shouted as the men on the rim hauled on the rope. Drumming my heels on the horse’s sides, I urged him forward. With a series of hops from his powerful hind quarters, we surged ahead. As the first mule cleared the rim, someone untied the rope and tossed it back down. Fortunately, it fell across my pommel. I grabbed it just as the slide began.

The last mule had just leaped to safety when the entire rock pile began to move. There was a deep rumbling sound and, like water, the surface of stones came cascading down on us. My horse screamed and tried to rear, but its hind legs were sinking between the shifting rocks. The momentum of the slide caused the horse to fall sideways, jerking me from the saddle as I clung to the rope.

I had a horrifying glimpse of the horse’s anguish cut short by a wave of dirt and rock that swept down, dragging the animal with it and burying it beneath tons of debris. Desperately, I gripped the rope as my body bounced like a child's marble when dropped on the floor. After what seemed an eternity, the roar and motion ceased.

"My God, Josey, are you all right?" I heard Carson shout.

"Stay there, Will!" I managed to respond. "Just pull me up with the rope."

I tried to get to my feet and walk up with some assistance from the rope, but the ground was still shifting. The result was that my friends hauled me from the canyon of the Purgatory like a sack of corn. My body was bruised all over and my ribs hurt when I breathed too deeply but, Will was right, it felt very good to stand in the late afternoon sun and be able to see for miles in every direction.

Captain Becknell scolded me. "You should've come up first. You damn near got yourself killed!"

In a wheezing voice, I tried to explain. "If I had gone first, we would have lost eight mules and their packs. This way we have only lost a horse and a saddle." A very good horse, too, I thought. I have always hated the suffering and sacrifice which we humans inflict on other creatures to serve our ends, but then, I was a young man afraid that my peers would think me too tenderhearted, so I said no more.

Becknell nodded. "That's true, but it's only by a miracle that you're not buried down there too. One more lost soul!"

"A miracle," I heartily agreed.

He looked at me sternly for another moment, then said to Carson, "Will, why don't you go cut one of the spare horses out for this boy. He doesn't look like he'd get too far walking and we've wasted enough time here."

There remained a few hours of light, so we pressed on toward the shadowy mass of the Ratones. The setting sun made the mountains to the west appear even taller. A chilly north wind riffled the tawny grasses and raced with a family of antelope startled at our approach.

It took two days of rock rolling, climbing, and struggle to get our party across the Raton Pass, but compared to the ordeal in the Purgatory, it was a pleasant diversion. Around us the air was filled with the scent and sigh of wind through the pines. Gurgling streams, like silver threads, laced the rocky heights and, from the pinnacle, we received a view that would gladden the heart of any New Mexican. Spread below us was a vast expanse of open plain like a golden carpet with a pattern of darker tree-lined creeks. On the western edge of this vast park, the red and green wall of the Sangre de Cristo Mountains marched majestically to the south.

From the Ratones, we rode out across the *Rio Colorado*. My companions were nervous. Several times over the preceding twenty years or so, parties of foreigners had tried to breach the viceroy's economic fortress and trade with New Mexico, only to end up stranded or imprisoned. Now that we were actually in New Mexico, the odds against our gamble on shifting political winds seemed infinitely greater. My own feelings were decidedly mixed. A part of me was delighted and wanted to spur my horse to a run that would carry me all the way to Santa Fe, while another part of me was fearful that I had placed my friends in serious jeopardy for my own ulterior motive of gaining safe passage home.

The day after we left the Ratones, we saw riders approaching from the south. At a distance, we could discern nothing of the horsemen's nationality so, as the Americans herded the animals together and primed their weapons, I rode ahead to meet the approaching band. At a hundred yards, I reined in, waving my hat and spinning my horse in delight. These were *ciboleros*, New Mexican buffalo hunters—my own countrymen.

Armed like Indians with lances, bows and arrows, these *ciboleros* sat their horses like men born to the saddle. Their bright woolen *serapes* flowed like capes and their ornate spurs jingled like tambourines with every step of their mounts. I stood in the stirrups and shouted my greetings. "*Hola, paisanos!* How good it is to see you!" The hunters reined their horses to a semicircle before me. A dark, stocky man with a full beard smiled in welcome.

"It's good to see Spaniards, again!" I effused, a foolish grin on my face.

With great seriousness, the man said, "But we are not Spaniards, *señor*."

"You're not?" My smile vanished.

"No, *señor*, now we are Mexicans." He and his companions all laughed at my confusion. "Forgive my little joke, *señor*. Spain is back in Spain now. Since the middle of September, this province is a part of the new nation of Mexico."

"Independence! It has come?" I laughed in glee, then grew serious as a new thought occurred to me. "Is there a new governor, now? Would he welcome trade from outside the province?"

The *cibolero* shook his head. "No, it is the same *gobernador*, Don Facundo Melgares. But he has pledged his loyalty to Mexico now. Maybe he will be glad to see traders from outside." He jutted his chin toward my friends in the distance. "Those, they are *Americanos*?"

"Yes, with trade goods such as would cost a fortune in Chihuahua!" I decided that I might as well begin to act like a merchant, since I had invested so greatly in the enterprise.

"*Oh, si?*" The hunter sounded interested. "Do they have guns so that we no longer have to hunt the buffalo with weapons such as these?" He waved at the bow hung across his back and the lance in his hand.

"No, but, if the governor permits, perhaps the *Americanos* may bring weapons on future journeys from the United Sates."

"It is good," he decided. "The people of Santa Fe will be very glad to see you, I'm sure. The *conducta* for Chihuahua only just left, and won't return until spring."

The *conducta* was the annual caravan of wagons bearing the exported produce of New Mexico along the old Camino Real. Forming south of Albuquerque, it departed in November, following the road beside the Rio Grande to El Paso del Norte and then south across the desert to Chihuahua. For many years a great trade fair was held in the city of Chihuahua itself, but this had been moved further south to San Bartolome when I was still a boy. I have been told that, at one time, half the Spanish population of New Mexico would accompany the caravan, filling hundreds of wagons, but dangers from Indians had curtailed that practice so that only men comprised the *conducta.* After making their purchases of manufactured goods, the *conducta* would return to New Mexico by March.

The *ciboleros* decided to ride with us for a while. I made the introductions of all the men, but conversation between the two groups consisted only of smiles and pantomime as neither knew the other's language. Naturally, I was kept busy translating all day long, so that by evening my voice was no more than a rasping whisper.

It was November now, barely two months since we had left Missouri. We angled to the west so that our trail would be closer to the shelter of the mountains, less exposed to perils from weather or warriors. An easy few days travel brought us to the Gallinas River, where we found a Spanish settler brave enough to risk exposure to the open plains. Luis Maria Cabeza de Vaca had only that year received a grant of land at that location known as the Spring of the Chickens, for the abundance of sage hens that frequented the site. With seventeen children and servants, Don Luis had already begun to raise buildings when we stopped for the night. *Ojo de Gallinas* today, of course, has the more impressive name of *Nuestra Senora de los Dolores de Las Vegas.*

My excitement rose as our trail turned into the valley of the Pecos. A relatively new town, San Miguel del Vado had been established by a group of *genizaros* at the crossing of the river and, at that time, had over one hundred houses and an impressive new church. At San Miguel, the *ciboleros* left us and returned to the east to hunt.

After a night as guests of the pastor of San Miguel,

we continued along the western bank of the Pecos. On our left rose the *pinon*-covered bulk of the Glorieta Mesa while on our right, the river hugged the feet of the Sangre de Cristos. We turned away from the river before reaching the crumbling pueblo of the Pecos, Cicuye, for our trail led west through the steep narrows of Glorieta Pass.

My friends teased me because I simply could not repress my excitement and talked constantly about the bright prospects that lay ahead of us—until we crested a rise and I fell silent, reining my horse to a stop. Before us lay a flat and dusty mesa. A cluster of some two hundred *adobe* homes glowed warmly like freshly baked loaves in the slanting afternoon light. From east to west a creek flowed through the village. Scattered amongst the houses, irrigated fields lay bare and harvested. The pungent perfume of pine smoke drifted to us from a hundred chimneys and the sound of church bells could be heard faintly.

Captain Becknell and Will Carson reined in beside me. They sat quietly as I struggled to control my emotions. It had been more than a year since I had been here. Finally, stating the obvious, I waved my hand at the town before us. "*La Villa Real de Santa Fe,*" I said. "Home."

Chapter Seventeen

The subsequent history of the trail to Santa Fe is rather well chronicled and I played no great part in that, so I will not linger over the details. I introduced Captain Becknell to the *Gobernador*, Don Facundo, and acted as translator as they arrived at an agreement. The Missourians were warmly received and their wares quickly purchased. The men were ecstatic with their profits. Becknell hastened back to Franklin with his rawhide bundles of silver coins by a shorter route suggested by the *ciboleros*. This came to be known as the Cimarron Cutoff and nearly cost the captain his life from thirst on a subsequent trip. In any event, Becknell was back in Missouri by late January of 1822.

Although New Mexico never had a great deal of hard currency, and most transactions were by barter, Santafeanos were willing to part with their coins for good quality manufactured items at a good price. And, despite an enormous profit, the Missourians were able to offer a better price than that permitted by the merchants from Chihuahua. Because of the monopolistic practices and exorbitant government taxes, goods imported from Mexico were always terribly expensive.

In fairness, I should point out that, until the American conquest in their war against Mexico, the trade from Missouri never amounted to more than a fraction of the commerce conducted with Mexico along the Camino Real. That road remained our economic aqueduct as it had for over two hundred years.

Although we were the first American party to enter Santa Fe, others came soon after us. Two more groups of traders arrived that same winter. I continued to keep in touch with the Carson family and with Captain Becknell. On his second trip to New Mexico, Becknell was the pioneer again in bringing the first wagons overland on the road. In the next decade, Becknell moved to Texas where he led a mounted militia known as the Red River Blues. He died there, peaceably, shortly before the terrible American Civil War began.

Ewing Young, with whom I was never terribly close, left the trader's life to become a famous fur trapper and explorer, leading expeditions into the Gila Wilderness, the San Juan mountains and as far as California. Unfortunately, he also had the dubious distinction of founding the first distillery in New Mexico, producing the infamous poison known as Taos Lightning.

I am afraid that I lost track of Marshall and McLaughlin. Young Marshall's sister had invested sixty dollars in her brother's historic venture as a pioneer of the Santa Fe trade. I could well imagine his toothy grin as he repaid her with nine hundred dollars of profit from that first trip of ours.

I, too, made money on the venture, some of which I invested with Becknell again in the Missouri trade, some of which went into transporting goods from Missouri to old Mexico and vice versa, and some of which went to recouping our family's fortunes and developing our land grant on the Pecos—but, I am getting ahead of myself.

I left the Governor's Palace that November 16, 1821 with a flutter in my stomach. It was time to go home. The sun was setting once again as I turned my horse up the Canyon Road and rang the small bell outside the large wooden *puerta del zaguán* of our home. After a wait that seemed interminable, a grey mustachioed face peered out at me through the dowels that covered the gate's aperture. "Who is it?" came a muffled voice.

"It is I, Paco, Jose."

There was silence, then the glisten of tears appeared in the old man's eyes. "Jose?" he asked, incredulous. "Don Jose?"

"Yes, uncle, it is I. I have come home."

"Dios santo y glorioso!" he exclaimed. Then, leaving me standing in the dusk, he ran off through the house, loudly proclaiming my arrival. I could hear questioning voices ringing through the rooms. After a few minutes, I distinguished my mother's voice above the confusion.

"Did you leave my son standing in the dust of the street, *viejo*?" Doña Maria Elena's voice scolded Paco as she hurried to the gate. "Open it! Open it, Paco! *Apúrate*!" With a squeal of complaint, the heavy gate swung inward and I led my weary horse in.

My mother stood at the head of a phalanx of people. She looked shorter and greyer than I had recalled. Behind me Paco closed the gate and came to take the reins from my hand. I gave his hand an affectionate squeeze before advancing to greet my mother. With tremendous effort, she retained her dignity long enough to give my cheeks a formal kiss, but the tears came quickly as I enfolded her in my arms.

There were many tears that night, and much laughter, as the entire household gathered round. Soon the *placita* was alight with torches and crowded with neighbors and relatives. The ovens were rekindled and my sisters brought baskets of food with their husbands and children. My limp and scars were duly noted and commented on with shaking heads and pursed lips. My highly edited version of my adventures was passed from person to person, and my homecoming became the occasion for a *fandango*, complete with musicians, that would be remembered for years.

But nowhere in this crowd of welcomers did I see Amada. After an hour or so, I was able to extricate myself from the center of attention and speak privately with my mother.

"And Amada?" I asked.

My mother's face assumed a sad expression and my heart stopped beating. *"Ay, la pobrecita!"* My mother shook her head. "She has not been well."

"She is alive, then?"

"Oh, yes, of course." My mother patted my arm reassuringly. "But she has not been well. She has no appetite, she's so skinny, you should see her Jose."

"Yes, I should see her."

"She gets headaches and breaks into tears for no reason. And angry! She gets so angry at herself for doing even the slightest thing wrong." Mother lowered her voice in confidence. "I hope that you do not mind, but she sleeps in your room now. She would not return to her room since . . . since . . ." Tears welled up in her eyes and I nodded in sympathy. "It seemed to comfort her to be in your room, so that is where she spends most of her time."

I frowned. "Does she know that I have come home?"

Doña Maria Elena shrugged. "I do not know. Her mind . . . she does not seem so aware of what goes on around her anymore."

At that moment a servant interrupted with a question from the kitchen and my mother left to attend the crisis.

I was stricken by the news of Amada's decline. Lighting a candle, I left the festive crowd and headed down the hall to the closed door of my room. I knocked and waited. There was no sound but the creak of the leather hinge as the door opened a crack.

"*Si?*" came a woman's voice. My candle illuminated only half of Lupita's face. Anger rose in me as I looked on her dark, hooded eye. So as not to implicate Amada for her apparent complicity in not denouncing Lupita for the murder of Esteban, I had decided to say nothing about what Jake had said to me in the Hidatsa lodge. Nonetheless the statement, "It was the woman!" continued to echo in my mind like a litany. I also decided not to explore another nagging thought, that perhaps I loved Esteban too poorly to pursue justice for his death. Instead, I had decided to allow the others to continue to think Jake had been the murderer.

"It is I, Jose," I said brusquely. "I must see Amada."

The eye opened slightly in surprise. There was a moment's hesitation, then the door swung open to admit me. The room was dark and stale. A single candle sputtered on the ledge of the small window. This room was typical of New Mexican homes in those days. Glass was a luxury seldom found, so the opening was covered with mica. Amada, in giving up her old room had sacrificed the light that flooded in through the glass that my father, at great expense, had imported for the windows in that one room.

I held my candle higher. The white-washed walls gave off a lunar glow in the faint light. "Where is Amada?"

Lupita pointed to the corner. I had not even seen her. A *colchón* was spread on the floor and, so thin was Amada, that I had not realized there was anyone beneath the bedclothes. Now, though, I could see her long hair spread across the top of a red and black blanket. Her face was turned to the wall. Above the mattress, in a niche in that wall, stood a sad-faced carving of the Virgin of Guadalupe. The wooden eyes of the *santa* gazed with pity at the young woman below.

I placed my candle on the dirt floor and knelt on a rug beside the bed. The sounds of celebration were barely audible here through the thick layers of *adobe*. "Leave us," I ordered Lupita.

"No," she said simply, to my surprise. "You should not be alone with her."

I nodded reluctantly. "Yes, you are right," I conceded. There was no reason to add scandal to whatever burden Amada already bore. Gently, I laid my hand on her blanket. The shoulder beneath was bony and sharp. So anxious was I to greet her that I decided to wake her. "Amada," I called softly.

"No, please, no!" Amada hissed. My blood froze as she jerked away from my touch and cowered against the wall. Her black hair clung tangled to her gaunt face and her eyes, terrified and unseeing, glared at me from their dark hollows. The blanket was clutched defensively to her chin.

Horrified, I glanced at Lupita for an explanation, but her face was a mask. "Amada, *querida*," I soothed, "It is I, Jose. What's wrong? It is only I, Jose."

The eyes came into focus and the expression changed to incredulity. "Jose?" came the weak voice. "You are not a ghost? Jose?"

I smiled. "By the mercies of God, I am not a ghost, Amadita. I am real. I am alive. I am here. See!" I held out my hand toward her as one might tempt a shy foal.

She looked at my hand in amazement then slowly, cautiously, she placed her hand in mine. Her fingers were cold. Carefully, I closed my hand on hers, applying only a soft pressure.

"Jose?" Her grip tightened. "Jose, you are alive! You have come back!" Tears spilled from her eyes and, with her free hand, she tried to cover her face. Her body shook with sobs.

I wanted to take her in my arms and comfort her but something made me hesitate. Instead, I lifted her hand and lightly kissed her fingertips. "I have come back," I confirmed.

It was a long time before she could compose herself.

"Thanks to God, thanks to God!" She tossed her long black hair behind her shoulders and pressed her hands to her cheeks. "I was having a bad dream—yes, a dream—that is all. Just look at me!" she said, then quickly added, "No! Do not look at me! Oh, I am so ashamed! What must you think!" As of old, she let her hair tumble forward to hide her face, peeking at me surreptitiously through its dark screen.

I laughed and sat back on my heels. "I think that the sight of you is like summer rain on the dry desert of my soul," I said, with a theatrical flourish. I grew serious. "But, tell me, Amada, what is wrong? Mother says you have been acting oddly and I can see that you are wasting away. What is wrong?"

There was a tremble in her voice. "Please, don't ask me, Jose! I really cannot say. But"—her tone changed—"I will be fine now . . . now that you are back." Something in her look warmed my heart.

Her expression grew concerned. "But you, Jose"—she reached out her hand to trace the scar on my cheek—"you have changed. You have grown older. Are you well?"

"I am fine. I have grown older, yes. I have seen and done many things, some of which I will tell you about in the morning." I rose to my feet, hiding the twinge of pain from my leg at the motion. "Now we must both rest. If the Lord permits, I will see you in the morning. May He grant you rest."

I picked up the candle and turned toward the door. So silent had she been, that I had forgotten that Lupita was in the room. The sight of her made me flinch.

"Jose!" Amada called.

"Si, hermanita?"

Her voice was low and earnest. "Thank you for coming back. Thank you!"

Confused by her intensity, I could only nod as I closed the door.

Despite my pre-dawn custom, I was not the first of the household to arise the next morning. My mother and Amada were both already in the kitchen when I entered. A place had been set and bowls of *chili colorado, frijoles* and *atole* sat beside plates piled high with *tamales* and *tortillas.*

"Good day," I greeted, "you are both up early this morning."

"Of course," my mother said. "You should learn, *mi hijo,* that women always work much harder than men. Isn't that right, Amada?"

Amada just smiled at my mother as her eyes greeted me. In the daylight, I could see how thin she had become. Her naturally slight figure was nearly emaciated, making her look like a young girl again but the skin appeared waxy over her protruding cheekbones.

"Have you eaten yet?" I asked with forced casualness as I sat.

"No, not yet," my mother replied. "But we will after the others have eaten, won't we *mi hija?*"

"Yes, *madrina,*" Amada replied in her soft voice. "I do feel hungry today."

Both my mother and I sighed in relief.

"I have some business to attend to still with the *Americanos.* But later I will sit down with Paco and find out how we are doing. This time, Mother"—I took her hand as she placed a cup of cocoa before me—"I am home to stay. I know my responsibilities."

Sniffling from Amada heralded the onset of tears so, to save her embarrassment, my mother said, "Amada, would you go check on my bread in the *horno*? It should be done by now."

"Si, señora." Amada dashed from the room, her apron to her face.

My mother just shook her head. "She seemed so much better today, Jose. She is so happy to see you again." She patted my shoulder, then fidgeted with her apron. "I must ask you. That man, that *Americano* who assaulted Amada and killed . . ." Her voice choked on the word. She turned away from me to compose herself. With her back still to me, she asked, "Is he . . . ?"

I completed her thought. ". . . dead? Yes, *Mamá*. Did I kill him? No."

"O, gracias a Dios!" she breathed the words as she turned back to me. "The blood of vengeance—of anger—you should not live with that on your hands, *mi hijo*. I am glad that you did not take his life."

"No, it was not my hand. It was the Arikara who killed him—Indians far to the north on a river called the Missouri," I explained.

"Ah, *si*." mother nodded. "*Los indios salvajes,* of course."

"Here is the bread, *señora*," Amada said quietly.

"Oh, *mi hija,* you startled me," my mother said, embarrassed at her 'savage Indians' remark. "Yes, the loaves look fine." She kissed Amada affectionately on the forehead as she took the loaves to a shelf to cool.

"Amada," I called, with an authoritative tone, "as the

new head of the household Garcia, I have orders for you. Come here."

She glided across the room to stand before me, a wary look on her face. *"Si, señor?"* she said seriously.

"First of all, you are to eat breakfast, and eat until you cannot stand. Garcia women must have much meat on their bones. Behold, my mother!"

"Malcriado, Jose!" my mother laughed.

"Second, when your wicked godmother releases you from your many chores, you are to sit in the sun of the *placita* and allow God's good air to bring color back to your beautiful face." My tone softened considerably toward the end.

Amada blushed and smiled. With a mocking curtsy, she replied, "At your orders, Don Jose."

"Good!" I smiled too. "And now I must go. Thank you both for breakfast. It has been a long time since I have eaten so well. Too long." I kissed both women on the tops of their heads before leaving.

My interview with Paco was discouraging. Although he had tried mightily, he could wield little authority in my name when it was generally supposed that I was dead. As a result, other men had infringed on our lands, merchants had refused us credit, and workers were reluctant to enter our employ. Our flocks had dwindled because of this reduced number of herdsmen. Some of our difficulties were also due to the change over from Spanish to Mexican authority. However, through the judicious use of my newly acquired wealth and many days in front of the *alcalde* and the council, I was able to reverse this downward trend over the next few weeks.

At the end of a day of argument and negotiation, I

was as fatigued as I had felt after scaling the Purgatory cliffs or fleeing the Blackfeet. Shortly before Christmas, I was slumped on a rolled *colchón*, my back leaning against the cloth that shielded the room's plastered walls, when Doña Maria Elena sought me out.

"Jose, why are you sitting here in the dark?" she asked.

"I did not realize how dark it had become. It was still light when I sat down."

"Well, dinner is ready. You should come eat."

"Si, Mamá." I lifted myself like an old man from my seat.

At the doorway, mother stopped me with a hand on my chest. "Jose, have you noticed Amada lately?"

I paused. There was concern in her eyes. "I thought she seemed to be doing better. She has filled out nicely and some color has returned to her face."

"That is true"—she nodded—"her body is much improved, but she is still very troubled in her mind."

"What do you mean, Mother?" I was disturbed by the news. I had had little time to spend with Amada since my return, but my thoughts were on her frequently. I had thought her much improved.

"Oh, when you are around she comes alive—she smiles and laughs a little. But when you are gone, the light goes out of her. She becomes very different. And at night"—she shook her head—"you do not hear her with your room so far away, but she cries and she has dreams . . . such terrible dreams."

"Have you talked with her? What does she say about this?"

"Nothing." She shrugged. "She tells me nothing. She will mumble an apology for disturbing my sleep or tell me not to worry, all the time hiding her eyes, her face from me. And Lupita"—she raised and dropped her hands in a gesture of futility—"it is like talking to the wall. She will tell me nothing."

I frowned. "Tell me about Lupita. How did she come to be Amada's *acompañante*?"

"It was your father's idea. Shortly before his death, he noticed that Amada was becoming a woman. You know," and she gestured toward her own ample bosom. "Anyway, he felt that she should have a chaperone. I don't know why. Amada never goes anywhere. Only rarely to the *plaza* to shop and then only with the other women. But he seemed concerned." Mother wagged her head in perplexity. "The Cordovas of Bernalillo had an Indian woman that the señora complained of. She thought she had an evil eye or something. We, of course, are not so superstitious." Unconsciously, she crossed herself nonetheless. "Thanks to God!

"Don Benito rode down to talk to Don Felipe Cordova and, when he returned, Lupita was with him. She has been very faithful to Amada, I must say, but there is something"—she groped for the right word—"*perturbado*, you know, disquieting about her."

"But father seemed satisfied with her?"

"Oh, yes, very!" Mother seemed surprised. "He would even tease her and joke with her, if you can imagine, and Lupita seemed to enjoy it. She showed great respect for Don Benito. For the rest of us she was as she is, indifferent. Although she did not like Esteban, God rest his soul. I would almost call her hostile toward him."

I nodded. "Well"—I patted her shoulder—"we should eat now, yes?"

"Yes, but you distracted me. I was telling you about Amada. You should talk to her. She is such a sweet child and I hate to see her so disturbed. She will listen to you. She is so"—Mother gave me a strange look—"fond of you."

"She is?" I asked, feeling very foolish.

"Oh, *no seas tonto*, Jose! You are not children anymore and I am not blind. I have known Amada practically since her infancy. I have always thought you two were a much better match than she and Esteban, God grant him peace. But your father had made his arrangement with her father and, of course, men may not change their word, or even their mind, no matter the realities," she said with scorn. "Come, the food must be cold by now."

If it was, I did not notice, nor did I notice if the night was dark or light, though I slept little. My mind was on Amada.

I came home earlier than usual the next day and slipped quietly into the *placita*. In obedience to my wishes, Amada sat on a bench in the sunshine, a *rebozo* wrapped about her shoulders to ward off the chill of December. Beside her sat Lupita. The two of them were cleaning seeds from a basket of dried red chilis, although Lupita seemed to be doing most of the work. Amada's movements were listless and her gaze wandered unseeing to a tile embedded in the ground. I was surprised and slightly touched at the sidelong looks of concern that Lupita gave toward her charge.

Clearing my throat to announce my presence, I walked into view. As my mother had said, Amada was like a dreamer waking. Her head came up, her back straightened and a smile appeared on her lips. Lupita, on the other hand, glanced at me coldly and continued her work.

"Jose," Amada chirped, "you are home early! How nice! Are you hungry? I will make you something." She rose to her feet, oblivious to the chilis which rolled from her lap.

"No, thank you, Amada. I can eat later. I would like to talk with you, though." I looked at Lupita and she returned my gaze with a look which one would give a chamber pot. A nearly imperceptible nod of her head gave me permission, then she resumed her work. With my hand on her elbow, I led Amada out of the hearing, but not the view, of Lupita.

"How are you feeling, Amada?"

Her eyes searched my face. "I'm feeling much better, Jose, thank you. You were right, I just needed fresh air and food."

I shook my head. "I did not mean physically, Amada. How do you feel in your emotions? Are you sad? Are you frightened?"

A guarded look came over her eyes and her hands fussed nervously with her shawl. "I'm fine, Jose, really." Her eyes refused to meet mine as she answered. "Let me fix you some supper, you must be hungry."

She started to turn away, but I caught her lightly by her wrists with my two hands to stay her. Her reaction appalled me. She froze in her steps, her chest and shoulders heaving under what seemed unbearable emotion. Her head fell forward limply and she pleaded, "Don't, Jose, please! Let me go!"

I released her as if my hands had been scalded. She leaned against the garden's *adobe* wall for support, her breathing labored.

"My God, Amada, what is it? Did I hurt you? I am so sorry!"

She shook her head. "No, it is I who am sorry, Jose. I didn't mean to frighten you." She pushed her hair back and composed herself. "It is foolish of me, but when someone grabs my wrists that way, I feel trapped, helpless and weak, too weak, almost, to stand."

Glancing her way, I saw Lupita staring daggers at me, the chilis ignored.

"What is wrong, Amada?" I begged with anguish in my hushed voice. "You are tormented in your mind by day and in your dreams at night! Please, let me help you!" I frankly suspected that she was preoccupied with a sense of guilt for not revealing what she knew about Esteban's death, and hoped that she might find relief if I provoked her into confession.

She drew the *rebozo* tightly about her. "Do not concern yourself with my welfare, Jose. You have so many other concerns. Please, don't let me trouble you."

"Trouble!" I tried not to shout. *"Dios santo, mujer,* but you do trouble me! You always have. No matter how long the time or how far the distance, the thought of you has troubled me day and night. For a long time I felt great guilt and tried to ignore my feelings, because you were to be my brother's wife. Even after Esteban died, I felt guilty, as if my thoughts—my desire—had somehow made his death come to pass."

There were tears in her eyes. Amada shook her head, a soundless 'no' on her lips.

"And now I have made you cry when all I really want is to bring you joy." I combed my fingers through my hair in frustration. "Amada, I love you! I have always loved you! I will always love you!"

I don't know what response I expected, but it was not the response I received. Her lips were parted and her eyes were wide as if in fear. Her whole body began to shiver as if with ague and she hugged herself tightly to control the trembling.

"You must not love me, Jose!" She began shaking her head. "No, not me! You must not!"

My frustration turned to anger—not anger at Amada, but at whatever the condition was that plagued her mind and emotions. "It's too late for that, my love," I growled. "Much too late." Slowly, deliberately, I grasped her shoulders and drew her into my embrace. She remained rigid and trembling, even as I kissed her head. Then, gradually, like melting ice, her trembling turned to sobs. Hot tears flowed, soaking my shirt front and finally, her arms went around my waist, tentatively at first, then tightly, almost desperately.

"Hold me, Jose," she whispered. "Oh, please hold me!"

I did, for what seemed like hours, as she wept in an anguish I could not have imagined. Her whole body was racked by an unfathomable sorrow. I murmured words of love and comfort to her, as you would to a child terrified of the storm, until the calm of emotional exhaustion finally descended upon her.

I had to know. "Amada." I lifted her face toward mine, my hand beneath her chin. "I want to marry you. Can you love me?"

Her eyelids were so heavy, I thought that she was about to fall asleep. “I’m no good, Jose,” she mumbled. “You deserve so much better.”

Again, I felt a flash of anger. “Answer me, Amada! Do you love me?”

With eyes of suddenly great clarity, but in a voice of weary resignation, she said, “Yes, Jose. I love you. Of course, I do. I have always loved you.”

“Then listen to me.” I held her at arm’s length. “I am going to tell Mother. We will make the arrangements. We will be married.”

If I expected some show of excitement, I was disappointed. She responded in that same maddening, lifeless tone. “Yes, Jose. As you wish.” With that she turned and walked back into the house, leaving me more confused than I had ever felt in my life.

Arrangements were made. A date was set for late January. As I watched her over those weeks, I saw Amada’s emotions swing like a pendulum from apathy, to fear, to exhilaration and back again. Sometimes she sought me out. Sometimes she avoided me. Mother, as well, complained to me of Amada’s extremes.

The sky was leaden and snowy on our wedding day. The church was filled with candle and incense and people. I have never seen anyone more beautiful than Amada as Paco brought her to stand beside me before the priest. We exchanged our vows and knelt side by side for the blessing. As is our custom in New Mexico, the rest of the day was a blur of festivities, food and dancing. It seemed that everyone in the region of the upper Rio Grande had braved the weather to be at our wedding.

It was late when Amada and I finally stood alone together behind closed doors. The room was warm and ruddy from the fire crackling in the corner hearth. We were both nervous, avoiding each other's eyes. I cleared my throat.

"Amada, please sit down. I have to talk to you." I pulled out a chair that had been placed in our wedding chamber. Seating her, I paced back and forth.

"What is it, Jose?"

"I should have told you this sooner, but I was afraid of your reaction. I'm sorry." A nervous smile twitched at my lips and again I cleared my throat. "I want there to be no secrets between us, so I have to tell you that I am not . . . er . . . without knowledge, shall we say, of a woman." With flushed face and downcast eyes, I told her about Chilsipee. "I'm sorry, I should have told you sooner."

"I see," Amada said flatly, nodding her head in an exaggerated show of understanding. It was then that I realized that she had had rather more of the El Paso wine than she perhaps should have. "We must be completely honest with one another, you say?"

"Yes, I think it would be best."

"Yes." Then she began to laugh, a normal laugh at first but it grew into a frightening, almost hysterical howl.

"Stop it, Amada!" I pleaded, gripping her shoulders tightly. "What is it? Why are you laughing so?"

"I, too, must be honest, dear Jose . . . dear, dear Jose . . . and tell you that I am not without . . . knowledge"—she gave a burst of bitter laughter—"of a man." Amada looked up to see my reaction, which was slack-jawed amazement. "Yes, my husband, knowledge imparted by your own dear brother, my betrothed, Esteban." She practically spit the name.

My legs felt weak and I had to sit on the floor at her feet.

Calmly now, almost unemotionally, she began to tell me what I could never have imagined. "Almost from the day I arrived here, your brother began to . . . to . . . do things to me. I was so scared and so alone, I did not know what to do. And he would tell me that it was all quite normal and natural since we were to be married some day anyway." Growing agitated, Amada began to pull on a lock of her hair that had come loose from her comb.

"When I would protest, he would tell me that it must be a secret, and if I ever told anyone, they would hate me and he would have to hurt me very badly." Another burst of horrible laughter, like acid, burned my ears.

"Not that he didn't hurt me anyway over the years." Her voice rose now and trembled with suppressed anger. "Here!" She pulled the wedding gown off her shoulder. There was indeed a scar along her shoulder blade. "And here, and here, and even here!" Stupidly, I nodded. Yes, the marks were there—scars and more scars.

"And there are others, which I cannot show you." Heavily, she sat back on the chair.

My mind was in turmoil, but from the chaos came the relentless question that I had lived with for nearly a year. "Amada," I whispered, "what happened the night Esteban died? Amada! Tell me what happened!"

Her long silence made me think she had not heard, but with a blank stare and a lifeless voice, she began. "It was better after Lupita came. She kept him away. I think Don Benito suspected, that was probably why he was so kind to me—not because he really loved me, why should he—but he could not confront his own flesh and blood. How can you think the unthinkable?"

"Then the night of my *quinceniera*, Lupita was busy in the kitchen. I went back to my room to change. I even felt happy that evening, despite that pig *Americano*." She laughed lightly at the memory. That night, and not, this, her wedding night, was before her eyes now. My brother, and not I, was with her.

"Esteban came in. He had been drinking. He pushed open the door and strutted in like a rooster. 'It's been a long time, *India*,' he said. He never used my name, it was always just *India*. 'Too long,' he said and he grabbed me." She flinched and rubbed her arm where his hand had been, in her mind the pain was fresh.

"I tried to push him away. 'Can't you wait?' I said. 'I'm fifteen now and we will be married.' He thought that was very funny. 'Married!' he snorted. 'Now that my father is not around to make me, do you think that I would marry you—*una India bronca*?' He laughed and it was like a shower of needles falling on my heart."

She grasped the seat of the chair tightly as if she might fall off. "Even as he laughed, he grabbed me again and tried to force me down." She closed her eyes and rocked in agony. "In my mind I called for Jose, I called for my mother or for Lupita, but my voice remained silent and no one heard. I could not really call. They would all hate me for being so bad. Esteban grabbed me by my hair and pulled. I flailed my arms and lost my balance. I fell onto the *colchón*, and there, before me, was the candlestick. I grabbed it and rose to my feet."

As she said it, she leaped from the chair, knocking it over with a crash. “He was mocking me. ‘Oh, are you such a fine lady now?’ he said. And he began to recount the things which he had done to me. I had to silence him! He had to be silent! Make him be silent, silent, silent!” Her eyes closed tightly, her hands covered her ears and her voice rose to a hissing whisper.

I leaped to my feet as if released from a spell. Throwing my arms around her, I hugged her tightly, her voice muffled against my chest, her hands beating on my shoulders. Her frenzy continued for what seemed an eternity. Tears were streaming down my face, and I could only repeat her name as her anger turned to tears and she slid weakly down my body to the floor. There on the hard-packed earth, she curled on her side, her arms about her chest, her wedding gown bunched around her waist, and she wept. “Don’t let him touch me! Please, don’t let him touch me!” she whimpered.

It was that lost and lonely little girl, scared, wounded and rejected, that I picked up in my arms and lay gently on the bed. Wrapping her in blankets, I held the trembling body of my brother’s killer, my beloved, my wife.

Chapter Eighteen

One of the greatest curses of old age, is the ability to remember, with terrible clarity, every mistake of one's youth. Now we possess the wisdom and experience to make proper decisions in circumstances that, in our youth, prompted us to act out of ignorance and passion. And though the memories are as clear and vivid as the hour just passed, they are as immutable as the seasons' order.

I arose that next morning still numb with shock. It had not been a restful night for either of us. Amada had quivered and cried and wrestled with her demons even in sleep. My demons had permitted me no sleep at all. I sat up and, in the pre-dawn light, I studied the slight young woman who was now my wife. Her sleep was untroubled now and the pain that usually pinched her features was absent. She was very lovely with her hair in disarray and her body curled like a child's.

The resemblance to Chilsipee was even more striking at this time, which brought even greater turmoil to my mind. I had loved what I saw of Amada in Chilsipee and cherished what I saw of Chilsipee in Amada, and yet, I had to admit, after the revelations of the night before, that I did not really know Amada at all. Nor had I truly known the brutality of my brother Esteban, nor the moral cowardice of my own father. It caused me to question what I really knew, to a certainty, about any human being including myself. And yet, though my mind was a maelstrom of questions and doubts, in my heart there was a certainty, as fixed and permanent as the North Star in the vast, shifting night sky, that I loved this woman, Amada, whoever she might be and whatever she may have done. The realization of this truth was a source of both comfort and confusion. And yet . . .

Amada stirred and turned onto her back. With feline grace she stretched. Her eyes, still heavy with sleep, half opened and she smiled. "Jose," she purred with pleasure, reaching her hands toward me. Abruptly she stopped. The guards of fear and wariness leaped to their posts in her eyes and her hands retreated to clutch the blanket beneath her chin.

I could think of nothing to say. Like a man after a night of drinking, my mind felt slow and stupid and painful. My face must have reflected both longing and confusion. I looked away. Stiffly, I rose from the *colchón* and blundered around the room searching for clothing to replace my rumpled wedding suit.

Amada's voice was flat and emotionless. "I'm sorry, Jose. It was your wedding night, you had the right."

I turned to look at her. "The right?" I said in disgust.

"No one has the right to do with you only according to his own will."

She sat up and shifted to lean against the wall, her legs hunched to her chest, only her head visible above the blanket. "Oh, Jose, you are so . . . different." She shook her head sadly. "You are too good."

I gave a scornful laugh at the thought. "I think what you mistake for goodness is only stupidity," I said bitterly. "Like Don Quixote, I see giants where there are only windmills."

"You must despise me," she said, her tone part statement, part command. "Since we did not consummate the marriage, I am sure you could obtain an annulment. You can send me away somewhere. You can. . . ."

"Despise you?" I dropped to my knees before her. "I love you, Amada! I just don't know you!"

"I am as you see me," she replied in a trembling voice, "no more than that." Bravely, she tried to banter, though her voice broke. "I can not be your Dulcinea, Sir Knight."

I bowed my head, eyes closed, as I struggled to control my thoughts and emotions. "I can live without my illusions, Amada." I looked at her directly. "I can not live without you."

Eyes brimming, she sought refuge behind her hair. In a tiny voice, she said, "I'll try, Jose. I swear to you, I will try."

She did try, and that effort was painful for me to see. By day, she was attentive and considerate to the point of annoyance, like an over-eager puppy anxious to please, but at night she could not manage to overcome the feelings of revulsion that stirred in her abused body to engage in any of the intimacies of marriage. She would try to feign passion, but the trembling of her limbs and the cringing of her flesh betrayed her, and I would give up my gentle efforts to demonstrate my affection and quietly kiss her goodnight. I pretended not to notice her stifled sobbing as I turned away.

I confess that I stopped trying before she. Though I was never unfaithful, increasingly I found pressing business to call me away from home all day and even overnight. It was futile, of course, for the thought of her never diminished in my mind. Yet, when I was home, silence, like the seed of a rank and poisonous weed, continued to grow between us. Though spring softened the land, the cold, dark winter of our souls only deepened.

Captain Becknell returned to Santa Fe, this time with three wagons loaded with goods, the first to cross the plains. Our reunion was a bright light in my darkness. He visited in our home and was charmed by my shy, dark wife, teasing me in private because there were no signs of an heir beneath Amada's narrow waist. My melancholy only deepened when he left.

In April, my mother came to me. "Jose, I've been thinking. Your sister, Olivia, has been pestering me to come live with them, and I have been thinking, perhaps I should. I could help her look after the children and, that way, you newlyweds could be alone." She folded her hands in her lap, but they refused to be still.

I frowned. "But this is your home, Mother. Do you want to leave? Olivia is only just next door."

She avoided my eyes. "Well, perhaps it would be easier for you and Amada if you had more privacy."

I sighed and laid my pen aside. "Are we driving you from your own home, *Madre*?"

"Oh, *mi hijo*!" she said in exasperation, rising to her feet. "This house has known sickness, tragedy and hard times, but it was always a home. Now, though, there is a sadness, like a drought, that is drying the life from this place." She looked at me squarely. "You are like a stranger and Amada . . . she seems more alone now than when you were gone! What is it, Jose?"

"I can not say, *Mamá*. I simply can not say." My fingers drummed on my knee.

"You must talk to her, Jose. Please! Amada is your wife, you are one flesh, as God would have it. You must be of one mind as well. The world is too hard to face alone."

I could only nod, my head bent. Mother looked at me as if she would say more, then turned and left with short, fast steps. All afternoon I sat, deep in thought. The band of light from the window moved across the wall behind me from west to east, faded into shadow, and still I sat.

My solitude was pierced. "Jose," Amada said from the doorway in her sad, soft voice. "Your dinner is ready." She turned to leave.

"Amada, wait. Please, sit with me, just for a moment."

Amada, without expression, dutifully came and sat where I indicated. She looked not at me, but out the narrow window where the light green buds of a peach tree glowed in the last light of day.

"I have been thinking, we are still losing far too many sheep. Some to wolves, some to Indians"—she glanced at me, then back out the window—"some to our less honest neighbors. And, under the Mexican law, we must make improvements to our land grant soon or lose our right to the land." I took a deep breath, letting it out slowly. "I don't really need to be in Santa Fe any longer, so I have been thinking, perhaps it would be wise to move"—Amada was looking at me now—"out to our land where I can grow crops and supervise the flocks in person. We can build a new home there, away from everyone else. We could take just one or two of the servants. But mainly, it would be you and me, Amada. It would mean much work, hard work, this starting over, but it could make things better." I was not speaking about our livestock. "Would you like that, Amada? Do you want to try with me, again?"

I could see only half of her face, the side toward the window, the rest was in shadow. Her eyes were downcast, and a single tear traced a glistening path down her cheek. With great dignity, she slipped from her chair and knelt before me, laying her head against my knee.

"Yes, Jose," she whispered. "I want to try."

Thus we sat in silence, my hand upon her hair, until the darkness was complete.

Preparations were quickly made and by May we were ready. We loaded two wagons with tools, supplies, bedding, clothes and whatever weapons could be spared. Amada and I rode in one wagon while the inscrutable Lupita and Paco's fifteen-year-old grandson, Manuel, drove the other. Doña Maria Elena, fearful for our safety, yet hopeful for our success, wept as she embraced us all and called God's blessing on our venture.

Amada sat twisted around, waving, as long as my mother was visible, but once we'd turned the bend, her back straightened, her jaw set and she never looked back again as the wagon bounced over the rutted road. Most Spanish women would have covered their heads and muffled their faces from the dust and glare, but Amada seemed to revel in it. Her hair danced in every breeze and the sunlight glistened on her face as on burnished bronze.

As it had so many times in my past, our trail lay south and east toward Glorieta Pass and the Pecos valley. Our mules were strong but slow and we made from only ten to fifteen miles a day, sleeping at night beneath our wagons. This was a familiar way of life for me, but for Amada, it was an epiphany. I had not stopped to realize how cloistered her life had been in my mother's house. Now, she saw and inquired after every bird, beast and bush that we passed. I answered to the best of my ability and indulged her childlike petitions for riding and shooting lessons. It was poignant indeed to see this daughter of the world's finest horsemen, clinging in trepidation to the back of a plodding horse beside our wagon.

We spent one night at the Pecos pueblo where our fathers had arranged our fates and were both filled with sadness and nostalgia. Our spirits lightened as we left early the next morning, following the river northward into the narrowing valley. For once in our acquaintance, even Lupita seemed content, looking about in silent placidity at the beautiful country. Manuel was one of those quiet, serious youngsters whose shyness made him seem aloof and mature. He tackled every chore with determination, only rarely gracing us with a bright smile when I would tease him about something like his nascent mustache or coltish long legs.

The valley rose and the mountains around us grew more towering. From short *piñon* to tall pines, we ascended until we came to a broad and grassy park. From the northwest, a smaller stream flowed to join the Pecos. We could see a flock of sheep grazing on the tall alpine grasses and wild flowers. Above us, a few fleecy clouds raced across the deep blue sky.

"Oh, Jose!" Amada laced her arm through mine in a gesture of such natural affection that my eyes stung with tears. "It is so beautiful!" she marveled, hugging my arm to her body.

"It is also, my wife, your new home." I watched her reaction. Her lips parted, her eyes grew round, and she looked again, drinking in the beauty of the place.

"What is that stream called," she pointed.

"That is the Espiritu Santo, the Holy Spirit. Further north, the Mora River flows in from the northeast. I thought we could build our house in that sheltered area between the Espiritu and the mountains, looking south down the Pecos. What do you think?"

She nodded enthusiastically. "Yes, oh yes! It will be a beautiful house, won't it Jose, to match this blessed place, yes?"

"Yes." I smiled at her. "Wherever you are, there is beauty."

Her expression grew serious and she lowered her eyes. The pressure on my arm increased.

We slapped our reins and continued across the meadow. A sheep dog bounded toward us to take a defensive position before the flock. I was annoyed that no shepherds had as yet hailed us or even made themselves apparent. As casually as I could, I checked the priming on my rifle, just in case Indians were the explanation for the missing men. The creek was running full with spring melt, so crossing was an exhilarating experience. Both wagons managed without mishap and we continued to the spot we had chosen for the house. Reaching into the wagon bed, I pulled a roll of paper from my case.

"Manuel, Lupita, come here! I want to show you something." When everyone had gathered round, I unrolled the paper, weighting its corners to the ground with stones. "This is the house we will build here," I said proudly.

My companions were gratifyingly appreciative of my design. I had decided on a small replica of the Indian pueblos. The building would be a rectangle open to the south. The northern segment of the house would be two stories tall while the east and west arms would be a single story each. A defensive wall with a gate would form the southern perimeter. The house would focus on that central *plaza* while only small windows, like gun ports, would open to the outside.

"We'll build with stone and *adobe*, of course," I explained. "With all these tall pines around us, we should be able to build real furniture, just like the *ricos* of Albuquerque." I rested my hand on Manuel's shoulder. "What do you say, *amigo*, would you like to become a carpenter?"

"*Pues, sí patrón*." He smiled. "Was not our Lord also a carpenter?"

We unloaded the wagons and made our camp for the night. With instructions to Manuel to keep his gun near, I took advantage of the light remaining to search for the shepherds. It felt good to sit astride a saddle again, after so many days on the wagon's unyielding seat.

I found a shepherd asleep in the shade of a tree and, with stern words, sent him to fetch his companions and their flocks so that I could gauge the extent of our property firsthand in the days ahead. That night, we stayed awake longer than usual beside our fire, excited by our plans for the future. Perhaps it was the cold, but Amada seemed to lie closer in my arms that night.

The days and weeks that followed were filled with the joy of work that was new and good. Though late in the season, a garden was cleared and planted with seeds from home. The foundation was dug, trees felled and peeled, rock brought from the river, and *adobe* mixed. We soon had hundreds of bricks drying in the sun. As the shepherds straggled in, I put the fear of God and Don Jose in them and sent them back to their pastures with a gift of tobacco for each.

Though the days grew longer, we still worked past sundown or, 'from can't see to can't see' as the Americans say. By summer, the outer wall was up and we moved within its protective confines. By autumn, the first floor was finished and we moved indoors. The second story would have to wait until spring.

The fatigue and lack of privacy throughout the warm months had made any intimacy between Amada and me difficult at best. As the days went by, though, I was gratified to see her blossom in her new environment. Smiles and laughter came more readily to her and her sleep was more tranquil. Her face took on a healthy glow from the constant exposure to the sun, and the work caused her body to grow stronger and more mature. Though we were seldom alone, I sensed a new trust that she felt in my presence.

She had developed rather well as a horsewoman, but I was still surprised when she came to where I was working one morning in October and suggested we go for a ride. "We've had no time off since we came here, Jose. Please, just today? We can work twice as hard tomorrow," she reasoned.

I had to concede. I saddled two horses and helped her into the saddle, resolving to teach her how to mount by herself in the spring. We followed the Espiritu Santo upstream. As Amada looked at the wonders around us, I marveled at the wonder that she had become. Fluid and relaxed, her movements were an unconscious complement to her horse's. She sat erect and confident, her long hair sparkling in the light like black crystal. At her request, we turned into the trees and climbed the valley's western side. When it became too steep for the animals, we tied them and continued on foot to a ledge that jutted clear of the trees. There we sat, breathless and content, with a magnificent view to our homesite and beyond.

Amada lay back, her hands behind her head, to gaze at the clear sky above us. A light breeze stirred in the pines, causing them to sway and sigh gently. She closed her eyes and smiled. "Are you happy, Jose?"

Looking out over the glorious mountains, I nodded. "Yes, I think I am. And, you?"

She looked at me. "Yes, I really think I am. Thank you for bringing me here."

"It was nothing. You were right. We needed a day off."

"No, I mean here to live, here in this place." She shifted onto her side, elbow bent, and her head resting on her hand.

I smiled. "It is good here." Unconsciously, I had been rubbing my leg, which ached from our climb.

Amada saw it. "Does your leg hurt?"

"Oh." I was surprised. "Only a little."

"Here, let me." Rising, Amada knelt astride my outstretched legs at my knee and began to gently massage my injured thigh. Her hair brushed across my face. There was a growing tightness in my chest, a tingling awareness of her body close to mine.

My hands went around her and I lay back with her in my arms. I kissed her and she responded with an urgency she had never displayed before. Through her clothing, my fingertips explored the contours of her back.

My hand moved across her flat stomach and then I felt the change in her breathing from passion to panic. I drew back and allowed her to roll away from me.

"No, please! I'm sorry! Oh, I'm so sorry!" She crouched, looking at me, an expression of misery on her face. "I wanted you, Jose, I really did. I thought maybe this time . . . But then that feeling—that awful, drowning feeling again . . ."

I stretched my hand out toward her, reaching but not touching. "It's alright, *querida*, really! I want you, it's very true, but I love you more. I will wait. I will outwait your fear."

She kissed the palm of my hand and placed it against her cheek. "I love you, Jose. I do so love you."

I rose to my feet and helped her up. "We had better start back before the weather changes. It will be winter soon."

Hand in hand we returned to our horses and rode back to the house.

Night-time frost soon painted new colors on our valley. The red and gold of oak and aspen stood out in gorgeous relief against a background of deep green pine. The mountain peaks donned caps of snow and we our woolen *serapes*. Manuel left with the shepherds to help drive a portion of our flocks to lower pastures and was gone for two weeks. We missed his help and steady good nature but, when evening came, we particularly missed his soft voice and skillful guitar playing. I tried to coax a few songs from his guitar while he was gone but my efforts only caused Amada to giggle and Lupita to find other chores to do.

Snow in the high country pushed the wild animals down to the valley. Amada noticed the migration first. She ran into my workshop, breathless and excited one evening, causing me to reach for my gun.

"No, no, Jose, leave the gun and come quickly, you must see!" Grabbing my hand, she led me at a run back outside the wall, slowing to a stealthy walk as we approached the trees. Eyes wide with wonder, she pointed, then covered her mouth with her hands to prevent any involuntary expressions of awe.

A family of deer stood browsing at the meadow's edge, their tawny coats making them nearly invisible against the autumn leaves. "*Mira, la chiquita*!" Amada whispered. There was indeed a young fawn among the group, its delicate jaw chewing in circular imitation of its elders. While the animal tableau was beautiful, I was more stirred by Amada, who was so completely enchanted by the scene. In my heart, I thanked God for His creation and for the healing He was performing in both Amada and me.

Manuel returned with packages and news from Santa Fe the day before our first snow. It began at sundown and, since there was no wind, we all went up on the roof to stand in the hush of the soft, white flakes as they settled like blessings on the land. The fire seemed warmer and Manuel's voice sweeter, as we sat before sleeping that night.

A few days later, I was out early with my bow and arrows, hunting for an elk to fill our storeroom for the winter, when I came upon moccasin tracks. My every instinct was immediately aroused and I debated whether to follow those tracks or return to warn the others. I knelt for a closer look. The tracks were clear and fresh in the new snow. I could see that there appeared to be four sets, one or two adults and two or three children. My ambivalence was from the small size of the second adult's tracks. I frowned. One did not take a family to hunt or war in such weather. By the pattern, the moccasins appeared to be of Apache design, always a cause for concern in New Mexico. There were drops of blood among the footprints.

I followed the tracks carefully to a dry ravine. Rather than enter the ravine directly, I climbed quietly along the rocky verge overlooking the brush-filled break. A soft murmur of voices made me stop and crouch. As slowly as I could, I advanced around a boulder and peeked toward the sounds below me. It appeared to be a family. Two small children huddled, shivering beside the carcass of a sheep—one of ours, I assumed—while a small woman bent over the prostrate body of a man I could only partially see.

Silently, I nocked an arrow and crept closer. Drawing back on the string, I was about to reveal myself when I heard the muffled cry of a baby. The woman moved out of my sight to hush the infant and I could see the man, grimacing in pain on the ground. A bloody cloth was clutched against his shoulder, and his head was turned to study his wound. I waited until the woman reappeared, a cradleboard in her arms, before standing and calling to the family. "*Hola*!" I said in Spanish. I knew no Apache at that time. My drawn bow remained pointed at the man who stared at me with angry eyes.

A small hunting bow lay near the man. I indicated that he should toss it toward me. When he growled and appeared ready to resist, I deliberately shifted my aim to the woman. Fear surged across his face at that and he uncoiled his muscles, passively throwing his weapons at my feet. I relaxed my bow and retrieved his. In sign language, I indicated that I would not hurt him or his family. He seemed not to understand my meaning or perhaps he did not believe me, because he tensed again at my approach, casting helpless looks at his defenseless family.

In my *parfleche*, I had some pemmican and some jerky which I offered to the woman and children. Though their hunger was obvious, they only looked at the food, immobile and shivering. I crouched beside the man and carefully lifted the bloody cloth. A terrible, gaping wound had torn into his flesh from a lance, the point of which remained imbedded in his shoulder. He had lost a great deal of blood. He would soon die if left there in the cold.

Slowly, in sign language, I explained that he would

have to trust me or he and his family would die. I repeated the signs twice and finally, he nodded. I then explained as best I could that they would have to come with me to my lodge, where they would be safe. That too, I repeated. He closed his eyes, his breathing labored and considered. Nodding his head again, he turned to his wife and spoke gently. The woman gave a sharp inhalation of fear, but she too nodded, then went to her children.

The Apache was so weak, I really feared he might die before we reached the house. Leaning most of his weight on me, we staggered painfully down the valley. He never cried out but, so close was his face to mine, that I could hear the grinding of his teeth as he bit back the pain. Manuel spotted us at a distance and came on the run, hesitating for an instant when he saw the tribe of my companions, but then quickly moved to help. Between us we carried the man into the main room and laid him on a blanket beside the fire.

Amada and Lupita had left their task of shelling corn and hurried to us when we entered the gate. The children had insisted on dragging along the carcass of the sheep, so ingrained was their ethic to not waste food. Lupita quickly relieved them of their burden, then shooed them like chickens before her into the house. Amada threw her own *rebozo* around the woman and her baby, leading them behind us into the warmth.

Until then, I had really failed to appreciate the better qualities of Lupita's character. With absolute efficiency, she scooped water from our barrel into a kettle, then set it to boil on the fire. Pushing me aside, she bent over the wounded man and examined the shoulder. "The point is caught against the bone," she diagnosed coolly. "If it goes forward, it will break the bone. It must be pulled back." With that, she stood and went to rummage among the kitchen utensils.

Amada, meanwhile, had given warm tortillas to the children and their mother, who devoured them ravenously. The baby, warming in the fire's glow, began to cry, so the woman lifted her blouse and pressed its hungry mouth to her breast. Amada came to stand beside me, looking at the wound for the first time. "Will he die, Jose?"

"Only God knows," was all I could answer.

Lupita returned with a knife usually used to carve mutton. As she turned the blade in the flames, she explained, "The lance point has been in the body for several days. The flesh has begun to close over it. It must be cut away or it will gangrene. Then the point must be pulled out."

When the blade was hot, Lupita indicated that Manuel and I should restrain her patient, then she lay the sharp edge to the puffy skin. The man flinched and groaned but, by tremendous will, tried to cooperate with our efforts. After carving away the offended flesh, Lupita cleansed the area with the hot water and stanched the bleeding with clean wool. Though she said nothing, perspiration beaded her leathery face as she explored the wound with her fingers. The man writhed in silent agony.

Lupita sat back on her heels with a sigh. Looking at me, she said, "I am not strong enough to dislodge the point." Unstated, her conclusion hung in the air. I must try.

I washed my hands and knelt beside the shoulder.

With silent prayer and closed eyes, I probed tentatively until I felt the point. Yes, it was solidly wedged. I hooked my finger around its edge and strained, succeeding only in adding my own blood to his as I gashed myself against the razor sharp point. Astonishingly, the Apache was still conscious, though his half-closed eyes seemed clouded and unfocused. His family and mine stood above him, all our muscles straining in sympathy for his pain.

"Manuel, in our tools should be a pair of blacksmith's tongs. Bring them, please." The situation required unorthodox remedies. When he returned, we plunged the tongs into the kettle. They were ready before I was. I looked around at the circle of concerned faces, the children wide-eyed, the adults squinting with worry. I took a deep breath. Using both hands to guide the *tenazas*, I clamped their jaws upon the cursed lance point and, while the man's body arched in extremity, I pulled with all my strength. There was a sickening screech of metal on bone and the point surrendered. It was out. The Apache had fainted.

Fortunately, Lupita stepped in to finish the ministrations, because I too felt faint. Staggering outside to the cold air, I vomited and leaned against the gritty wall, grateful that no one had followed me out. In a while, I composed myself and returned to the room. A blanket covered the man whose face was ashen and pale beneath its coppery surface.

Manuel approached me, the lance point in his hand. "What should we do with this, *patrón*?" he asked.

"Save it. If he lives, he may want it for his medicine

bag." Manuel looked at me oddly, but shrugged and nodded.

All night and all the next day, the man wrestled with the death angel as his wife sat beside him, mopping his face, diverted only by the need to nurse the baby. The children, wary at first, soon accepted Amada's good intentions and followed her wherever she went, a serious expression indelible on their faces. They were a boy and a girl, probably five and four years old respectively. In our concern, none of us had much sleep. The only one who seemed unaffected by exhaustion was Lupita.

Late in the afternoon, Amada sat singing the children's song *Don Gato* to the uncomprehending but attentive children. Manuel was with the animals and the wife sat in patient attendance on her unconscious husband. Lupita was stirring a kettle of beans at the fire, when I approached her.

"Lupita," I said, squatting beside her, looking at the beans, not her. "I owe you an apology." She continued stirring. "I thought that you had killed my brother." I spoke softly, so that only she would hear. "I know the truth now. Thank you for protecting Amada."

Lupita still did not look at me but she did stop stirring. "You are not a bad man." That was all she said but, coming from her, it was the equivalent of a medal of commendation. She resumed her stirring. I nodded, and left her to herself.

Late that evening, the man spoke. Only his wife heard it, but we heard her reply and saw her quickly return the baby to its cradleboard and bend over her husband.

Limply, he lifted his good arm and tenderly touched her face. Lupita quickly examined his wound, felt his forehead, and nodded in satisfaction. "He will live."

And he did. In fact, Eagle's Cry and his family lived with us all winter though he recovered quickly. Over the weeks, he taught me Apache, for which I have often since been grateful. Soon after his recovery began, he told me, in a mixture of sign, Apache, and Spanish, how he had come to his frightful plight.

The Jicarilla Apache were surrounded. Pressure from Comanche, Ute, Navajo and Spanish over the years had driven them from an extensive range of mountains and plains in northern New Mexico to a scattered few embattled rancherias. As part of a despicable program to pacify the Apache, an earlier *visitador* of the Interior Provinces, Bernardo de Galvez, had instituted a program of keeping the Apache supplied with plenty of alcohol. Mexican *aguardiente* had proved debilitating enough, but in recent years, American mountain men had used Jicarilla Apache scouts to locate beaver in the mountains and found it expedient to pay them with whiskey. The result had been the near destruction of their society.

American whiskey had made strong incursions into the life of the rancheria of Eagle's Cry. On the evening of our first snowfall, a drunken brawl had ensued involving both Apache and mountain men and Eagle, though not drinking, had been wounded when he tried to keep a fellow Jicarilla from entering his wickiup to search for more whiskey. Appalled at the debauchery to which his people had fallen, Eagle's Cry had preferred to flee, wounded, into the storm rather than stay. He had hoped to reach another band of Jicarilla less depraved or even the distant Mescalero or Chiricahua. His injury proved too severe, though, and he was preparing to die when I found him.

When he was strong enough, we moved the family into an empty room of their own, though they usually joined us for meals. Amada spent a great deal of time with the children, which seemed to give her at least as much pleasure as it did them. The first Spanish they learned was "*Tía* Amada". More important, I think, they taught Amada how to play, returning to her a small portion of the childhood she had missed.

On Christmas Eve, my hunting produced a fat elk, and I returned to find our home decorated for the holy day as well as our primitive means allowed. Amada always loved Christmas. The image of the baby Jesus, cold and rejected among the animals, always brought tears to her eyes. Christmas Day, we prayed, sang songs, and feasted on elk, corn, beans, chili, and onions with cups of hot *atole* afterward.

Leaving the warmth of the hearth, I went out into the freezing night. Climbing the ladder, I stood on the roof and drank in the beauty of the moonlight on the snowy ground. A halo, like a frozen rainbow, circled the nearly full moon. As is my custom when I am alone, I spoke to God, thanking Him for sustaining me through so many hazardous circumstances, most of which were precipitated by my own foolishness, and bringing me to that blessed place. And yet, I had to confess, I was not entirely content.

I thought of Eagle's Cry and his family and I turned my face to the north. The North Star twinkled brightly.

Somewhere, I thought, beneath that star, Chilsipee sits beside a fire with a child I will never know. This thought triggered a twinge of self-contempt in me. *Are you feeling sorry for yourself, Little Spaniard? Little Fool, may God bless them and keep you from hurting anyone else.*

"It's cold out here, Jose."

I spun around, startled. Amada stood wrapped in a blanket. I reached out my arm and she came to nestle against my body. "The moon is so bright you could read a book standing here," I said.

"Why would you want to do that, when your eyes could be filled with all this?" she teased, gesturing toward the magnificent valley. After a comfortable silence, she asked, "Why do you suppose God would come to earth, to suffer so much as a human being?"

I shook my head. "Probably to tell us in person, what we refused to read in all this." I, too, swept my hand toward the moonlit panorama.

Amada turned her head and pressed her face against my *serape*. "My nose is frozen."

I nodded. It was very cold. "We'd better go in. My leg is aching."

"Is it?" She looked up at me, eyes bright with moonlight. "I will massage it for you tonight." She looked at me a long time to be sure that I understood her meaning.

"That would be wonderful," I responded, in a choked voice. With my arm around her, we walked to the ladder and climbed back down to the warmth of our home and our marital bed.

Chapter Nineteen

The winter was long and hard, with snow piling deep in the high country but, as always, a day came when the breeze was from the south and the tinkling music of a million icicles melting could be heard in the imagination if not the ear. We could hear the tinkling of the flock leaders' bells as the sheep returned to the higher pastures. With the end of winter, we also said good-bye to Eagle's Cry and his family, who went in search of a new people. Amada was sorry to see her two young friends leave, but she was comforted by that spring's new life both around and within her.

I made a trip to Santa Fe to check on certain affairs of business. Doña Maria Elena wept with joy when she heard that Amada was going to provide her with a new grandchild. I rushed through my business and pushed my horse to a lather, so anxious was I to return to my wife and home. Amada was radiant and more at peace than I had ever known her. Even Lupita was susceptible to smiles that season.

When the time came for shearing, our valley became a bleating sea of wool. The sheep had wintered well, and the lambing had increased the flocks greatly. I have never shrunk from labor, but I must confess that sheep shearing, for me, is a veritable torment. The aching, cramping muscles from the endless bending, reaching and cutting, had everyone exhausted. It also made me careless.

I, of all people, should have known the importance of vigilance but, after more than a year of peaceful pursuits, I allowed the herdsmen to serve only indifferent guard duty.

We had been shearing for two or three days and the warm air was thick with wool and dust and bleating cries. The shearers and I were stripped to the waist and rivers of sweat coursed down our dust-caked bodies. There was a great deal of good-natured shouting among the men and I was not sure that I actually heard the gunshots. Nonetheless, something made me straighten up to ease my aching back and I saw Javier, who was on guard duty, running from a distance. He was shouting something I could not distinguish. Even before I saw them, a surge of fear coursed through my body.

"Amada!" I yelled, turning to look for her. I saw her walking down the slope from the house, one hand holding a bucket, the other her slightly rounded belly. She looked up in alarm at my voice. "Get back in the house!" I shouted. Just then the riders burst from the trees with a chorus of yelping cries.

Everything was in motion then. The shearers jerked

to attention and began wading through the milling sheep to reach their weapons. Poor Javier was quickly run down, a lance through his chest as he turned to defend himself. I scrambled toward the house, relieved to see Amada disappearing through the gate. When I reached the house, she met me, handing me the loaded rifle.

"No," I panted. "You keep that. I'll get my bow." I could fire a dozen arrows in the time it would take me to reload the rifle. "Stay inside and bolt the door." I heard her say, "Jose . . ." but did not wait for the rest.

Rushing back through the gate, I saw the attackers already among the sheep, gleefully shooting at men and animals without distinction. They had many firearms which they used to deadly effect, dropping many of our men before they could reach their weapons. Angrily, I fired an arrow at the nearest enemy. It went wide. "Calm down, you fool!" I scolded myself, speaking out loud. My next arrow found its mark, hitting the man squarely in the chest and knocking him backwards off his horse into the roiling sea of sheep. "That's better," I said.

Manuel reached the gate, his left arm hanging limp and bloody. "Inside quickly, *mi hijo*!" I instructed. I let fly another arrow and another horse rode free. Two more of our men reached the gate and scrambled through. Looking around, I could see no more of our people standing. A bullet dug into the *adobe* beside my head. I backed through the *puerta* and helped the men to close and bar the gate. Outside, the shrieking continued above the bleating of sheep and pounding of hooves.

I quickly assessed the situation. It was not good. To our good fortune, there were six of us safe inside the walls. Amada and Lupita were in the house. The two shearers, Manuel and I were in the courtyard. To our misfortune, Manuel was badly wounded and the shearers had no weapons. I tried to think. I had my bow, Amada had a rifle, and as well as I could envision, every other weapon lay useless outside with the attackers.

As if to remind me of their presence, I heard a scraping sound and looked up to see a man coming over the eight-foot wall. Quickly, I nocked an arrow, stepped away from the wall and shot him just as he stood up on the height. He tumbled forward into the courtyard.

"Felipe! Octavio!" I called to the terrified shearers, "help Manuel to the house then keep your eyes on the wall! Alert me if anyone tries to come over! I can't watch all directions at once." They nodded and rushed to Manuel, glad of having something specific to do.

"No, *patrón*," Manuel shouted back. "I am fine. Let me stay and help you!"

The door to the main room opened and Lupita bustled out. When Amada tried to follow, Lupita snapped at her, "Stay!" Amada obeyed. Stooping beside Manuel, she examined the shoulder.

"How is he?" I asked, my eyes on the tops of the walls.

"It was a bullet. It passed all the way through. Not too much blood," she reported. As ever, she seemed calm, regardless of the circumstances.

I nodded. "All right, you can stay Manuel. Lupita, back inside please."

"*Sí, patrón*," she answered.

I actually had to stop and watch her reenter the house. She had never before addressed me as *patron*. My astonishment was interrupted by a rain of arrows.

The men outside were arching a volley of arrows into the courtyard in the hope of blindly hitting someone. They succeeded. Octavio cried out, an arrow in his back. He fell to his knees and hunched forward in pain.

"Quickly, against the front wall!" I ordered. Felipe helped Octavio and I helped Manuel as we rushed to the tenuous shelter of the wall. We would be safely within the angle of the arrows' flight there. With my back pressed against the *adobe* I looked at the man I had shot from the wall. He had a brown beard.

"This is not an *Indio*!" I cried. The others looked as well. "This is a *Norteamericano* mountain man!"

"Not all, Don Jose," Felipe informed me. "Some are *Indios*, some are *Norteamericanos, como ese*." He nudged the body with his toe as one would prod a piece of garbage.

That made no sense. Perhaps the Indians would see me as a trespasser, but what argument had I with these mountain men? Surely they did not covet my sheep! "How many were there, Felipe, could you see?"

Felipe shrugged. "More than I cared to stand and count."

"I think maybe ten or twelve, *jefe*," Manuel suggested.

I had shot three, which still left more than I wanted to deal with. Another volley of arrows thudded harmlessly into the yard. My quiver only had two arrows left, so I scurried around the yard, quickly reaping the enemy arrows, before returning to the safety of the wall.

Crash! The *puerta del zaguán* shuddered. Crash! The blow came again. They were using one of the timbers meant for the construction on the second story, to batter the gate.

"Arm yourself with something, anything!" I ordered, then ran for the ladder. From the front of the roof, I would be able to get a clear shot at anyone in front of the gate, making myself a rather easy target in the bargain, but something had to be done.

I scrambled up the ladder as another crash echoed across the courtyard. Leaping to the western roof, I sprinted to the front, drawing my bow as I ran. Without aiming at individuals, I let fly as many arrows as I could, as quickly as I could, in the general area of the gate front. From their screams, I knew that I must have struck several, but I also knew that I was a dead man. As if in a dream, I saw the muzzles swivel upward in search of me. The tongues of flame, the puffs of smoke and I was falling before I ever felt the bullets hit.

I lay on the dry ground of the courtyard and heard a roaring in my ears. From a distance, came the splintering crash of the gate as it buckled. The screams of my unarmed companions violated my ears. Fingers of blackness plucked at my consciousness but I rebuked them, rolling onto my side. From that angle I watched as the attacker lugged the timber across the *placita* to the door of my house—the door that shielded my Amada.

My arms betrayed me as I struggled to my knees. Numbly I watched as the barrel of my rifle thrust from the shuttered window and spit death at the enemy. *Yes, my beloved, fight them! Do not ever be the victim again, my Amada!*

One man fell, but the rest persisted. Crash! Crash! Crash! The door shattered. A ragged cheer went up from the men. I sank back on my heels. Blood flowed in warm streams down my arms. One more crash and the door toppled inward. Through the ruptured opening flew Lupita, her butcher knife flashing in every direction. The men fell back before her fury, but not for long. A rifle fired at close range slammed her against the wall. A bloody stain marked her slide to the earth.

The dark fingers clutched at me, toppling me sideways to the ground. In absolute impotence, I watched the men enter the room and emerge a few moments later with a struggling Amada. At the direction of a man with a straw-colored beard they dragged her toward where I lay.

A face thrust near mine. "You still alive, Spaniard? Good!" Absaroka Jake straightened up and directed his friends. "Prop him up, boys! I want him to be able to see real good."

"Amada," I whispered as rough hands leaned my back against the wall. My head fell forward weakly and a hand grabbed my hair to hold it up.

"Jose, oh, my poor love!" I could hear Amada crying for me.

"You're a scrappy little greaser, I'll say!" Jake continued. "I guess you thought you'd fixed it with your 'Rikara friends to rub ole Jake out, didn't ya? But you didn't figger on my partner Ed Rose comin' down behind me by a day, did ya? He stayed clear of them Injuns and fished me off'n a snag in the river more dead than alive."

Jake was pacing back and forth before me, a terrible, mad expression on his face. "Ole Rose patched me up and floated me down to Fort Recovery where I heard about you stealing my peltries!" His voice rose in anger and he kicked me, though I could not feel it. Amada struggled against the hands that pinioned her but could not break free to reach me.

"I lost your track from St. Louis, Spaniard, lost it for near two years. Then I come back to Taos 'n heard how you got rich leadin' Becknell from Missoura. Yore a famous man, Don Josey!" Jake snarled, punctuating his address with more kicks.

"Now I aim to see you dead fer what you done to me, Spaniard, but I'm real gratified that you ain't gone yet." I was not so sure that I agreed with his diagnosis. I was rapidly losing consciousness.

"Bring her here!" Jake snapped. I struggled to fight the darkness. In a nightmare, I watched Jake grab Amada by her wrists and push her to the ground.

Amada tried to look at me and I tried to stay conscious, but my eyes were relentlessly closing. "I aim to make her pay too, boys!" Jake added and began to laugh.

I slumped to my side, but my head was twisted so that I could see his face. There was a series of dull, thumping noises then, and the laugh in Jake's throat became a cough. His leer twisted to pain and surprise, and the last thing I saw was a fountain of blood gushing from his mouth. The last sound I heard, was Amada's scream. Then there was darkness.

Then there was a light. As if I was looking through the wrong end of a telescope, the light seemed distant but inexplicably attractive. From a distance, from within that light, I heard Red Hand's voice repeating once again, "Peace, peace, *paz, paz . . .*" My father's hands were strong and comforting on my shoulders. Soft warm hands were holding mine. I looked to my right and Chilsipee smiled at me with her impish grin. I looked to my left and Amada smiled shyly through her veil of hair.

The light was closer, and so inviting, like a warm *colchón* at the end of a too long day. But there was another voice now, beside Red Hand's. I looked to the left and there were tears in Amada's eyes. She was calling me, calling me from a great distance. I was confused. I was weeping. I longed for the rest of that peaceful light, but Amada was calling me. She needed me. I had to go to her.

"Jose, Jose!" It was Amada's voice. My face was wet. I must be lying outside, I thought, and it's raining—warm rain. I should get up and go inside. "Jose, Jose."

I opened my eyes. I was within the tent of Amada's hair. Her face hovered above me, distorted by grief, and a steady sprinkling of tears pattered down on my face.

"Amada?" I whispered.

Instantly she stopped intoning my name and opened her eyes. "Jose?" Her head whipped up and she informed someone else, "He lives."

How odd, I thought. She's speaking Comanche.

Another face, a painted one, took the place of Amada's above me.

"Little Spaniard?" it asked.

Well, yes, but who are you? I rolled my head to the side and blinked. A dozen Comanche warriors stood looking down at me.

I looked up again. "Amada?"

"Si, mi amor, estoy aqui!" Amada's lovely face was above me again, her hand was on my cheek.

"Amada? Am I dead?"

She began to laugh even as her tears resumed. "No, Jose. You're alive! You're alive!" She punctuated her words with kisses to my face. "Alive! Alive! Alive!"

Gingerly, the men picked me up and carried me through the carnage of the *placita* to my *colchon*. Gently, Amada began to bathe my wounds. "The bleeding has stopped, Jose, but you have lost much blood. It is a miracle that you are alive! A miracle!"

The painted young face was before me again, looking over Amada's shoulder. There was something familiar about it. "Windy?" I whispered, in awe.

The young man cast an embarrassed look toward his companions, then nodded. Tapping his breast, he said, "I am now called, Strong Wind that Blows the Enemy Away, Little Spaniard."

With effort, I smiled. "Yes. A good name. A name of much *puha*." I shook my head in wonder, but stopped quickly because of the dizziness it induced. "But I thought you were dead!"

"The rest, they are all gone," he said. "But I survived. A band of Yampareekuh found me lying beside my parents and took me from that place. I have an adopted family now."

Amada, who had lost much of her command of the Nermernuh language, had nonetheless understood most of our conversation. She had stopped nursing me and was looking at Windy in wide-eyed wonder.

"Warrior," I addressed Windy, "you still have blood relatives." I nodded at Amada. "We are truly brothers again. This woman is my wife. She is your sister." Windy stared as if at a ghost. Amada, in her excitement, looked as if she were about to hug her twin.

"Amada," I cautioned her in Spanish, "remember that he is Comanche!"

"*Si*, Jose," she said, composing herself to a more dignified state, she nodded to Windy and resumed tending my wounds.

Windy stood up and moved away from the *colchón*, his eyes shifting from Amada to me and back. He paced in agitation, then seemed to make up his mind. Returning shyly to our side, he studied Amada. "Our parents would not speak of you, but the Little Spaniard would tell me about you when he was with us. He talked of you a great deal." With great formality, he said, "I am pleased to see you, my sister." Then he smiled, and looked happily at his companions who nodded their approval.

I had been fortunate to be shot with bullets that passed through me rather than arrows that would have lodged in my body or I would have surely bled to death.

My chance conversation with the Comanche at the Big Timbers of the Arkansas two years earlier, had eventually resulted in Windy hearing that the Little Spaniard who had been in Four Bears' camp, was alive. Now seventeen years old and a proven warrior, Windy had convinced his companions to make a detour from their hunt, to seek out the Little Spaniard. Questions at the Pecos pueblo had led him to our home at a most opportune time. They had entered the *placita* in time to see Amada thrust to her knees. They had rightly deduced the situation and let fly a well-aimed volley of arrows.

The casualties were great. Eleven renegade Indians and outcast mountain men lay dead. All of the shearers were dead. Manuel was seriously wounded, but would quickly recover. Lupita, Amada's guardian angel, had died defending her beloved charge. A few years later, I chanced to be in Bernalillo and I asked the Cordova family what they remembered about Lupita. From them I learned that Lupita had been a young wife and mother when a Spanish expedition had attacked her Yaqui camp in the usual reprisals both sides inflicted on each other with Old Testament regularity. In the raid, both her husband and her baby girl had been killed. Lupita had been captured and given to a Franciscan mission after some barbaric treatment at the hands of the soldiers. Ultimately, she arrived in Santa Fe and found her lost daughter in Amada. Lupita had the place of honor in our new little cemetery—our *Jardin de las Cruces.*

Windy stayed with us only a few days, until I was stronger but promised to return, which he did regularly for years. On his way back to the *llano* he left word at Cicuye of what had occurred and, within two weeks, my brothers-in-law, Paco and several of our servants had arrived to help us rebuild.

It took me several months to recover my strength, but by the time our first son was born, I was able to ride and to work almost as before. Manuel recovered even quicker than I and, before the year was out, was asking permission to go on frequent trips to Santa Fe. It seems that a certain young woman had caught his eye. I did not object, as his romance provided me with a ready courier to the capital.

Doña Maria Elena insisted on sending a servant out to help Amada care for the baby and even made the long trip out herself to help with the delivery. I think it was the only time she ever set foot outside of Santa Fe.

Christmas of 1823 put me in a nostalgic mood. Manuel sang, and we ate like kings, but our minds were heavy with the memory of those gone. After dinner, I again climbed to the roof, this time two stories high. As on the year before, the moon was bright, and the sky calm and clear.

"Lord," I prayed, "this living—it is not an easy thing!" I shook my head. Closing my eyes, I breathed deeply of the freezing air, scented with pine smoke. Like a compass, my gaze was drawn to the North Star. "Thank you," I whispered, thinking of all that I had been blessed with and all that I had survived, by the mercy of God.

"It's cold out here, Jose!" Amada came to her accustomed place beneath my arm.

"Yes," I agreed. Pointing to the North Star, I asked, "Do you see it?"

Amada nodded.

"The heavens revolve, the earth turns, but it never moves, it never changes, and no matter how lost you get, if you can keep your eyes on that star, you know that sooner or later you can find your way home again."

Amada was looking at me rather than the star.

"I understand. But that star is too far away for me—so far and so cold in that black sky." Her arm went under my *serape* and around my waist. "Thank you, Jose," she said softly.

"Why do you thank me?"

Amada simply smiled and shrugged. Pressing her nose against my shoulder, she said, “My nose is freezing.”

I kissed her nose. “It is cold.”

“How is your leg?” she asked, in a husky voice.

I looked at her and smiled. With my arm about her, we went back down into our home together.